BARE KNUCKLES

The foreman lay in the dust of the street, his face beaten and puffed, his hair matted with sweat and grime. And over him stood Will Lockhart, swaying with a deadening fatigue that barely left him on his feet.

"Why'd you do it?" the man asked him.

"Well," Lockhart said, "you might say on account of some good wagons of mine that burned up. Or you could blame it on a rope that dragged me a ways on the ground. But you'd be real close if you asked me about a brother of mine. Yeah, I guess I'd have to tell you. Because he's dead…"

THE MAN FROM LARAMIE

T. T. Flynn

LEISURE BOOKS NEW YORK CITY

A LEISURE BOOK®

April 2009

Published by special arrangement with Golden West Literary Agency.

Dorchester Publishing Co., Inc.
200 Madison Avenue
New York, NY 10016

ISBN 10: 0-8439-6098-1
ISBN 13: 978-0-8439-6098-3
E-ISBN: 1-4285-0654-3

Visit us on the web at www.dorchesterpub.com.

THE MAN FROM LARAMIE

Chapter One

They had been at the salt lagoons three sweating, vigilant days now, loading the four big freight wagons. The heat this third day had a brassy scorch as Will Lockhart climbed the lava cone that lifted raw and steep at the east end of the lagoons.

He climbed with steady, thrusting steps, a long man burned dark, his bleached denim pants crusted white with dried salt. When he halted on a slab of gas-pitted lava below the jagged peak, the gray shirt was plastered darkly to his sweating back. Sucking great breaths, he looked southwest over the arid plain to the wreckage of two burned wagons.

When his own four wagons had reached the lagoons, smoke wisps had still curled lazily from that fire-blackened wreckage. The dead teamsters had been callously burned, too. Apache! Again— Apache! And the same howling fury could return. Will Lockhart's watchful glance tilted down to his four wagons and the five men loading coarse damp salt.

Ready by sundown, he guessed. The crystallized shore salt and glassy lagoons had a glinting, evil shimmer which made him squint.

Six bridled mules were picketed near the wagons. Twenty-six other mules, chain-hobbled and listless in the molten heat, had scattered out on scanty grass and the thistly growth called *sisaña*. The mules, Will decided, were ready. He looked south, and his narrowed gaze tightened on a far, diaphanous lift of dust.

The flat planes of his dark-burned face stayed composed and intent as Will watched. Finally he called down through cupped hands to the wagons, "Visitors south!"

Smiling faintly, Will watched the five men drop shovels and break for the picketed mules. One man moved leisurely, almost disdainfully. That one, Will saw, was Charley Yuill, an odd mixture of Scot father and Indian mother.

"Probably from Fort Roxton!" Will called, and started down.

The men straggled to meet him, unshaven, too, their clothes stiff also with white, dried salt. Charley Yuill, his mahogany skin tight over the wide cheekbones of his Indian blood, and whisker bristle a startling, challenging red, gave the others a faintly derisive look and asked, "Do we fort up or run?"

Will grinned. "Charley, we load salt. One rider is scouting ahead of that dust. I'll watch him."

Shovels were banging again on the wagon side-boards when a rider came on the trot down the last long arid slope, and became a broad-shouldered lieutenant out of Fort Roxton.

Will Lockhart noted the straight back and fine tawny mustache. He gestured a greeting as the lieutenant swung down and swiped a perspiring face with a blue neckerchief end.

"Lieutenant Evans, commanding a patrol out of Fort Roxton." It held a trace of pompousness.

Evans knocked dust from his black felt hat and placed the hat back on his head firmly, precisely, without rake, Will Lockhart's interested glance noted. Mildly, Will said, "I'm Lockhart— My wagons."

He watched Evans's frowning estimate of wagons, mules, and men, and made an abrupt decision. *No humor. Knows the book, and that's how it'd better be.*

Will wryly reflected on the folly of men while Evans nodded indifferently and bluntly demanded, "How well are you men armed?"

"Three rifles and four handguns."

"For six men?"

Will nodded, and Lieutenant Evans censured him with brusque annoyance. "Hardly a mile from where two wagons were attacked and burned four days ago. And not enough weapons to protect yourselves."

Will's gaze took on bland irony. "Now," Will murmured, "we have you, Mr. Evans. And your command."

Evans's stare fixed alertly on him, and ruefully Will decided, *No fool on regulations.* Silently he damned the slip of tongue which had said, "Mr. Evans," in the easy manner of rank to rank.

Evans said irritably, "The Apache is getting hold of the latest repeating rifles. And you men are here like sitting ducks."

"One of my drivers is quarter-Zuni, quarter-Apach'," Will said easily. "He thinks some young Mescaleros out hunting their manhood blooded on those two wagon drivers, then pulled fast for the home wickiups, satisfied."

Evans snorted.

Will casually added, "I agree with Charley; waste of time to patrol through here now."

Lieutenant Evans gave him an affronted look and

a curt "Haven't asked your opinion. I'm told sweet water can be found by that volcanic rise."

Will nodded. Suspicion was stirring in Evans's stare, and Will guessed what it might be and tightened warily against it as Evans said slowly, "I can't place you—Cavalry, wasn't it?" Evans's aloof inspection of the dirty, brine-crusted figure before him suggested distaste that yellow stripes could come to this.

"Why place me?" Will said indifferently. Resignedly he wondered if this man's affronted curiosity meant trouble later on.

Evans persisted, "I take it you work for Alec Waggoman's Barb Ranch?"

"No," said Will briefly. "I'm renting salt rights here from Half-Moon Ranch."

Evans's perspiring face reddened. "Why tell me something which obviously can't be true?"

For an unbelieving moment Will waited for a smile, a gesture—anything to change the man's meaning. None came. Outrage filled Will's stare. His fast-reaching hand caught the blue blouse and gilt buttons over Evans's chest. A yank brought Evans forward off balance; then Will's contemptuous shove sent Evans back an unsteady step.

"Don't call me a liar!" said Will calmly, coldly.

He watched Evans's hand drop instinctively to the black holster belt and revolver. Then training held Evans motionless in purpling rage.

"Damn you! If you were an officer—"

Will finished curtly, "You'd think twice before questioning my word."

"We're escorting a young lady as far as the salt lakes here!" blurted Evans in fury. "She told me Barb Ranch has leased all this land—these salt lakes, too—from a man named José Gallegos, who owns the Gallegos Grant!"

"This is Gallegos grant land," Will conceded. "Half-Moon has leased it for years. Five days ago I rented salt rights from Half-Moon."

The shaking fury still held Evans. "The lady's word satisfies me!"

"Be civil about it next time," Will advised. He wheeled toward the wagons, leaving Evans there with shredded dignity.

The teamsters had witnessed the clash and stopped work. Their expectant grins turned uncertain as Will told them brusquely, "The lieutenant says Barb Ranch has leased this land. Stop loading until we know where we stand."

Charley Yuill scratched the flaming red whorls of his jaw stubble and looked askance at the loaded wagons. "A lot of diggin' there," said Charley ruefully. "Plenty sweat—Do we have to unload?"

"You might," Will admitted. He turned to watch Lieutenant Evans striding toward the volcanic cone. Taking out tobacco and papers, Will started a smoke and moved away from his men, held now by a puzzled thought— If this was Barb land, why had Half-Moon rented salt rights to a stranger like himself five days ago?

Will shrugged; he'd get at the truth when the lady arrived. In that mood he watched Evans climbing the lava cone, and guessed ironically the sweating effort would consume some of the man's wild anger.

Then Will watched keenly while a small detail of troopers came down the long arid slope, following shallow wheel ruts which curved past the lava cone and struck off north.

Ten troopers, corporal, and a sergeant, Will counted. Mauled by the sun, dust flouring their faded blue trousers and blouses, and every man-jack of them, Will guessed, recalling with sweating envy the cool shade behind Roxton barracks, and cooler, foaming beer in Roxton town, a scant mile from the post.

Then amusement stirred in Will's gray eyes as he noted the lone buckboard the detail was escorting. The driver was a girl, small-built, slender, riding the buckboard's jolting seat under a man's incongruously large high-crowned straw sombrero.

The sergeant's gaze was shuttling from Evans's waiting horse to the lieutenant's figure nearing the top of the lava cone. Now the sergeant's gravelly tones called, "Hyaaalt! . . . Di'm'nt! . . . 'Tease!"

The buckboard came on to Will before the girl pulled the bay gelding and claybank mare to a halt. Dust covered her denim skirt and jacket and masked her small face with a grayish film. She'd perspired and swiped a jaunty smear around her mouth.

"A big escort, ma'am," Will drawled, "for one small buckboard and lady."

She said calmly, "They were coming this far, so I took the short cut to Coronado. I'm carrying mail."

Will's eyebrows lifted. He eyed the brown tarp lashed over the buckboard's load, and guessed, "You're Miss Barbara Kirby— Making a trip for your father."

Knowing a little about Miss Barbara Kirby, and more about her father, Will guessed why she flushed as she looped reins on the seat iron and stood up.

He stepped to the wheel and handed her down.

Barbara Kirby thanked him and slapped her dusty jacket and skirt with grimy hands. Her oblique glance made Will conscious of the rough whisker bristle and rime of salt brine, stale sweat, and caked dust which made him a completely filthy stranger. Smiling faintly again, he said, "I'd guessed Miss Kirby was a big one, a fire-eater."

She gave him a direct look. "Where," she asked coolly, "were you discussing Miss Kirby?"

"Merely overheard the name in Coronado, ma'am," Will said hastily, vaguely. "I'm Will Lockhart."

Barbara Kirby's red underlip had pushed out a little in warning signal. "Where, in Coronado, Mr. Lockhart, did a stranger like you hear my name?"

"I can't recall," Will evaded, and his thought was rueful, *Should have known better*. This Barbara Kirby, challenging under the oversized sombrero, had spirit. Her eyes were a clear blue-green. A ringlet of brown hair at her dusty temple was alive with coppery highlights. Will guessed uncomfortably, *They've rubbed her father into her too much.*

He changed the subject, saying bluntly, "The lieutenant tells me Barb Ranch controls these salt lakes now."

"Yes."

"How long has Barb leased here?"

"A week, at least." Barbara Kirby was surveying him coolly. "Aren't you digging salt for Barb?"

"For myself," Will told her. "With Half-Moon's permission. I meant to sell the salt to Darrah's store, in Coronado." He wondered why her look grew guarded. Her quick question was odd, too. "Did Darrah agree to buy from you?"

"We had some talk about it. You're certain about Barb leasing all this?"

"Quite," said Barbara Kirby with increasing reserve.

She looked toward the lava cone. Lieutenant Evans had been searching the distance through a small field glass, and now was descending. "Trespassers," Barbara Kirby said without expression on her small, dusty face, "are never welcome on Barb land. I wish you luck."

"For the kindly thought, ma'am, thanks," said Will with faint irony. "I'll expect luck."

She said briefly, "You *are* a stranger," and turned to her team, plainly dismissing him.

Will walked back to the wagons and told the men tersely, "Seems to be Barb salt we've loaded." Barbara Kirby was leading her team toward the sweet water flow, and Will said, "Charley, help her."

After that he rolled another smoke and pondered what to do. He'd heard about Barb Ranch and the almost legendary Alec Waggoman who owned Barb. There was more to the mix-up in ownership than he could sort out now, he decided. The wagons were loaded. They should stay in this sun-blasted, desolate spot until Alec Waggoman was contacted. Either that, or unload the thousands of pounds of coarse salt.

Frowning over the problem, Will watched the troopers take horses over to the sweet water. The buckboard pulled away, rounding the lava cone and heading north. Charley Yuill came back to the wagons, grinning.

"A honey, wasn't she?" Charley asked. "Treated me nicer'n she did yellow legs."

"It's your red whiskers, you bobtailed Scotsman," Will said good-naturedly.

Charley could mimic perfectly his father's burr. "A bra lassie, mon," Charley said, and then sobered. "I heard the lieutenant tellin' her his patrol stopped here. But up there he sighted a party of cowmen heading this way from Coronado. Barb riders probably, he said, and she'd be safe from here on."

"Barb riders?" said Will alertly. He guessed, "She'll meet them and tell them we're here." His thin smile followed. "We'll soon know whether we unload or not."

Barbara Kirby, driving north across the broken, sun-scorched plain, identified eight riders heading for the salt lagoons. They swerved to intercept her, and Barbara pulled her team to a halt.

Silently under the broad straw sombrero she watched them surround the buckboard with a swirl of trampling horses and hot dust.

Every horse was a fine horse, carrying Alec Waggoman's renowned Barb brand, the curve, the point, and down-slashing barb of a great fishhook. A shark hook, some men bitterly said. Every man was armed. Barb men always carried guns. Barbara's greenish eyes watched the leader wheel his long-backed gray gelding to the buckboard's left side and give her a jocular greeting.

"How's Cousin Barbara today?"

He was Dave Waggoman, Alec Waggoman's only son, and his covert amusement watched Barbara's red underlip push out slightly in warning temper. Aloud, Barbara innocently wondered, "Dave, haven't you more nursemaids than usual?"

One of the men sniggered. Dave's smile thinned. "Sharp-tongued as ever."

"It's the people I meet," said Barbara calmly. She glanced beyond Dave, at a massive thick-necked man with short dark beard, whose heavy hand was curbing a restless, broad-chested sorrel flecked with foam. "Bullies like Vic Hansbro," Barbara added coolly.

Chapter Two

Vic Hansbro, the Barb foreman, eyed Barbara with impassive dislike and spat to one side, eloquently. Grins among the Barb men wiped away as Hansbro's flinty gaze swung to them.

Dave Waggoman was close-knit and wiry, with a tight mouth having a hint of Barbara's full red underlip. Dave's eyes were a hot restless blue, and the restlessness was on Dave's thin face, too, mirroring his short temper.

Dave asked now, "Where's your father?"

"He's busy."

"Doing what?" asked Dave slyly.

Barbara gathered the reins and her temper. Dave knew well enough what Jubal Kirby was probably doing. So did the other grinning Barb men. Dave saw she meant to drive on and ceased his baiting and said, "I hear wagons are loading salt at the lagoons."

Reluctantly Barbara nodded. "Isn't there salt enough for everyone?"

"It's Barb salt now," Dave said past tightening lips. He wrenched the gray horse away, temper and aggressiveness setting mulishly on his face. The lot of them departed in another burst of dust.

Barbara drove on, thinking now of the lanky sun-blackened stranger with the brief, ironic grin. He hadn't seemed to know much about Barb or Dave's destructive temper. Soon now he would know. Barbara found herself regretting it. Dave had never been much comfort as a cousin. To a stranger trespassing on Barb land, Dave could be grave trouble.

Coronado lay among cedar-dotted foothills west of the great upthrust of Coronado Peak. The smashing heat slacked off in the foothills and the buckboard team trotted more briskly. Barbara sat straighter when the first log and adobe houses of town appeared, and in a few minutes she reined the team off Palace Street into the alley behind the small frame post office.

Aaron Sadler, the postmaster, a graying man with dry zest in keen hazel eyes, stepped out the back door and observed, "Made it with your hair still on, I see."

Barbara pressed fists into her stiff back, stretching, grimacing, and said, "Troopers from Fort Roxton were patrolling to the salt lagoons. I took the short cut that way with them."

"I thought," said Aaron tartly, "you'd growed into sense. Drivin' where two men was kilt the other day shows I was mistook." Aaron estimated the tarp-covered load. "Big mail?"

Barbara chuckled. "Something free for everyone. Bags of printed matter from Washington."

Aaron groaned. "Again?" He helped Barbara down and watched her belt dust from the denim skirt with the big straw sombrero. "Run on now," Aaron said. "I'll unload an' take your team to the feed corral."

Carrying the straw hat, Barbara walked home, cramped muscles limbering into light, brisk steps. Her father had lived in better homes than the small clapboard house with sun-warped shingles and faded yellow paint. But it was home, the picket fence neatly whitewashed and flower beds a riot of color. Barbara called gaily in the front door, "Hi-a, dad?"

Deserted rooms swallowed her greeting. *And he promised not a poker game while I was gone,* Barbara remembered in indignant resignation. In her own small room, she sailed the big hat to the figured counterpane, of the small brass bed and glanced in the mirror of the walnut bureau which had been her mother's. Barbara groaned at the dusty smear around her mouth.

Half an hour later, bathed and wearing a white cambric suit and small jaunty white chip hat trimmed with a red silk bow, Barbara walked briskly out of the house, her face sun-browned and animated.

On Palace Street the dipping sun was nudging indigo shadows over the silvery dust as Barbara crossed to a store building freshly painted light gray, its high false front boldly lettered:

> *Frank L. Darrah*
> *Merchant*
> *Supplies   Contracts*

The well-stocked store had uncluttered aisles, with an office at the back partly screened by overhead poles holding polished bridles and harness, brightly-tinned hand lanterns, and colorfully patterned blankets.

An under-counter cash drawer to the left rang its flat tinkle warning of disturbance as McGuire, the clerk, made change. Two bonneted ladies there turned to watch Barbara Kirby's slender, white-clad figure enter the office. Their smiles were knowing.

In the office a stooping figure was placing a green-painted cash box in the large iron safe. Barbara's mirthful question, "Counting your pennies again, Frank?" brought him around in pleased surprise.

Frank Darrah was a solid young man with the smooth, pinkish complexion of one more often at ledgers and sales than abroad in violent sunlight and scouring wind. Barbara met his kiss willingly. Frank's hands, confident and possessive, held her arms a moment before dropping away.

"I missed you," Frank said. His blond, crisp hair was closely combed. He wore the salt-and-pepper suit well.

Smiling and a little breathless now, Barbara told him, "Frank, you're always a comfort." Her quick warm thought was, *And I'm always proud of you.*

Four years ago Frank Darrah had come to Coronado with meager capital. He had prospered amazingly. Ambitious, industrious, Frank was everything her father was not. Frank was steady. Frank was dependable. Barbara had the almost humble thought, *I'm lucky, lucky.*

Frank moved past her and closed the office door, saying wryly under his breath, "Mrs. Anderson just came in. She gossips."

"Who doesn't?" Barbara wondered lightly. She picked up a pencil from Frank's orderly roll-top desk, and turning the pencil absently in her fingers, casually asked, "Didn't you tell me confidentially last week that Barb was leasing around the salt lagoons?"

Frank's forehead puckered. "Did I?"

"Yes. And when I passed there today, four wagons were loaded with salt. The man said he was selling to you."

"I buy anything which sells at a profit," said Frank, smiling.

Barbara hesitated. Why, she wondered now, speak of it at all? *I have to know,* Barbara decided almost fiercely. She asked, making it sound casual and perplexed, "If Barb owns the salt now, how could you be buying it, Frank? The man didn't know Barb had leased the lagoons. He said Half-Moon had given him permission to dig salt. Lockhart is his name."

"I remember him," Frank said readily. "A jackleg teamster who hauled some of my freight from Colfax." Half smiling in a quizzical way, Frank explained, "I see what must have happened. Half-Moon, you know, has been leasing around those lagoons for years. The other day I learned in strict confidence that Barb had quietly leased that land. I couldn't tell Lockhart, of course. He must have gone to Half-Moon for permission to dig salt." Frank shrugged. "Evidently Half-Moon hadn't discovered the new lease had been turned over to Barb."

This, Barbara realized with relief, was the way worry started. Of course, Frank had been entirely innocent of misleading Lockhart. Sobering, she said, "I met Vic Hansbro, Dave Waggoman, and six of their men riding to the lagoons. Dave had heard someone was loading salt. He was angry. And you know Dave's temper."

Frank nodded and shoved hands in his coat pockets and turned to peer through the door glass into the store. His profile was gravely thoughtful.

"Dave Waggoman's temper may get him killed at any time," Frank said slowly. "Then you'd be heir to Barb. Ever think of that?"

Barbara said quickly, "Of course not!"

"You would inherit," Frank reminded.

"Dave will marry and have children who'll get Barb—and I can think of better things to talk about," said Barbara positively.

Frank turned to her, smiling sheepishly. "It merely occurred to me— Did I say you're lovelier than ever today?"

"That's better," said Barbara, smiling absently.

She was still thinking, for no good reason, of the ironically smiling, sun-blackened stranger named Will Lockhart, and wondering what the Barb men would do when they reached the lagoons.

Will Lockhart also wondered about the Barb men as he smoked thoughtfully on a high wagon seat and counted eight riders approaching from the north, where Barbara Kirby's buckboard had vanished.

Will shifted on the seat, eyeing Lieutenant Evans and his troopers a long mile away at the wreckage of the two burned ranch wagons. Evans was a perplexing problem. The man had a tenacious, monumental self-esteem, which would stubbornly try to place this Will Lockhart who'd sparked a vague memory. The clash which had occurred between them would only make Evans press his memory harder.

A thought brought Will's gaze to his five men waiting uncertainly by the bedrolls and smoke-blackened cooking-pots. "Put your guns away," he told them.

Reluctantly they obeyed. Will rolled another smoke. Steamy heat came off the damp salt filling the deep wagon bed. The sun had a searing glare on the shore salt and glassy lagoon brine. Near by the raw lava cone bulked somberly against the dry, sisaña-dotted landscape.

For a thousand years, Will mused as he waited, the Indian tribes had come to those lagoons for salt and ceremonial worship of Old Grandmother Salt. In Spain, long ago, a royal king had granted all this land to one family. Half-Moon Ranch had leased here for years. Now Alec Waggoman's great Barb Ranch seemed to hold the lease.

The eight riders came sweeping around the lava cone to the salt-filled wagons. Horses bearing the bold Barb brand, every man armed, Will noted as they pulled up at the wagons.

His glance briefly weighed one huge, powerful man with short dark beard, and went on to a younger wiry man whose hot, challenging look was taking in the scattered-out hobbled mules, the loaded wagons, and waiting men.

"Who's Lockhart, who owns this thieving outfit?" the hot-tempered demand came from this younger, wiry man.

Will took the cigarette from his mouth. "I'm Lockhart."

"I'm Dave Waggoman! This is Barb land! Barb salt! What are you doing here?"

"Digging salt," said Will mildly. "I didn't know Barb held the lease here until the troopers and Miss Kirby told me. No harm meant. If there's a charge, I'll be glad to pay."

Dave Waggoman hesitated. His glance went to the bearded man. "Vic, that's one way of handling it."

Will had heard in Coronado of Vic Hansbro, the Barb foreman—heard nothing good about the man. He was not surprised at Hansbro's curt argument.

"An' next time, Dave, they might not be caught. Next time might not be salt— Might be cattle."

Will negligently flipped his cigarette toward Hansbro's powerful, lather-flecked sorrel. His reminder held a restrained patience. "We're here for salt. Any man who calls me a rustler is lying."

A kind of startled interest alerted every Barb man as Hansbro drew the holstered gun off his hip. Disgustedly Will guessed, *He baited me and I took it.* Calmly Will said, "You don't need that."

Hansbro laid the gun barrel on his saddle horn and spoke to Dave Waggoman. "Alec always handled men like this. Had to."

Dave's mouth thinned angrily. "Well, handle them."

"Fitz," Hansbro said without turning his head, "you don't miss often with a rope."

The man who kneed his horse forward was short, sallow, and grinning as he expertly shook out his rope loop. Will stood up, warning, "Don't try it!"

He stepped off the wagon, and saw the fast flirt of Fitz's wrist, and threw up both arms to knock the rope loop away. His right wrist struck only the inside of the loop, and as Will's feet hit the baked earth, a spur rake drove Fitz's horse lunging against a swift dally on the saddle horn.

The rope loop snapped in tight below Will's hips, jerking him down in a sprawl. He was dragged through the dead ashes of a cook fire before Fitz got the horses under control.

"Hold him," Hansbro ordered briefly.

Will lay on his side for a moment and spat dirt and sucked in a great breath. In utter waiting silence, he rolled face down, pushed back to his heels, and came upright, the rope still tight about him. A dark and overwhelming wrath filled his stare at Dave Waggoman and Hansbro.

"That was a mistake," Will said thinly.

Hansbro told Fitz, "Jerk him down again if he needs it." Then with a complete lack of visible anger, Hansbro spoke to the Barb men. "Burn the wagons. Shoot the mules."

Will heard it in complete disbelief. "You'd shoot good mules?"

Hansbro's flinty regard swung to him. "Anyone invite 'em on Barb land?"

The Barb men went about it efficiently. One man yanked a wood ax from leather loops on a wagon. Vigorous swings splintered the sun-dried sideboards into kindling. Fires were built under the front axles of the wagons, where the salt dampness had not reached. The flames caught quickly in the dry wood.

Charley Yuill picked up the black hat which had been knocked off Will's head. Charley's dark eyes were glowing as he brought the hat to Will. Charley looked along the taut rope to the revolver barrel Fitz was resting on the brass saddle horn.

"A richt likely mon tae meet wi' another day," Charley murmured in his father's thick burr, which Charley could turn on and off effortlessly.

Fitz glowered suspiciously. And then Will's coldly satisfied wrath broke on the moment. "The troopers are coming back. Now we'll see."

Chapter Three

A deep-rooted pride held Will as he watched the small column of disciplined troopers sweep back to the burning wagons. There came law and order and all that was fine, all that was proud.

Lieutenant Evans's lifted arm halted the column a hundred yards away. Evans came on alone, his frowning glance roving over the scene.

"What is this?" Evans called.

Vic Hansbro answered from the saddle in a kind of contemptuous calm. "We've caught trespassers on Barb range."

Standing in the rope loop which Fitz kept tight, Will spoke in restrained fury. "I've offered to pay fairly for a mistake. They insist on shooting my mules. Will you stop this?"

Dave Waggoman had reined over beside Hansbro. Now Dave flung out with suppressed tension, "This isn't the army's damn business!"

"I'm aware of the army's business," said Evans disagreeably. He looked at Will Lockhart and the five angry, helpless drivers standing in the swirling smoke. "What about Lockhart and his men?"

Hansbro said indifferently, "They can ride away."

Will tried again. "Lieutenant, they intend to shoot our mules!"

Evans answered him with stiff disinterest. "Private quarrels are matters for the local sheriff and territorial courts."

In completely unbelieving wrath, Will reminded

hotly, "They're going to butcher good mules! And you mouth nonsense, Evans, about regulations and courts!"

He could see Evans's anger break redly around the tawny mustache. But Evans kept his words coldly, stiffly formal. "My orders, Lockhart, don't include meddling in private quarrels, short of threatened murder."

Contemptuously Will ended it. "The hell with you!"

The rest of it was ruthless.

Evans drew his men off another hundred yards and held there aloof. The first slapping gunshots flattened across the shimmering lagoons, and Will turned his back. Charley Yuill, standing close by, watched the mule slaughter without expression.

Smoke from the blazing wagons whipped about them. A front axle burned through and the loaded wagon crashed down, splintering wood and driving red sparks through the mushrooming billows of smoke.

A nightmarish quality threaded the smashing gunshots and wild braying of terrified mules. Finally the last of it fled in diminishing echoes across the baked plain, and the steady crackle of the burning wagons was almost peaceful.

The troopers departed and Hansbro rode to Will and gazed down at Will's dark stare. Something in Will's black silence goaded Hansbro's temper.

"There's a mule for each of you to ride away!" Hansbro snapped. "If you're caught in these parts again, you'll get worse!" He wheeled the foam-spattered sorrel away, calling to his men, "Let's go!"

Fitz slacked the rope and Will stepped out of the loop and watched the Barb men leave—fine horses—efficient men—the full ruthlessness of Alec Waggoman's great Barb holdings. Another wagon crashed down in a geyser of sparks and smoke. One of Will's men began to curse thickly.

Good mules, Will thought helplessly. And then, *So this is Barb?* And a revealing thought struck him. Young Dave Waggoman might have settled reasonably. But Hansbro had crowded Dave. Hansbro was the man, not Dave Waggoman. Will turned as another of his men queried, "Now what?"

"There's a mule left for each of you," Will told them. "Pack out anything you can take."

From a leather money belt, damp with perspiration, he counted their wages. They took the eagles, double eagles, and damp greenbacks as he'd known they would, being hired drivers without stake in his fortunes.

Four of them rode south without looking back. Charley Yuill stayed, hunkered impassively beside his bedroll. When he and Will were alone, Charley's question was musing. "Well, Cap'n?"

Will's boring look considered the man.

"I hired you in Silver City four months ago," Will said evenly. "Never saw you before. Why call me 'Captain,' now?"

Charley reached down and scratched a bare, dirty ankle. He looked dominantly Indian now, impassive, deliberate.

"I was scout last winter at Fort Kilham when the supply train was ambushed in Dutch Canyon," said Charley, unblinking, almost dreamily. "I went out with the relief. The Apach' had used new repeating rifles. One dead officer I remembered. He'd had orders to report to Kilham, they said. The train had been goin' his way. Hadn't had his commission long. He'd bellied behind a dead hoss. The empty shells showed he'd earned his rank right there."

Charley picked up a pebble and cocked a pensive look at Will. "A bra laddie, that young Lieut'n't Lockhart."

After a moment Will asked levelly, "What's on your mind?"

Charley murmured, "I hit Silver City an' needed a job; you had one." Charley jiggled the pebble slowly. "Four months we been jackleggin' around the edges of the Apach' country. You turned down two freight contracts I know of that'd've took you the other way. At Kilham, someone said the young lieut'n't had a brother at one of the upper Missouri River forts—a cap'n Lockhart." Charley sighed softly. "Ain't anyone curious where the Apach' gets those fine new repeatin' rifles an' plenty shells?"

After a moment Will's gesture was resigned. "You bobtailed nosey Scotsman. You red-whiskered fake."

"Ain't I now?" assented Charley placidly. He scratched his red whisker stubble and grinned.

Will hunkered at the other end of the bedroll, looking almost Indian himself, withdrawn and expressionless. His slow words were bitter.

"The man who sold the guns to the Apaches really killed him, Charley. Killed other good men, too. And butchered more than a few women and young ones."

Charley brooded over the pebble in his motionless fingers. "Do they come back to him nights, Cap'n—specially the mothers an' cryin' kids—askin' him if the money was worth it?"

After a long moment Will said softly, "Charley, I'll ask him."

Charley turned his head. His eyes were luminous, questioning. Will returned the look, searching now for what lay deep in Charley Yuill. He made a decision, and in the way of a man who boldly backed his own judgments, spoke frankly.

"Two hundred rifles and ten thousand rounds of forty-four caliber ammunition were shipped from New York to New Orleans by steamer, Charley. The man who took delivery in New Orleans hadn't a gun or shell for sale when asked."

"Long way off—New Orleans," Charley commented mildly. He swiped at a drift of smoke in front of his eyes.

"A longer way to the gun factory," said Will slowly. "But the guns get out here. That seemed the best way, Charley—start looking at the factory. Took friends, letter writing, help. And finally a clerk in that New Orleans business told a friendly stranger who bought him drinks after work, that the boss had a cousin living in the West. Letters came now and then—from a town named Coronado. From a man named Darrah. A letter with that information reached me at Colfax."

Charley asked quickly, "Did we haul—"

"No," Will denied. "No guns in that freight we hauled from Colfax to Darrah's store. But if those rifles are heading this way, they'll be along any time now. Any day."

"Two hundred new rifles. Ten thousan' shells," said Charley softly. "A lot of killin' there, Cap'n, in the wrong hands." Charley shook his head. "That Frank Darrah in Coronado didn't seem like a man who'd do it. He's well thought of."

"Could be a mistake," admitted Will readily. "But if Darrah's the guilty man, he'll have a greedy streak down deep. It will be a weakness to trip him."

"He'd need help to trade with the Apach'," Charley muttered. "And if he guesses what you're up to—" Charley pulled a suggestive finger across his throat.

Will grinned faintly.

"Might happen, Charley. I've stayed away from the army in these parts until today. Now I find that Lieutenant Evans has heard my name somewhere, or seen me. He's trying to place me. If he does, he'll talk."

"Go to the colonel at Roxton an' have Evans shut up," Charley suggested.

"I'm on leave, acting unofficially," said Will dryly. "I doubt if the colonel would approve what I'm doing in his district. Want to scout toward the reservation for me?"

Charley's slow grin was finally satisfied. "Sure thing, Cap'n. What'll you do?"

Will explained. "Hauling salt was an excuse to stay near Coronado and Frank Darrah. I'll ride back to Coronado."

"Barb men won't like it," Charley reminded. "Hansbro warned you."

Will shrugged and stood up. "Darrah's the danger. If that New Orleans shipment comes to him, he'll have to make a move." Will rubbed a palm over his jaw bristle. "I'd feel better knowing what Darrah's been doing these last few days."

Frank Darrah, in Coronado, was measuring bolt cloth against a yardstick tacked to the counter edge, and relishing even this small sale of six yards of blue dotted swiss to Mrs. George Freall. The swiss had moved slowly. A commotion in the street drew Frank's glance through the front store window at his left, and he frowned.

Kate Canaday, who owned Half-Moon Ranch, was arriving in town as usual, her team in a fast run and her old topless buggy flanked by a swirl of tongue-lolling hounds. Frank always bristled instinctively at the sheer gusty impact of the woman.

The buggy made a dust-roiling stop outside the store. A rifle scabbard was strapped to the whip socket, a canteen was lashed to one side of the seat, a rolled yellow slicker tied on the other side. Kate Canaday left a man's gray hat on the seat and her agilely descending bulk tilted the buggy step down.

Margaret Freall, a thin woman of sallow elegance, tightened lips as Kate Canaday stamped into the store and came to them, asking gustily, "H'lo, Maggie. How's George?"

"Quite well, thank you, Katherine."

Kate Canaday's broad weathered face had a rough, lumpy, amiable look under an iron-gray, wind-blown pompadour. She wore a man's red wool shirt and brown skirt, and her expression became grimly humorous as she regarded Margaret Freall.

"Maggie, you look liverish. Whyn't you hole up on Half-Moon with me fer a spell? A lion hunt up to timber line'd work that liver-look offa your face!"

Margaret Freall's smile was pained. "I don't hunt, thank you, Katherine."

Kate's gusty chortle was full-hearted and knowing.

"You don't hunt, Mag? Why, you never missed a heel-smell trackin' down George Freall. I bet Jubal Kirby a box of Manila cheroots George'd get away, an' did I get skunked! Mag, you treed Georgie like a red-bone houn', an' dragged him down an' made him like it. Ain't a sister this sida Santa Fe coulda done so well."

Frank Darrah broke the package string with a jerk. *Worse than a bunkhouse roughneck,* he thought irritably. *Enough to drive trade away.*

Margaret Freall hurriedly picked up her package, and her strained smile and pallid flush departed hastily. Kate Canaday's knowing grin followed her out the door.

"Nothin' wrong with Maggie Freall a whisky quart wouldn't cure," Kate said amiably. She pulled a folded paper from a pocket of the red wool shirt. "Here's a list of stuff the wagon'll pick up tomorrow. That Lockhart feller come in yet with his salt?"

Frank left the penciled list untouched on the counter. "I have my doubts he will, Miss Canaday." A swift question on Kate's weathered face convinced Frank, *She still hasn't heard.* Casually he said, "You know, I suppose, that Alec Waggoman has leased that land. Some of the Barb men rode to the salt lakes today." Then pleasurably Frank watched a strained and bitter calm set on the woman's broad, lumpy face.

"So Alec skunked me on that Gallegos land!" Kate muttered. "An' me like an ol' fool figgering it didn't matter whether I seen José Gallegos a few days early or late about renewing the lease. The old weasel never peeped he was dickerin' with Barb."

Frank waited with pleasant patience. He'd never seen the big, booming woman quite like this, stricken and subdued.

Kate was muttering to herself. "Alec knowed he

was gettin' my best winter grass. Twenty-eight year battlin' that old pirate. Shoulda lined him in a rifle sight long ago!"

Kate hauled at a buckskin thong looped around her neck, dragging out a fat silver watch. "Late," she said absently, and dropped the watch back inside the shirt. Then Kate shrugged, drew a deep breath, and said loudly, briskly, "Well, git that stuff together for the wagon tomorrow."

Frank reminded, "Your bill is rather large now."

"What if 'tis?"

"I'm afraid I'll need something on account."

"So now I got you to worry with, too, Darrah?"

"Business, Miss Canaday, is business."

"Business, young feller, is a pain in the gizzard! You git that order up! I got the eatin'ist cowhands this side El Paso!" Kate stalked out wrathfully.

Across the store, McGuire was making a show of straightening canned goods on a shelf, all ears, of course. Frank listened to Kate Canaday's loud voice outside ordering the dogs quiet. Through the window he watched her stand indecisively, then cross the street with long mannish strides. An irritable suspicion grew in Frank that he was going to fill her supply list on credit. Big Kate Canaday knew too many people in the Territory. Too many liked her. And she was too friendly with Barbara Kirby.

He was glowering at McGuire's suspiciously uninterested back when the sound of horses in the street drew his glance outside again. In a kind of fascination, Frank watched Alec Waggoman and three Barb hands pass the store. That powerfully built man with white handlebar mustaches, bold nose, and craggy face, always gave Frank a feeling of insufficiency.

Alec Waggoman rode the muscular steel-gray gelding like a border chieftain of old, a man so accustomed to power he no longer bothered to be conscious of the fact. Waggoman waved the cowhands on, and reined to the bank hitchrack and leisurely dismounted. The bank door was closed, its green shade drawn inside, but Waggoman's heavy, leisurely steps crossed the boardwalk and his fist hammered on the door.

The green shade presently was lifted a little at one side. Then the door was unlocked. Alec Waggoman stepped confidently in and the door closed again.

Frank stood some moments behind the counter in deep thought, then walked back to the glassed-in office at the rear. From a pigeonhole of the roll-top desk he took a brown envelope and intently went over the papers inside.

Satisfied, Frank thrust the envelope in his coat and caught his narrow-brimmed gray hat off the rack by the door. He paused a moment at the small mirror there, adjusting the hat carefully and centering his black cravat. His expression had a renewed complacence as he left the office and called to McGuire, "I'm going out."

He crossed the street and rapped on the bank door.

Chapter Four

Frank Darrah had to knock twice on the bank's front door before George Freall peered again past the edge of the green shade, then opened the door as he had for Alec Waggoman a short while before.

Smiling and confident, Frank said, "Is Alec Waggoman too busy to talk a few minutes? Save me a trip out to Barb if he can."

Freall's, "Come in, Frank. Alec and me were just yarning," was pleasant.

Back of the bank counter and high, ornate grill, George Freall's office was small and plain, like Freall himself—a pine desk, two wooden chairs, hatstand, bookcase, and a black-framed engraving above the desk.

Alec Waggoman, munching a half-smoked cigar gone dead, was lounging comfortably back in Freall's own swivel chair. *Like he owns the place*, Frank thought; and entirely fitting, too, seeing who Alec Waggoman was.

George Freall said tactfully, "Frank's got some business with you, Alec. I'll step out a few minutes."

"Stay," Alec Waggoman said briefly. He surveyed Frank noncommittally from eyes that had an opaque look under heavy white brows. Frank had a renewed, baffled feeling about the man. Waggoman's eyes were curtained eyes, revealing nothing, asking nothing. The man's "Well, Darrah?" past the cigar was dry and neutral and not greatly interested.

"This won't take long," Frank promised, smiling, as he dropped on the scuffed pine chair beside the desk. He had a thought which had come to him before: behind those sweeping white mustaches, Alec Waggoman had the face of a stone man.

It was a chiseled sort of a face, a carved, eroded kind of face, chipped here, dented there, the whole of it powerful, commanding, almost majestic. And today an odd, vague shadow of sadness seemed to lie on the craggy face. Frank's wry smile almost followed the thought. Alec Waggoman sad? This man who'd achieved everything worth while in life—land, money, power?

Thought of what this one old man had accumulated held Frank Darrah for an instant of unrestrained envy and admiration. Then with smiling confidence he spoke of his business.

"I've filled a few quartermaster contracts: lumber, corn, oats, and so on to the various forts, when I could locate supplies and bid low enough. You may have heard so."

Waggoman said briefly, "Yes."

Frank was opening the brown envelope. Each detail of this interview had been carefully thought over. "I might do a fair business in salt—if I can lease the one good salt source in this part of the Territory."

Alec Waggoman's craggy face did not change expression. But past the cigar he rolled to the corner of his mouth, Waggoman drawled, "How'd you know I had salt to lease?"

Frank hesitated, then admitted, "I tried to lease from old José Gallegos. He said to speak to you after the first of this week."

"You tried to lease out from under Kate Canaday?"

Frank held his smile. "I merely tried to lease. Gallegos owns the land."

"You tell anyone I got the lease from Gallegos?"

Damn the man, Frank thought uncomfortably. No telling what he knew. Man felt like flushing guiltily. The truth was obviously necessary.

"Only Miss Kirby, in confidence, sir."

"You courtin' Barbara?" Behind the sweeping white mustaches, the craggy face still lacked expression.

Frank had the feeling he was close to perspiring. *Damn the man.* Alec Waggoman's dislike of Barbara's father Jubal Kirby, was known. What Alec Waggoman thought of Barbara herself was not known, uncle though he was to Barbara. The wrong answer now might draw Waggoman's displeasure.

George Freall's amused chuckle in the doorway was no help. "If Frank ain't sparkin' Barbara, then every lady in town has guessed wrong, includin' my wife."

Frank admitted then, smiling, "Barbara is very attractive."

Alec Waggoman slowly took the cigar from his mouth and asked noncommittally, "What's your proposition about salt?"

"This contract seems fair to me," Frank said, opening the document.

Alec Waggoman waved the paper away. "Just tell me."

"Perhaps I'd better read it."

Waggoman nodded, settled himself more comfortably in the chair, and listened silently while

Frank read down the paper. When he finished and looked up, Waggoman's half-closed eyes gave the look of out-ranging thoughts. Finally Waggoman turned the swivel chair to George Freall's desk and picked up a black wooden penholder.

"I'll sign," he said shortly, and reached to the small glass inkwell as Frank rose hastily and moved to his elbow with the contract.

The pen point slid off the right side of the rounded inkwell. Waggoman stabbed again, and the pen point struck to the left of the small opening with its dull collar of dried ink.

For an instant Frank was bewildered. Then the amazing truth crashed at him. *The man can't see! He must be almost blind!*

The improbable idea was staggering. In a kind of breathless, chilled fascination, Frank watched Alec Waggoman's other gnarled hand reach deliberately for the small inkwell and bring it forward with a grip so crushing the knuckles stood out pallidly.

"Put your finger where I sign." The tone was controlled, grating only slightly.

Mechanically Frank complied. He tried to keep his finger from trembling as it touched the document. *No one knows this! It's never been mentioned.* And it certainly would have been talked about. Loss of Alec Waggoman's keen sight would be important news through all the Territory.

Frank realized he was blocking George Freall's gaze from the doorway. *Does Freall know?* Frank swallowed. His throat had dried, tightened. In all probability, he decided, not even George Freall suspected.

Alec Waggoman was a canny man. Lack of sight was a devastating affliction for him. The day word flashed out that Alec Waggoman—the great Alec Waggoman—was half-blind, that day three long, ruthless decades of old scores would stir and take life.

They'd be after Alec Waggoman quickly. After Barb. They'd move in like pack wolves racing to hamstring a great lamed buck. In his day, building, expanding, holding Barb, Alec Waggoman had been completely ruthless. He'd get no better once he was considered helpless.

The pen made a dull clattering sound as Waggoman threw it down. His tone held an even harshness now.

"Darrah, you'll make money out of that salt. I've been watching you. Now take an older man's advice. Salt's one thing even a cow an' a damn' sheep have to have. Don't get too greedy."

Frank was folding the signed lease. "I'll remember, sir." He wondered if the slight tremor in his voice was noticeable.

Waggoman had leaned back in the creaking swing chair, his opaque gaze hooded, brooding. And now Frank understood the odd, curtained look, the shadowy cast of sadness. Carefully he said, "Thank you, sir. It should be profitable for both of us."

He wondered if he didn't hear a faint irony in Waggoman's, "Let's hope so," and didn't really care. He had Waggoman's signature. He had knowledge now about Waggoman's sight.

Undoubtedly, Frank guessed as he emerged from the bank, he'd left too hastily. But his pulses were rioting; he had to get off alone with this bursting torrent of thoughts.

They were overwhelming; they pushed and

prodded. *Something will happen now.* The logic was inescapable. Couldn't be long now until Dave Waggoman had Barb. All of Barb. And Dave's uncontrolled temper might get Dave killed at any time. Then Barbara would inherit.

The thought held a dangling, glittering promise. Alec Waggoman's great Barb Ranch to Barbara Kirby! Complete fruit of a strong man's ruthless, industrious lifetime thrown as a fabulous gift to small Barbara Kirby. And, of course, to the man who was married to Barbara—who loved Barbara—and that had been so easy. Barbara might have been ugly, awkward, repulsive. Looking at it now, Frank could detect something like destiny which had carried him to this ratty frontier town, put his interest on Barbara Kirby, led him to the bank just now.

Frank realized he'd crossed the wide street without noticing. He paused on the boardwalk under the overhead sun roof, and tried to force some measure of calmness to his racing thoughts. Then with deliberate stolidness he walked to his store, went back to the tall iron safe in his office, and put the brown envelope and signed contract behind the safety of metal.

He started to sit at the desk and was too restless. He was pacing slowly back and forth when the measured trampling of passing horses sent him to the office door. "Who's passing?" he called to McGuire.

"Some Barb men," the clerk said carelessly.

"Dave Waggoman?"

"Yes."

Frank Darrah was conscious of a quick and secret regret. The tall, smiling wagon freighter named Lockhart had seemed capable of violence if crowded. And Barb always crowded. Tempers might have flared dangerously today at the salt lakes. Dave Waggoman had been keyed to it when he walked out of this office yesterday at dusk.

Now Frank Darrah stood indecisively, and finally started out again, telling McGuire curtly, "I'll be at McGrath's."

In this last hour of glassy light, saddle horses lined the long tie rail of McGrath's Bar. The Barb horses were there, frosted with dust and lather. Inside the slatted swing doors, Frank found the usual late afternoon din of talk and yeasty haze of tobacco smoke laced with the richer mixed odors of whisky, beer, leather, and sweat.

This spacious log-walled saloon was a rendezvous for a hundred miles in any direction. One met here cowmen and merchants and traders, lawmen, prospectors, drummers, troopers, and politicians. Sooner or later everyone moving about the Territory stopped at McGrath's. Frank Darrah had used the place to his profit, never drinking much and always listening carefully.

He found Dave Waggoman breasting the bar halfway back. Vic Hansbro loomed at Dave's right shoulder, a huge and powerful figure, bearded and silent. There was open space at Dave's left elbow and Frank stopped there. His drinking preference was known. A hustling, white-aproned bartender slapped a bourbon bottle, glass, and water before him without asking. Dave, moodily turning an empty whisky glass in lax fingers, glanced indifferently at him.

"They were there—four wagons," Dave said shortly.

Frank asked carefully, "Any trouble?"

An aggressive arrogance hardened Dave's tone.

"We burned his damn' wagons. Shot his damn' mules. Told him to keep going."

The complete ruthlessness of it held Frank silent. "Lockhart," he ventured finally, "won't trouble you again."

He was conscious of Dave's fine serge pants and expensive boots, the bright silver on Dave's holster gun and the massive silver buckle of Dave's shell belt. Always Dave wore expensive clothes with a swagger, as if taking carelessly for granted all the wealth and power of Barb. That was the way it should be, Frank reflected. Who owned Barb had everything. The thought was heady.

Cautiously Frank said, "I've been talking with your father. He seems in fine health."

"Why shouldn't he be?" Dave was indifferent.

Vic Hansbro turned his head, staring across Dave, as if only now aware of Frank Darrah. Hansbro's question came casually out of the dark, chopped-off beard. "You interested in Alec's health?"

A quick caution touched Frank. He met Hansbro's stare, wondering if the man had some covert knowledge of Alec Waggoman's sight. Smiling, he said, "Always interested in the health of friends." The vague bristle of warning persisted, and Frank brought into sharp focus all he'd ever heard about Hansbro.

Moodily Dave reached for his bottle, and Hansbro spoke under his breath warningly, "Slow there."

"Tend to your own drinking," Dave retorted sulkily.

"Alec's in town." Hansbro had gone quietly persuasive. "We oughta take on some grub. He'll want us to ride back with him."

Indecisively Dave eyed the bottle, and said irritably, "I'll have this one first." He did so, and tossed a gold eagle on the bar, scooped up his change, and said irritably, "Well, let's eat."

As the two men walked out, Frank considered an astonishing fact: *Dave didn't want to— Hansbro made him—*

He paid and moved toward the door, pondering this new, important knowledge, and an unexpected handclap on the back almost drove an annoyed oath from him.

"My boy, 'tis a miracle, no less!"

Frank thought dismally, *How much will this cost me?* His smile was an effort as he turned. "Hello, Jubal."

Barbara's father had a bush of rumpled hair— Irish-black hair—and a clean-shaven look of raffish, ingenious charm. Jubal was chewing a clove; his hand had dropped to Frank's arm with a proprietary grip. Knowing grins along the bar made Frank's smile more strained.

Jubal Kirby always reduced Frank Darrah to a smolder. The man was worthless, unreliable, good-for-nothing. Yet everyone liked Jubal. His raffish twinkle usually started other men smiling. The completely flamboyant and airy lack of responsibility in the man became, against all reason, a kind of virtue. Jubal's humor and anecdotes were inexhaustible. He'd been the gayest of blades, prodigal with money. Now he had no money—and Jubal seemed to enjoy life even more.

Smoldering now, Frank thought, *No wonder Alec Waggoman hasn't any use for him.* And because of Barbara, Frank knew he must stand smiling, ignoring the grins at the bar.

He said significantly, "Barbara's back. She came by way of the salt lakes. Fortunately nothing happened to her."

Slowly Jubal put another clove between his lips. A vague unease seemed to touch him briefly. "Barbara see any trouble at the lakes?"

"She didn't speak of it."

Jubal's lingering gaze became blandly innocent. At times Jubal seemed to have an oddly smiling, Buddhalike understanding which made Frank vaguely uncomfortable. He had the feeling now. Holding the false smile was an increasing effort.

"I'm needed back at the store," Frank said bluntly.

Jubal moved with him, holding Frank's arm in the irritating, proprietary way. All Jubal's smiling and raffish geniality had returned.

"As I said, my boy, miracles are with us. Would you believe when I stepped away from the table back there, a trifle short of cash at the moment, I held jacks-up and three in the hole?"

Frank muttered, "Hardly a miracle."

Jubal chortled. "The miracle, my boy, was in seeing you at that exact, heart-rending moment. There you stood, a fine handsome young man of tact and generous understanding—"

Frank wanted to swear and pull away. He muttered instead, helplessly, "How much, Jubal?" And he almost groaned at the amused, assured calculation Jubal turned on him.

Moments later, outside on the boardwalk, Frank did curse softly, helplessly. His hand touched, almost unbelievingly, the new leanness of the leather wallet inside his coat. His thought was spiteful. *If he weren't Barbara's father—*

Then, with dismal acceptance, Frank decided

once again that this sort of thing was business. Money lent Jubal was a business loss against the time Frank Darrah was married to Barbara, and Jubal no longer needed to be cultivated. *Then*—

Frank was relishing the thought as he stalked across the street intersection. And then Frank stopped in the street dust, staring ahead with startled surprise.

Kate Canaday had backed her old buggy away from the hitchrack at Darrah's store. She'd halted there, and from the buggy seat was talking with a big, sun-blackened man on a bareback mule.

Frank moved slowly forward to the boardwalk. Lockhart's wagons had been burned. His mules had been shot. He'd been warned out of the Coronado country by Dave Waggoman and Vic Hansbro. Yet, there was Lockhart now, dropping off his mule as Frank watched, and crossing the street toward a group of men loitering on the boardwalk in front of Kitty's Home Café.

Dave Waggoman and Hansbro were in the group, their backs to the street.

Frank opened his mouth to warn Dave. Then he remembered Dave's wild temper—Dave's present surly mood—

In complete and silent fascination, tense with sudden hope, Frank Darrah stood there on the street corner and watched Lockhart's advance toward Dave and Vic Hansbro.

Chapter Five

Will Lockhart had been listening to the big woman with the lumpy, weathered face say bitterly, "Friend, I got skunked worse'n you!" And his roving glance had halted across the street on two men emerging from Kitty's Café, joining a group of ranchmen and townsmen there on the boardwalk.

A deep wrath had flared in Will's stare. Kate Canaday had seen the fury take hold of this unshaven stranger in salt-stiffened overall pants and faded gray shirt. He'd been talking quietly, reflectively; now, with abrupt but odd courtesy for a mule skinner, he said, "Pardon, madam," and dropped lightly off the bareback mule.

Kate had turned hastily on the buggy seat and looked across the street. Her involuntary "Slow down, friend!" had burst out as Lockhart rounded the back of the buggy.

Lockhart kept going.

Kate muttered, "The blamed mule-head ain't even got a gun!"

She sat hatless and indecisive on the open buggy seat. Then, grimly, resignedly, Kate caught up the reins and hauled the team into a turn. Her work-roughened hand reached for the carbine in the scuffed leather scabbard lashed beside the whip socket.

Will Lockhart was aware he was being hasty and reckless. But the slaughtered mules by the glaring shore salt of the lagoons were too vivid in memory.

His hair and clothes still reeked of the burning wagons. Ashes of the dead cook fire he'd been dragged through at a rope end were ground into his clothes as a reminder. Barb had done all that.

But Hansbro, the Barb foreman, had really decided it. And a cooler calculation backed Will's anger. He'd be run off the Coronado range now, he suspected, if Hansbro's virulence was allowed to dominate. And he had to stay, watching for those cases of fine new rifles from New Orleans.

Hansbro's gun sagged carelessly in its holster. The man would use it, and have help, too, from Dave Waggoman and other Barb men. Will made a calculated gamble that even Barb might hesitate to kill an unarmed stranger openly here in town. A bearded man looked inquiringly as Will stepped up on the boardwalk. A second man glanced idly as Will said, "Hansbro—"

The Barb foreman turned. His look narrowed in recognition. His rough "I told you—" got that far when Will hit him.

Hansbro could never have been struck so brutally. He'd tried to dodge, and the blow smashed the bearded corner of his mouth. The sound was meaty, squashy. Hansbro's head was driven far over to the opposite shoulder. Incredibly, almost, the immense, muscular bulk of the man staggered back on high boot heels and pitched backward off the boardwalk.

Hansbro's wide shoulders and broad back slammed down hard on the street and skidded in a gray roil of dust. Will went after him as stunned incredulity held every witness. Most of them were unaware the drop-off at the walk edge had partly betrayed Hansbro.

The Barb foreman was tremendously powerful. Even now, wind knocked out and half-stunned, Hansbro groped for the holstered gun. Will kicked mercilessly at the wrist. His instep and bootheel smashed into the back of Hansbro's large hand, and Will callously drove the foot down hard, grinding the sharp heel.

Hansbro screamed as flesh and bone were savaged between hard leather and sun-baked earth. He tore the hand away, losing skin and releasing the drawn gun.

Hansbro rolled violently as Will kicked the heavy revolver far out in the street. This was something Hansbro could understand. This sort of cruelty was Barb's own language, and the town could read it, too.

Hansbro slapped palms on the earth and thrust upright, scrambling to his feet, reeling away. He shook the right hand and red droplets flew off the mauled flesh. Hansbro was fouled with street dirt and had lost his hat. His dark hair and chopped-off beard had taken on a wild, bristly look.

Will glimpsed Dave Waggoman stepping off the boardwalk, hand on his gun. Then a rifle laid its flat slapping report on the scene. The bullet spattered dirt near Dave's feet and Dave leaped back. Kate Canaday's gusty voice boomed genially, "You think I can't chip off a toe, Davey boy, try again! Let 'em alone!"

Kate stood in the open buggy, her iron-gray pompadour wind-blown above the broad face, the carbine held carelessly ready. She looked big and bellicose now.

Fleeting humor touched Will's mouth. The big blunt-spoken woman was like bugles arriving as a

skirmish grew sticky. With better spirit Will ran at
Vic Hansbro's bristling frenzy and dodged Hansbro's wild blow. The huge bleeding knuckles skidded over Will's left ear. Even that close miss caused
a numb feeling, as if the ear had almost been torn
away.

Close to the man now, Will struck right fist, left
fist into Hansbro's middle. It was like battering a
wall. Hansbro grunted explosively, grabbed him,
and started a knee kick, and Will stamped viciously on the man's instep.

The new agony made Hansbro gasp. Will
shoved fists together and drove them together into
Hansbro's belly. He leaned against Hansbro's
great pumping chest and took a frenzied clouting
of Hansbro's hamlike fists on head, neck, shoulders. Arching his back, Will brought up both fists,
up fast in a sledging strike into Hansbro's beard
and throat and underjaw.

He never guessed it, Will thought unbelievingly.
All his cording wrath had backed that sledging
strike into Hansbro's throat. It flung Hansbro tot-
tering again, gasping, strangling.

Will was sweating. His chest sucked great
breaths as he stalked the man with malignant calculation, knowing now that Hansbro thought
slowly. But the man was durable and dangerous.
Certainly Hansbro was merciless. With a kind of
chill satisfaction, Will gauged him fully. Give
Hansbro an exact order and he'd do well enough.
But hide the plan, move fast, strike fast, unexpectedly, and Hansbro erupted in sheer fury of mass
and muscle.

Now, gagging from the throat blow, Hansbro
plunged forward in a kind of berserk frenzy. Will

dodged fast and struck the bearded cheekbone. Hansbro's wide-swinging fist slammed Will's chest with paralyzing shock. The fast-pounding heart inside seemed to flutter and stop. The sensation was dismaying.

Will staggered back, and somehow kept going back on his feet, back into the middle of the wide street. He saw Hansbro's bearded mouth, bloody and frenzied, open in a kind of confident snarl. Hansbro ducked his head and rushed to finish it.

The paralyzed feeling ebbed with agonizing slowness. Rubbery weakness loosened Will's knees. He let the knees buckle and saw Hansbro's exultation blaze as Hansbro swung a tremendous, looping blow—

Will's wobbly crouch barely slid aside. Then, desperately, he came up, striking up more desperately, and Vic Hansbro's bearded jaw ran squarely into the blow. The impact shuddered back through Will, and Hansbro's bulk veered away from the blow, dropping forward in a heavy, clumsy-looking dive. The man's big hands and arms were not breaking the fall.

Will dropped his hands and watched in fascination. The bearded face struck first. Hansbro's huge body drove the face plowing through the street dirt, and then Hansbro lay there, sacklike, unmoving.

Wet with sweat, panting heavily, Will stepped close, noticing now the crowd gathering from both sides of the street. He bent and hauled the limp figure over and silently looked down at it. The face was a caricature of Vic Hansbro. Mouth, nose, and forehead were cut and abraded. Red droplets oozed through dark beard hairs matted with dirt.

Will felt no pleasure. Wrath had burned away in

the fight's fury. A beating, he knew soberly now, could not right what Hansbro had done. And Hansbro would remain the same man. *Had to do it*, Will argued to himself.

Hansbro would probably try to kill him for this. But, Will guessed, even a killing wouldn't exorcise Hansbro's lasting humiliation at being mauled and beaten barehanded while much of Coronado watched. In this glassy hour of early twilight, here on Palace Street, in Coronado, the myth of Vic Hansbro had suffered irreparably.

What it would do to Vic Hansbro inside was anyone's guess.

Will glanced around as Kate Canaday's amiable jeer reached along the street from the buggy where Kate stood holding the rifle.

"How's that, Alec, for lettin' gas outa a big, whiskered balloon? Shoulda been you, ye horn-faced old connivin' bull!"

Chapter Six

Kate Canaday had said, "Alec!" *Alec Waggoman?*

Will's narrowing gaze went to the broad-shouldered man with impressive white mustaches who was stepping off the boardwalk past Dave Waggoman.

This, then, was the rather fabulous Alec Waggoman—this big man who ignored Kate Canaday and walked leisurely, solidly out into the street. Spectators had quieted. The same tight interest caught Will Lockhart as he studied Alec Waggoman's uneven and powerful and bold-nosed face. *A man*, was Will's instinctive thought.

The hard, calm look of power was there. And much more, Will saw immediately. All the delegated power of Barb had never given Vic Hansbro's bearded ruthlessness that almost majestic look of shadowed serenity and assurance, that look of strength taken for granted.

Waggoman's gaze touched Will briefly with an odd, peculiar, baffling blankness. Will waited then, watchfully, his sweat-beaded chest sucking great breaths.

Silently Waggoman looked down at Hansbro's mauled face. He turned and considered Will's sweating exhaustion. His question was evenly put. "Why?"

"You're Waggoman, of Barb?"

"I am."

Will said with rough disinterest, "Ask your son. Ask your foreman."

Alec Waggoman said evenly, "I'm asking you."

Will said then, coldly, "For twenty-six mules of mine they had shot at the salt lakes today. For four wagons of mine they had burned. For a rope that dragged me on the ground. Any other questions?"

A flick of emotion touched the rocklike face. Dryness entered Waggoman's comment. "Handled you roughly, I take it. Do I know your name?"

"Do you? I'm Will Lockhart."

"No," Waggoman denied. "Never heard of you." He stood for another silent moment, and again Will had the puzzled feeling this man existed behind the veiled opaque gaze which completely hid the real man.

Calmly Waggoman said, "A mistake has been made. In the morning, tell George Freall at the bank the fair value of your wagons and mules. He'll pay you." Another flicker touched the craggy face. A slight gesture indicated Hansbro. "I see you've already collected interest," Alec Waggoman said dryly.

Will heard it with a kind of disbelief. He saw spectators look startled and unbelieving as Alec Waggoman walked back to Dave Waggoman, who was watching sullenly. Waggoman's brief order to his son was obviously meant to be overheard.

"Get Hansbro and the men back to the ranch without more trouble. Anyone who doesn't make it peacefully is fired."

Waggoman stepped up on the boardwalk, and Will noted how men made way for the tall, white-mustached figure. None attempted to halt Alec Waggoman for talk or argument, and Waggoman ignored them. He had the look of a man who moved alone—a big, isolated figure.

Will walked slowly to the buggy, noting amazement also on Kate Canaday's broad face. Something had just happened, Will guessed, which not even Kate Canaday could understand in Alec Waggoman. He was breathing easier now, and he spoke gratefully to the big woman.

"Ma'am, I thank you."

The buggy creaked as Kate sat down hard on the seat. Under her breath, Kate muttered, "Climb on your mule, young man, an' ride a ways with me. There's talkin' we need to do!"

Frank Darrah had watched the fight from the boardwalk across the street. Its fury had been breathtaking with promise. For tight seconds Lockhart had seemed beaten by Hansbro's sledging fists. Now, in the amazing aftermath, Frank watched Will Lockhart walk unchallenged to the bareback mule, tiredly haul himself up, and accompany Kate Canaday's old buggy and scatter of hound dogs out of town.

Nothing about Lockhart had suggested the merciless reduction of Vic Hansbro. When Lockhart's four wagons had brought freight from Colfax a few days ago, Lockhart had seemed only a quiet, readily smiling stranger. Now Frank remembered the steady gray eyes and to-the-point orders Lockhart had given his drivers. Frowning, Frank speculated on why the man was accompanying Kate Canaday.

The small crowd was dispersing. Dave Waggoman and several Barb men had gathered in the street around Vic Hansbro. Watching them, Frank remembered that Barbara Kirby had brought mail from Roxton Springs. He crossed the street to the post office.

Others had thought of the mail, too. Waiting in a line before the wicket, Frank heard the further astounding news that Alec Waggoman was paying Lockhart for the dead mules and burned wagons.

After a moment, Frank thought he understood. The idea brought a kind of heady elation. Paying Lockhart was clear indication of Alec Waggoman's new helplessness. A legend was toppling. A giant was falling. Else why should Alec Waggoman placate a strange jackleg teamster?

Frank's turn came at the wicket. Aaron Sadler gave him a small bundle of newspapers and letters, and Frank walked out, preoccupied with his thoughts. Vic Hansbro would be in a killing mood now. Dave Waggoman's temper would be smoldering.

The top newspaper Frank idly unfolded as he crossed the street was the Silver City Globe. He read: *Indians Massacre Family on Upper Gila.* Almost violently Frank rammed the newspaper in his side coat pocket.

From the letters, he plucked and expectantly opened an envelope sealed in blue wax and mailed in New Orleans. The first lines of the letter registered as he entered his store. Frank moved mechanically back to the office, reading the letter, and the words seemed to shout derisively at him.

. . . writing you via a St. Louis packet leaving today. A clerk I had not suspected was caught this morning pilfering my office desk. He confessed that a stranger had tempted him with money to scan letters recently arrived from the West. I fear the worst from this inquisitive stranger and hasten to inform you. Perhaps the recent shipment has

reached you in good order as you read this. Or will shortly. . . .

Frank looked up haggardly and found himself in his office, and closed the door quickly. His throat was dry and rough as he read the letter again. And now fear was a pricking chill. The presentiment of disaster was sickening. Frank dropped into the desk chair, tossed the rest of the mail to the desk, and stared sightlessly at it.

Three years ago when he'd first realized the enormous profits in purveying rifles and ammunition to the tribesmen, he'd weighed the risk carefully. Safe enough, he'd decided, for a cool, calculating man who needed money to expand other business interests. He'd made the profits; he'd expanded. Someday, of course, the rifle trade would have to stop. But not quite yet, he'd thought only this morning. Frank's sweating fist crumpled the letter. Then violently he tore the letter into bits.

His fortunes were soaring suddenly to a peak. He'd discovered Alec Waggoman's eye trouble. Barb, incredibly, might come now to Frank Darrah's ownership. And now a treacherous clerk in New Orleans had opened the way for disaster. Frank groaned. Ruin—if gun sales to Indians were ever traced to him— *Damn that clerk*, Frank thought wildly. *Damn him! Who can a man trust?*

The carefully planned, circuitous path of the gun shipments through New Orleans undoubtedly was being puzzled out by someone. And the stranger who'd bribed the clerk in New Orleans might be traveling west now toward Coronado almost as fast as the warning letter had come.

Then Frank sat rigid again, gripping the chair

arms in a new surge of panic. Suppose some other man were already here in the Territory? Possibly here in Coronado today—watching Frank Darrah? Frank stood up and looked wildly around. Then distractedly he began to prowl the office, trying to think. What strangers had been in town lately? Who had seemed to be watching Frank Darrah? Perhaps bribing McGuire— Undoubtedly McGuire was treacherous also. Already McGuire might have gone through papers here in the office. A new thought came to Frank and he halted in mid-stride.

Merchandise from the East arrived steadily at Darrah's store. Whose business was it, really, what Frank Darrah received and held for sale? If he made a mistake and overstocked on rifles and shells, for instance, whose business was it? The past would be hard to trace to him. Only what Frank Darrah did in the future could be dangerous. Frank laughed shakily and sat at the desk again. Now he could think and plan. He sat motionless in deep thought, and finally he began to open the rest of his mail.

One brief letter from Albuquerque Frank studied intently.

> . . . *beg to advise we dispatch tomorrow 11 wagons ass'ted freight to Colfax and Roxton Springs. Freight consigned to you will be unloaded as per yr. usual order at Roxton Springs by Sat. latest, if undelayed. About 2 wagonloads, mostly Eastern freight, in this shipment to you . . .*

Frank moistened dry lips. The shipment of rifles and shells might be on those wagons. But now panic was absent as Frank considered the problem intently, coolly. Finally he stepped to the office door and called curtly, "McGuire! We're closing early! Bring the cash here now!"

Frank closed the door, thinking he'd never again trust McGuire. Or trust anyone. He sat down at the desk again, lighted a cigar, and turned his thoughts with pleasurable anticipation on Barbara Kirby. Barbara had become the complete key to his plans. Frank sat thinking with complacent assurance about Barbara and what must be done quickly now.

Night hung blackly outside the kitchen window as Barbara Kirby dried supper dishes at the zinc-covered sink board. She had eaten alone, pondering news a neighbor had brought at dark. A stranger named Lockhart had beaten Hansbro, the Barb foreman, with bare fists, while Kate Canaday's rifle had held others out of the trouble. The Barb men had burned Lockhart's freight wagons at the salt lagoons and shot his mules. And, most astounding of all, Alec Waggoman had promised to pay Lockhart for the wagons and dead mules.

Thinking of Will Lockhart now, Barbara smiled faintly. At the salt lagoons today, Lockhart's sun-blackened, ironically smiling confidence had had the look of latent violence. Barbara held the towel motionless on the scalded willowware plate as knuckles rapped the front door.

Frank Darrah's "Barbara?" called hopefully.

"Come in, Frank!" Barbara was untying the red-bordered gingham apron when Frank came smiling to the kitchen doorway.

"Wish this were our kitchen," Frank said, watching her.

"Dishes," reminded Barbara dryly, "would still have to be washed."

She was glad now she'd kept on the white cambric suit. Lifting the lamp from the table's red-checked oilcloth, Barbara suggested, "It's cooler on the front porch."

Frank had shaved and changed into his best blue broadcloth suit. He seemed to have a small, secret air of excitement. Barbara put the lamp on the small marble-topped table by the front room window, and when they stepped out on the front porch, Frank guided her down the worn wooden steps to the gravel walk.

After the heat around the kitchen wood range, the night felt cool and fresh. Barbara drew a deep breath, noticing how bright the stars were in the jet sky. Insects chirping in the grass and flower beds made the dark yard restful and intimate. Frank seemed to sense it, too. His arm slipped around her waist. Then, surprisingly, Frank blurted, "Can't we be married right away?"

"For goodness' sakes!" Then Barbara's half-laughing thought came, *What an answer!*

Frank's arm had tightened. He said, "I mean it!" Taking her hands, facing her, Frank asked, "Haven't I waited long enough?"

Barbara almost observed tartly, "Too long." But she said, instead, the thought that was never far from her mind. "Jubal needs me."

"Your father can live with us," Frank said readily.

"He wouldn't."

"Whatever he wants," said Frank largely. "Barbara, I have to go away for a day or so. Can't we settle this before I go?"

Barbara heard herself—and it was like listening to an uncertain stranger talking— "I couldn't possibly in less than two weeks—"

Chapter Seven

The ring Frank slipped on her finger was a perfect fit, and completely unreal. All of this was suddenly, fantastically unreal. Barbara lifted the hand in the starlight. Frank struck a match. The wavering yellow flame glinted coldly back from the large solitaire, and Barbara said impulsively, "Frank, it's beautiful!"

Past the match flame she could see Frank's satisfied smile. With a kind of shock, Barbara realized, *In two weeks—married—*

Frank dropped the match and kissed her again. "Barbara, we'll do everything! Have everything! Nothing can stop us!"

Frank's elation sounded like Jubal Kirby's grandiose plannings of the past. But Frank wasn't like Jubal. Frank was steady. Frank was careful, dependable.

Barbara asked curiously, "Where are you going on your trip?"

Frank said readily, "To Roxton Springs, first. I'm leaving tonight."

"Tonight? Do you have to go tonight?"

Frank laughed easily. "Not the first time I've driven all night on business."

He was like that, Barbara thought; Frank was industrious, ambitious. But—married in two weeks? Two short weeks— In her own small bedroom an hour later, Barbara stood motionless before the oval mirror of her walnut bureau, her thick brown hair brushed loosely over her shoulders. She held her left hand up again, studying the undoubtedly expensive diamond.

Aloud, experimentally, Barbara said, "*Mrs*. Frank Darrah—"

Barbara turned her head as footsteps came on the porch and cautiously entered the house and paused. Jubal Kirby's question in the front room had never sounded airier. "Still awake?"

Tartly Barbara answered, "Don't you wish I weren't?"

Jubal opened her bedroom door and looked in. He was smiling. His black hair was rumpled and inclined to be curly. And as usual, Jubal had the infuriating, ingenious look of a man whose conscience was limpidly clear.

Coldly Barbara reminded, "So you didn't feel well? So I had to make the trip to Roxton."

Jubal stepped in. His unabashed gaze had an unholy gleam of eternal youth. Barbara tried to hold resentment as Jubal surveyed her with smiling pride. She knew what he was thinking. Jubal often said it to her. *Like your mother—sunshine and laughter—too young, too pretty to be my daughter—*

What could you do when your father thought such things? Said such things? When he really believed each word? Almost despairingly at times Barbara knew what you did. Always you dissolved completely, continuing to love the lovable, raffish, and unreliable man fiercely, protectively.

Jubal's always interested and keen glance noted Frank Darrah's diamond on her finger. He paused between the door and small brass bed. His smiling glance asked a silent question.

Barbara told him almost defiantly, "Frank asked

me tonight. We're going to be married in two weeks."

Jubal's smile lasted another moment, then folded in and disintegrated. He sat heavily on the bed and stared wordlessly across the round brass footrail. The spicy odor of cloves, the infuriating yeasty fragrance of McGrath's Bar were on him. But Jubal was entirely sober, and on his face now lay something stricken.

Slowly Jubal inquired, "Love him?"

Some held-in fiend deep in Barbara lashed back in long-suppressed bitterness. "Does it matter? Frank's steady and reliable! He's successful! He's dependable! He's—" Barbara bit off the rush of scalding bitterness and miserably watched Jubal sit there for a long silent moment.

Slowly Jubal stood up and came to Barbara's side and peered into the bureau mirror.

Her mother's mirror, Barbara recalled poignantly. How many times had Jubal stood like this beside her mother, looking at the two of them in the mirror?

Jubal's remark was gentle. "Enough fine qualities to make any girl happy." He sounded absent, and he turned back to the bed and slowly began to empty his pockets.

Barbara's lips parted in amazement as Jubal tossed yellow gold eagles and larger double eagles and green currency on the figured counterpane of the bed. His brown suit had looked rumpled and sagging. Pockets stuffed with money had been the reason.

"A little luck, finally, at McGrath's," said Jubal in the absent tone. His smile returned, strained-looking now as Jubal tossed a final flutter of bills on the pile. "Now you'll have as fine a wedding as any girl ever had," said Jubal quietly. He stepped over and kissed Barbara lightly on the cheek, and murmured, "Happiness, Barbee, all the years ahead."

Her "infant" name did it. Barbara reached quickly, holding to him tightly, fiercely, silently, Jubal's arm went about her understandingly. Neither spoke. They both were smiling when Jubal stepped back and admitted, "I'm sleepy, too."

In the doorway Jubal faced around and inquired casually, "Going to have Kate Canaday at your wedding?"

Barbara said quickly, "Of course. I thought I'd ride out to Half-Moon in the morning and tell Kate."

Jubal looked pleased. "Kate's always been partial to you." He hesitated, and said slowly, "Kate's levelheaded. Her advice would be as good as your mother's."

It was an odd remark from Jubal. Trying to sleep, Barbara guessed that Jubal wanted her to take Kate's advice. But what advice? Kate couldn't help but approve of Frank Darrah. Puzzled lines creased Barbara's forehead in the dark. Almost, it seemed, Jubal thought otherwise about Frank Darrah. But why should he? No one else in Coronado did.

Will Lockhart, the next morning, swung lightly onto a counter stool in Kitty's Café and ordered an immense breakfast—flapjacks, ham and eggs, fried potatoes, hot biscuits, and a great slab of apple pie.

His face was bruised. He ached from yesterday's savage brawl with Vic Hansbro. He felt fine.

Over the pie and coffee came a reflective, amusing thought. This keen, surging anticipation was a hunter's reaction. It always came after a frustrating trail brought the quarry finally in sight. Then all was forgotten but the kill. The exciting kill.

Will had the feeling this morning.

Dark resentments had driven him since the Fort Kilham wagon train had been shot to a shambles in the Dutch Canyon ambush. Now most of the roweling uncertainties had faded. Here in Coronado lurked the shabby truth of how those waves of Apaches had brought fine new repeating rifles against the Kilham wagon train—how the bursting pride, the instinctive valor, and bright eager dreams of young Lieutenant Lockhart could have been blotted out in an unnecessary hour.

Last night Will had scrubbed clean in the back room tub of a barber shop, had a shave, had a haircut. His canvas duffel bag with scanty belongings had been left at the Trail House, Coronado's only hotel, while his wagons went to the salt lakes.

This morning he had pulled on clean denims and blue cotton shirt—clothes which would never pass parade muster under some stuffy colonel's critical stare. Will grinned at the thought.

He finished breakfast leisurely, pondering the reasonable certainty that Frank Darrah was the man he wanted. The talk with Kate Canaday after the fight yesterday had riveted his conviction that Darrah was the man.

But guilt had to be proved. The shipment of new rifles from New Orleans would probably do it. If they came. And if coming at all, that rifle shipment must now be nearing Coronado.

At eight o'clock—bank opening time—Will thrust his cigarette sizzling into the coffee dregs and swung off the stool.

The buxom redhead who was Kitty took his two silver dollars at the cigar case by the door. Her question was amused. "Do you eat this big every morning? Or only after fights?"

Will chuckled. "Only when the cook is as pretty as this cook. And can cook like this cook."

Her ready laughter came back. "For that the house treats."

Will scooped up the cigar she pushed out on the glass. He saluted her with it and walked out smiling. And when he was gone, the lean, listening customer on the front stool spoke with morbid relish.

"He better get serious about that Hansbro. You watch."

Will had somewhat the same thought as he paced the boardwalk to the bank. Even yesterday, as the huge bearded foreman of Barb sprawled inertly in the street dirt, Will had guessed there would be more to it. A thought now made him smile faintly. This trouble with Hansbro and Barb would at least obscure his interest in Frank Darrah and the shipment of rifles.

He found the bank open. Short minutes later he sat in the banker's small plain office and said, "Alec Waggoman said to see you."

George Freall, a pleasant, plain man with thinning brown hair, relaxed back in his swivel chair and nodded. "Four wagons and twenty-six mules, wasn't it?"

"Correct."

"Alec signed a blank check yesterday," said Freall readily. "This morning I stopped at the feed corral and talked prices of wagons and mules. I filled the check in. Suit you?" He reached to the desk and handed Will a check.

"More than I paid," said Will quickly, looking up from the check. "Knock off about three hundred."

Freall refused the check. "Alec will be satisfied." A mildly surprised warmth entered George Freall's closer appraisal of this stranger beside his desk, this tramp wagon freighter, here briefly and then gone on the long rough roads in the way of his kind.

A long, lean-jawed young man of indolent power and smiling reserve was what George Freall saw. The denim pants, blue cotton shirt, and taut-skinned face scoured leathery by weather were marks of a boss teamster. But the calm look of poise and reserves of strength in every clean line were oddly different. A direct and smiling and vastly human understanding filled the steady, gray-eyed scrutiny which rested on Freall himself.

To George Freall came a flash of insight, puzzling in a way. He sensed depths of experience and understanding in this man, forged into the calm of self-awareness. In Lockhart, a warmth, a sincerity, and a spontaneous humor evidently took life without cynicism. Savoring what was good, Freall guessed. Weighing events calmly with that smiling, indolent self-assurance. A man, Freall decided now, who had mastered himself, whose smiling reserves would not be mastered. *Hansbro found it out*, came with a kind of satisfaction to Freall's mind. He felt impelled to speak.

"Some say Alec Waggoman has been a hard man. More often he's been fair. Always kept his word."

Will made no comment.

Freall added musingly, "A man had to be hard in those days."

Will made a dry guess. "You like the man."

Freall said, "I've damned him, too." He studied

Will, a plain banker with shrewd eyes. "You got caught in a leasing mix-up between Barb and Kate Canaday. Where were you meaning to sell salt?"

"Darrah's store."

"Darrah say he'd buy?"

Will nodded, and Freall casually inquired, "When'd Darrah say so?"

So that, Will guessed, *is the fish you're trying to hook? Now why?* He said thoughtfully, watching the banker, "The day before I started to the salt lakes. That's why I rode out to Half-Moon and rented permission to dig salt. I had a buyer. I had work for my men and wagons."

Freall said blandly, "Plain enough." And revealed nothing with the remark. A shrewd man, who deftly changed the subject. "Want cash for your check?"

"Some pocket money. I'll deposit the rest." Will stood up and Freall got to his feet with a narrowing, contemplative question. "You're staying in Coronado?"

"Why not? Barb put me out of business until I get more wagons and mules."

Freall's nod agreed. His remark was sober and unexpectedly personal. "I've studied Vic Hansbro for years. Barb is his life."

"Waggoman," Will murmured, "must be a good man to work for."

"Not Alec—it's the ranch." And to Will's inquiring gaze, Freall explained, "Hansbro was the foreman while Barb grew big. He never could have built Barb himself, and knew it. But as Barb foreman, Vic Hansbro grew important, too. More important than he'll ever be again without Barb. Alec Waggoman can die. Barb goes on."

Irony came into Will's faint smile. But George Freall remained sober. "Alec knows it. I've seen him laugh and ask Vic what he'd do if a new owner fired him."

"And—"

"Vic thought he was smiling back at Alec. But Vic looked like a big dog snarling when his meat was threatened." Freall shook his head over the memory.

Will said bluntly, "You're trying to tell me something."

"You whipped Vic Hansbro. It's never happened before. And it was over Barb business. So you whipped Barb, too, in Vic's mind."

With faint temper Will reminded, "Waggoman ordered no more trouble. Who's running Barb?"

"Sometimes," said Freall slowly, "I wonder. Alec goes away on long trips. More and more Barb is left to Dave and Vic Hansbro. Dave will own Barb someday, of course. But—"

Will prodded, "So Dave Waggoman and Hansbro cut the cookies now? And I'd better pick up my crumbs and move?"

"Suit yourself."

"I'll stay."

Freall shrugged, and Will asked a final, curious question. "Why bother to warn me?"

In that, Freall finally found humor.

"Not every man would knock three hundred off the check." Freall's smile was lean. "A banker gets a liking for a good note or an honest man. Step out to the counter, Mr. Lockhart, and I'll open your account."

Chapter Eight

This shaded east side of Palace Street was still cool when Will left the bank, thinking of Freall's words. So the Barb trouble had not been settled by Waggoman's check. Barb, it seemed, was no longer only Alec Waggoman.

A fabulous character had aged. A giant had wearied of the game. Dave Waggoman and Vic Hansbro were beginning to take over. And in the way of human nature, a little taking-over was always stretched. And stretched. By men like Hansbro. By hotheads like Dave.

Absently Will bit off the end of the redhead's cigar. Young Dave might have compromised reasonably at the salt lakes. But Hansbro's will had dominated.

So there it was—Hansbro could handle young Dave Waggoman. And when Dave finally owned Barb totally, then Hansbro, in a way, would also own Barb by dominating Dave.

Will swiped a match against a wooden awning post and got the cigar going. Barb under Hansbro's fist after Alec Waggoman died—

Wry and ironic, Will's feeling came: *I'd not care to be Alec Waggoman with that at my back! Hansbro counting my time to the grave, Hansbro might get impatient!*

Across the rutted, dusty street, the new sun flooded the high false front and black-lettered sign of Darrah's store:

Frank L. Darrah
Merchant
Supplies   Contracts

And guns, Will added darkly. *Massacres!*

He crossed the street, and inside Darrah's store he paused, scanning this headquarters of Darrah's expanding affairs. From Kate Canaday yesterday, he'd learned more about Darrah. The man sold merchandise throughout this part of the Territory, taking payment often in cattle, sheep, wool, hides, grains, and beans.

All that, Darrah resold at further profit. In four years he had prospered greatly. He bid now on army supply contracts. He formed side partnerships with other men in such ventures as sawmilling, real estate, ranching, cattle, sheep—

And what difference between a quiet venture in sheep—and one in contraband arms? Only in the risk. Only in the enormous profit.

McGuire, the clerk, came forward, a stocky, brisk man wearing brown-cloth sleeve guards. His droll smile was likeable.

"I want a carbine and scabbard," Will told him. "What have you got?"

"Your choice," said McGuire largely, leading the way back and speaking over his shoulder. "Two Winchesters."

"Only two?"

"They're hard to get. Mr. Darrah picks up all he can."

Will tried the guns McGuire put out on the counter. "This one," he decided, tapping the first one.

McGuire was surveying him with smiling admiration. "Sure now," said McGuire's loosening brogue, "'twas a grand soaping you handed out yesterday. Did the old man pay like they say he promised?"

"He did."

When Darrah's freight from Colfax had been unloaded at the platform out back, McGuire had checked the lists, brisk and chuckling. Now, ducking below the counter, McGuire's voice floated up. "The devil's in your hip pocket, or left his luck there." McGuire came up with an armful of leather saddle scabbards and laid them out on the counter.

Will chose one. "And a box of shells." He glanced toward the office at the back. "Darrah here?"

"Ain't an' won't be. He rode to Roxton Springs last night."

"In a hurry, wasn't he? Riding there last night?"

"He was," agreed McGuire cheerfully.

"And what kind of business would push a storekeeper like that?"

McGuire picked up the money Will counted out. His bright black eyes rested on Will. "Mr. Darrah comes an' goes. After the fight yesterday, he read mail from Roxton, an' decided to close early and ride last night."

"How long will he be gone?"

McGuire shrugged. "If you're going to Roxton Springs," said McGuire casually, "you might mention to Mr. Darrah that the Half-Moon wagon came this morning. Loaded everything that was on the list Miss Canaday left, an' another list she sent."

Will gave the man a thoughtful look. Only this moment had he decided to go to Roxton Springs. But McGuire had shrewdly guessed it. Or was McGuire fishing to see if he meant to go?

"What makes you think I'll be in Roxton?"

"First stop away from Barb an' Hansbro," said McGuire with droll impudence.

But after his customer walked out, McGuire took a sheet of folded paper from a shabby billfold on his hip and furtively opened it on the counter. Early closing last night had prevented sweeping and tidying the store. This morning McGuire had been about to burn the contents of the office wastebasket when a single word on a torn scrap of letter paper had caught his eye: *pilfering*—

Only McGuire's secret conscience knew why he had picked out all scraps of the torn-up New Orleans letter, why he had pasted the letter together again on this sheet of paper.

> . . . *a clerk I had not suspected was caught this morning pilfering my office desk.* . . . *stranger had tempted him with money to scan letters recently arrived from the West. I fear the worst.* . . . *Perhaps the recent shipment has reached you in good order as you read this.* . . .

McGuire, an underpaid and overworked clerk who received scant politeness from Darrah, hastily returned the sheet to his wallet as another customer entered the store. McGuire's smile as he walked forward was broader than usual with an inner excitement, with anticipation.

Will Lockhart had walked directly to the Sierra Corrals, off the lower end of Palace Street. There, beside a long adobe barn where the sun-baked wagon yard and pole corrals held a stir of morning activity, he bargained with the owner, a burly man named Roberts, for a horse and saddle.

His selection was a star-faced roan gelding, short-coupled, powerful, with the rough look of mustang infusion. As they walked to the office to complete the sale, Roberts gave grudging admiration.

"Some woulda passed him. Best one I got on hand though." Roberts's speculative glance rested on Will. "In the market for mules now?"

"I'm looking."

"Take looking to find twenty-five or thirty good mules," Roberts stated. "Wagons won't be easy to find quick, either."

"No hurry," Will murmured.

Later Will saddled the gelding himself and rammed the new carbine into the new scabbard forward of the stirrup. The saddle purchased from Roberts had saddlebags. He dropped the box of shells into one bag and was preparing to step on the horse when a stranger with a long, leathery Texan look strolled across the yard.

"Lockhart?"

"Yes."

"I'm Tom Quigby, deputy sheriff."

"Howdy."

"I got in last night," Quigby drawled. "Heard there'd been a little trouble at the salt lakes an' in town here. Any complaints or charges?"

Will shook his head. The deputy's drawl leveled to an even tone. "Mostly I handle the law here. I like it peaceful."

Will glanced about the wagon yard and murmured, "Seems peaceful."

Quigby's "It ain't" lacked annoyance. "A man who tackled Vic Hansbro like I hear you did, knows the score." Quigby's glance rested on the new leather scabbard and carbine. "I know Hansbro.

And you, friend, ain't exactly a shy violet. Next there'll be a killing."

Will glanced down at his lack of cartridge belt and holstered gun. "You ordering a killing? Or warning me?"

He got then a better measure of Quigby. "Hansbro and the Waggomans will hear what you're hearing, Lockhart. Make charges against them now, or forget what happened."

"Waggoman has paid for my wagons and mules. I'm satisfied."

A faint puzzlement entered Quigby's look. "Any idea why Waggoman paid a stranger like you?"

"Never saw the man before. Decided he owed, I suppose."

Quigby considered the idea. His head shook slowly. His smile took a wry twist, not unfriendly. "Well, you've been warned. Leaving town?"

"I'll be back. And I'll not be interested in Barb. Or Hansbro."

"Glad to hear it." Quigby's wry, questioning smile lingered as he offered his hand.

Will met the clasp, liking the deputy. Then, riding to the hotel, Will was satisfied. His interest in Darrah was still unsuspected. Save, perhaps, by McGuire, the clerk. McGuire disturbed Will a little.

In his hotel room, Will took from the canvas duffel bag his rolled shell belt and revolver. He would have preferred leaving the weapon packed away. On his way out, he paid the room rent a week in advance.

After that he rode south on the Roxton Springs road, trying out the new horse. He liked its smooth, powerful lope, easy trot, quick understanding of his wishes. This was another day of open sky and the climbing sun's liquid blaze. Juniper and cedar here in the foothills, shin oak and piñon, gave greenness and dappled shade. Pulling the roan's lope to a walk, Will twisted a cigarette and studied the lay of the country.

East, over his left shoulder, towered the sky-reaching mass of Coronado Peak. Over that way Half-Moon and Barb straddled their runs of clear, cold mountain water, and reached up through the higher foothills to the yellow pines and loftier stands of spruce and Douglas fir.

Barb, the greater ranch, flung its long drift fences far out on the lower, sun-scorched grasslands which gave winter graze. Both ranches, Kate Canaday had said yesterday, had been started about the same time. Half-Moon by Kate's father. Barb by young Alec Waggoman.

In those early years, Waggoman must have been a man, Will mused now—a driving, determined, lusty young giant, fearing nothing, ruthlessy determined to build. A man to admire, even if one had disliked him. That last thought had run grudgingly through all Kate Canaday's remarks about Waggoman. A man to admire in those days.

Will shook the roan into another stiff lope, restless to learn now what had taken Darrah so suddenly through the night to Roxton Springs.

The narrow dusty road curved past the end of a rugged igneous dike. And midway of the open quarter-mile stretch, a woman was riding ahead of him. The next moment Will felt a quick, warm rise of anticipation. Barbara Kirby had not been on his mind. But there she was ahead, alone. The prospect was oddly pleasing.

Chapter Nine

Barbara Kirby recognized him warily as the blowing roan dropped to a walk beside her horse. Her "Good morning" was calm.

"Miss Kirby—" Will said, hat in hand.

Memory had tricked him. She looked less a small girl this morning. But the same small, square shoulders filled her lightweight wool jacket. Today her jaunty little hat of red-brimmed felt was entirely feminine. The coppery highlights he remembered ran liquid in her brown hair as the sun fingered it. And her calmness, he was aware, covered spirit and temper which could flare quickly.

He asked, "Riding to Roxton?"

"Only to Half-Moon," Barbara said.

Will grinned at her. "I *was* a stranger, wasn't I?"

Barbara laughed then and considered him. "And wise this morning to leave like this."

Will let her think it. A small silence held them as the horses paced together. He was glad now of the bath and shave and haircut last night. Barbara's first estimating glance had clearly noted the change in him. Then Will saw the diamond ring on her left hand and the edge of his pleasure dulled.

"I didn't notice your ring yesterday."

Barbara glanced at the hand. "I've only had it since last night. You've met him—Frank Darrah."

Will nodded. Barbara sensed some lack of enthusiasm and her glance rested curiously on him. But her comment when it came changed the subject.

"Did Uncle Alec pay you for your wagons and mules?"

Will said in surprise, "Is Waggoman your uncle?"

"Yes."

"The bank paid me this morning; more than enough."

"He can be like that," Barbara said. "And you're leaving now, so there'll be no more trouble."

"Tell him so," Will suggested. "Tell him I'm satisfied; I want no more trouble with Barb."

"We don't meet often," Barbara said. "If we do, I'll tell him."

That was all; Will touched his hat and put the roan back into the long lope. In his mind was the thought that twice he'd met Barbara Kirby now and this time her own trouble lay ahead. Her soaring hopes of a happy marriage were going to be smashed, if he were right about Darrah. She'd chosen the man freely. The good—the bitter—Will did not look back. He hoped now he would not meet Barbara Kirby again.

At Barb Ranch, in his large, quiet bedroom, Alec Waggoman cut himself while shaving. Razor in hand, he peered across the washbowl into the mirror, where the hazy reflection of craggy face, white mustaches, and foamy lather peered back. The cut was invisible, but a seep of red quickly stained the white lather.

Impassively Waggoman watched the spreading blotch. East windows admitted the bright early sun into the bedroom, yet Waggoman finished shaving and dressing with slow careful movements, as if shadows filled the big room.

The cook had beaten the iron triangle outside the

cookshack before Alec Waggoman emerged from the low, fortresslike stone house into the wide, sunny back yard. In front of him bunkhouse and barn, wagon shed, windmill, and watering-troughs, cookshack, and storage sheds enclosed the hard-packed yard like the uneven stockade of a fort.

It *had* been a fort; it was still a fort in a way, Waggoman thought with a flare of memories which brought his wide shoulders straighter. From a small one-room cabin on this spot, Barb had grown and defied the world.

The low racket of breakfast came out of the cookshack. When Waggoman opened the door and stepped in, momentary quiet fell. Then midway of the long crowded table came Dave's mildly sarcastic query.

"You try to cut your throat this morning?"

Waggoman's chuckle was easy as he took the vacant chair at the head of the table and fingered the cut chin. Over a shoulder he spoke to the cook.

"One egg fried hard, Joie. A piece of ham fried soft. That's all." He could have breakfasted on the gall of helplessness. But a man had to eat.

Vic Hansbro's bearded face was in its accustomed place at the far end of the table. The foreman was eating in dark silence. What Waggoman could see of Hansbro's face had a swollen, abraded look.

The first men finished and got up. Waggoman spoke to them without emotion. "No one goes to town today."

Hansbro's head came up challengingly. His protest sounded thick past puffy lips. "I got business in town."

"Put it off, Vic. Come to the office in half an hour. You too, Dave."

The blur of Hansbro's swollen face glowered indecisively. Then Hansbro's growled "Sure" ended it for the time being.

A little later in the office in the south wing of the big house, Waggoman paced back and forth slowly, remembering Hansbro's near challenge. Increasingly, a subtle arrogance grew in Vic. Almost as if Vic suspected.

From east windows of the office the great forested lift of Coronado Peak cut off the farther world, and compensated with soaring cliffs and high frowning escarpments and the dark folds and bends of the great high valleys. And not a hand's span of it he didn't know, Waggoman thought with an ache.

Peering through a window now with straining intensity, he could see only the peak's dark and massive blur. The shape without the substance.

South through the doorway glass one could see the vast down-roll of foothills to grassy meadows lost in the blue haze of lower distance. The haze now, when Waggoman looked, was not distance. This haze began on the wide porch outside the door glass and swiftly thickened.

The sun-washed and lovely land was still there. Eyes unborn would admire it. But Waggoman knew the bald, bitter truth. For him it had gone, save in memory. He did not bother to glance through the west windows at the ranch yard. Paper work waited on the roll-top desk. Dave should have done most of it. But Dave disliked paper work.

The plain, sunny office with potbellied iron stove, wood box and sandbox in a corner, had benches along one wall. Several wooden chairs sat about. A grizzly skin and gunracks were on the back wall. Shelves held brown paperboard file boxes.

Here men came for orders and favors, came to buy, sell, visit. Men had called this room the Eagle's Nest—and Robber's Roost, and names less complimentary. Waggoman's grave smile came under the white mustaches at the memories. He walked to the roll-top desk at the right of the door and sat down reluctantly. Light flooded the desk from the left and streamed over his right shoulder. But the tally lists he picked up were a blur of figures.

Some days his sight was a little better. But always now the bad days returned and grew worse. Last Monday he'd groped like a blind man. Waggoman put the tally lists down. His corded hands came up slowly and rubbed his eyes. *Blind. Helpless—*

He brought both fists down in a savage helpless strike to the desk that made papers jump. Then he sat staring at the blurred figures.

Matt Seldon, a better doctor than Coronado deserved, had explained it regretfully. *Cataracts.* Eye lenses were clouding, thickening. Like gradually boiling the white of an egg, Seldon had explained. Opaque curtains were closing out the world, relentlessly blotting out light and life and all that made the days keen and clean and worth while.

Eye doctors should be seen, of course—St. Louis, Chicago, Philadelphia, New York, Boston— There was a fine doctor, too, in San Francisco—

He'd gone to them. By saddle, by stagecoach and railroad palace cars he'd journeyed to those distant waiting-rooms. And always when the blurred fierce demand of his look had pinned the fine doctors down, Seldon's verdict was confirmed.

Waggoman drew a long slow breath. At least Matt Seldon could be trusted not to talk. Matt knew what it would mean. Waggoman turned his head as boot heels struck the porch steps outside.

Dave and Vic Hansbro came in together.

"Shut the door," Waggoman ordered briefly. He swung in the creaking swivel chair and regarded them. "We've all slept on it. Now what were you men doing at the salt lakes yesterday?"

Dave said sulkily, "I went after the fellow and caught him stealing salt."

"How'd you know he was there?"

"Frank Darrah mentioned Lockhart had gone to the lakes to load salt."

"Darrah, eh?" Alec Waggoman sat for a moment. "I see. Well, Darrah made a fool out of you."

Dave's angry "I don't see how—" was cut off by a curt "Be quiet! Vic knew better. And if you've got the stuff, Dave, to run Barb some day, you should have known. Now Lockhart gets his money at the bank this morning. That ends it."

Dave flared, "So *you* never cracked down on anyone?"

Alec Waggoman looked at his son in silence. Dave had been a handsome baby, he recalled. Dave was a handsome young man. Strong. Spirited. Much like his mother. And with her temper. They'd been proud of Dave. Looking back now, sadly, Waggoman couldn't recall exactly when he'd started to worry about Dave's wild temper and Dave's headlong insistence on having his own way, regardless.

Not bad, Waggoman sought reassurance in his knowledge of Dave. *Just wild. Never broke to harness.* He tried now, reasonably, mildly.

"Sure, Dave. I cracked down. When a man wanted trouble, he got trouble. When they tried to trick me, I broke 'em. Wasn't much law. It was the only way Barb could have been built and held."

Dave met it with hostility. "Now you're going soft. Buying peace."

Waggoman tried again. "Different times, different ways. Your job will be to run Barb profitably. You'll need peace and friends."

"A cow coddler?" Dave sneered. "Ducking trouble? Afraid to try anything you did?"

Waggoman sat motionless, the helpless feeling coming at him like a tide. *Got to make him see it!* Time was running fast now. Dave wasn't ready.

Slowly, bluntly, he tried.

"You're not the man I was, Dave. Try to copy me and you'll meet a better man. He'll turn your headstrong, stubborn ways against you. He'll break you. You're smart enough. Stop acting like a spoiled brat at times. Now get out and think about it. I want to talk to Vic."

Chapter Ten

Dave slammed the door as he went out. Vic Hansbro stared after him. "Rough on him, weren't you, Alec?"

"Think so?" A chill restraint in the question brought Hansbro's puffy face around uncertainly.

"None of my business," Hansbro muttered. Then Hansbro's bruised mouth opened silently as Alec Waggoman suddenly cursed him.

"You damn'd cold-blooded bully! Long ago you'd have been whittled to size if I hadn't close-herded you! Even thought for you!"

"Alec, I ain't got such talk—"

"Shut up! You could have stopped that trouble yesterday at the salt lakes! That stranger Lockhart didn't beat you half enough! I'd have crippled you!"

Hansbro's thick protest started again and another "Shut up!" silenced him. "Vic, listen carefully! You won't hear this from me again!"

Vic Hansbro blinked uneasily at the tall, rising figure which had given decisive orders as far back as Hansbro cared to remember.

"Better believe this, Vic! Starting now, I'm not keeping an oversize bully-boy to help Dave get into trouble!"

Hansbro's shocked disbelief burst out. "You ain't gonna fire me after all these years?"

"I'd fire you now if I thought it'd help Dave! I'm warning you now! If you're near Dave's next fool move and don't stop him, I'll bust you to a cowhand! If you help him, I'll fire you! Pull your pay and ride if you don't like it!"

"My God, Alec! I ain't quittin'! You know that!"

"I know it. And I know why, Vic. Now get out and think it over."

Hansbro's massive bulk shouldered to the door and stamped out. But he closed the door quietly. Waggoman marked it. Hard-faced, unreconciled, he turned back to the desk and the tally sheets, guessing Hansbro would rowel a horse off to the mountains in black rage. And it might be that Vic would return chastened, subdued.

Hansbro would have been further enraged at the calm knowledge of his intentions. At the horse corral in black silence Hansbro saddled his top horse, a magnificent roan. Dave came from the house and eyed the saddling with a thin, knowing smile.

"What'd he say?"

Hansbro jerked viciously on the webbed cinch strap and tucked the end in before he looked at Dave. "Ordered me to stop any fool moves you tried."

"Nursemaid?" Dave sneered.

"Got to humor him."

"Why?"

"He'll fire me."

Dave's grin took on a malicious edge. "He'd fire you quicker if he knew some of the tally counts were low."

Vic Hansbro glanced quickly around to see if they were overheard. His manner turned placating. "That was for you, Dave. You know it was. Everything'll be yours, anyway, one of these days. You swore you needed the money."

"And you took half," Dave sneered again. "Half,

Vic. Remember that when you try to tell me what to do. Alec won't like to hear you peddled some of his best beeves while he was away on trips. I don't even know who bought 'em. You handled it all." Dave's grin was amused. "Now sweat it out. And don't try to tell me what to do."

"Sure, Dave." Hansbro said it softly, thickly. He gathered the reins in one hamlike fist and watched Dave walk away, and Vic Hansbro was suddenly afraid of Dave.

Hansbro stepped on the roan and caught the braided leather quirt off the saddle horn. His savage slash drove the roan into a wild gallop. Alec Waggoman, in the office, heard the receding pound of hoofs and paused, listening, before bending over his desk work again.

He had to hold the papers close to his eyes. Six months ago it had been a full foot. The strain was great. Inner rebellion and a frustrating sense of helplessness finally became intolerable. Waggoman swung away from the desk with a growled oath. He caught his hat off the deer-horn rack beside the door and walked heavily outside to the edge of the yard, and called to the nearest figure. "Saddle my horse!"

Alec Waggoman rode down out of the hills, solitary and pine-straight in the saddle, somber and silent, his thoughts on the future, on Dave. The mountains were at his back. Before him the world flung out mile upon endless mile of foothills and deep washes, knife ridges and long reaches of grama grass. All the wild rough beauty of Barb.

He knew it was there; he could see it clean and lovely and enduring in the memories of the long years. A very little of it, tantalizingly, he could see now close beside the ranch road. Then the thickening blur took all the rest.

He had the memories, the long rich memories. But who had the future? Dave's future? Barb's future? And after the black shackles of full blindness fastened on him, who had Alec Waggoman's future? Waggoman's faint, ironic smile followed the thought.

His horse snorted softly. Its ears went forward. Unable to make out who was coming, Waggoman reined to a stop by the roadside and slowly rolled and lighted a cigarette. He heard the approaching strike of horseshoes against the road rocks, and finally the rider materialize into a woman.

As she neared the solitary horseman waiting forbiddingly at the side of the road, Barbara Kirby had the half-prideful, half-defiant thought that Alec Waggoman looked exactly what he was: a rocklike part of this wild, unyielding country where he'd carved out the great reaches of Barb. That bold-nosed, craggy face and iron-willed energy had always been a harsh contrast to Jubal Kirby's likeable, casual ways.

Now Alec Waggoman had a brooding look of challenge as Barbara rode to him. He waited, forcing her to speak first. And Barbara's own instinctive defiance sounded cooler than she intended.

"Good morning, Uncle Alec."

Surprisingly, a slow, grave smile spread under his impressive white mustaches. "Barbara! Coming to visit an old man?" In his lofty, detached way, Alec Waggoman had always seemed amused by her mildly defiant coolness toward him.

"I'm going to Half-Moon," said Barbara coolly. "But that stranger—that Will Lockhart—asked me to tell you he's satisfied with the money the bank paid him this morning. He wants no more trouble with Barb."

Waggoman's hooded look rested on her. His even voice asked, "Why didn't Lockhart bring his own message?"

"Would he have been safe at Barb?"

"He would." The veiled stare considered her. Waggoman's question was idle. "Was Lockhart going to Half-Moon?"

"He was riding to Roxton Springs, leaving these parts."

Waggoman's demand thrust like a rapier stroke. "If Lockhart's leaving, why bother to send me word he wants no more trouble? Why send you miles out of your way with an unnecessary message?"

"I don't know," Barbara admitted uncomfortably. "He didn't really ask me to come."

"You just decided to visit your Uncle Alec, eh?" Waggoman's smile took on edged humor at the thought. "Are you certain Lockhart isn't hiring out to Half-Moon?"

"He didn't speak of it." Barbara knew she was flushing. Defiantly she countered the tall old man eyeing her closely. "Are you afraid of Lockhart?"

His smile spread under the white mustaches. "What is fear?" His own dry answer said, "Not caution. I know Kate Canaday. After losing her lease on the Gallegos tract she'd not pass up a chance to hire Lockhart."

"Uncle Alec, why did you do that to Kate?"

Alec Waggoman's smile faded. The rocklike look dropped on him. Then, surprisingly, he said, "I was looking ahead. Barb will need that winter graze. If I died suddenly, Dave would never get it. I took care of the matter now."

He sounded almost, Barbara thought, as if the years ahead weighed on his mind. Knowing Dave all her life, Dave's small strengths and greater weaknesses, Barbara had an intuitive flash. This tall, somber old man was trying to reach beyond the grave and prop and bolster Dave.

He can't, Barbara thought a little sadly. *Dave won't change.* She argued, "Half-Moon needs that range."

Waggoman's faint smile returned. "Half-Moon still has Kate Canaday."

"Barb still has Alec Waggoman."

"And who knows tomorrow?" Waggoman said dryly. Then unexpectedly he said, "Yesterday I leased the salt lakes to Frank Darrah."

"Frank didn't tell me," said Barbara involuntarily.

"Should he have told you?"

"He could have mentioned it." Barbara was annoyed, without exactly knowing why. "Last night Frank asked me to marry him. We talked of other business matters."

Alec Waggoman showed no surprise. "Are you going to marry him?"

"Haven't you noticed my ring?" Barbara held up her left hand. Waggoman leaned over, peering. When he straightened and gathered the reins, his smile had an unusual warmth.

"So you're happy, Barbara? Now, please an old man, too, by riding with him to the Half-Moon turnoff."

He was a pleasant companion as they rode side by side. Barbara caught herself wondering, *Why can't he be this way all the time?* Not until later when she reached Half-Moon, did Barbara recall Alec Waggoman's conviction that Kate Canaday had tried to hire Will Lockhart.

Kate's Half-Moon headquarters was a rambling log house, log bunkhouse, barn, and outbuildings. Kate's pack of hound dogs streamed out in full clamor as Barbara rode up. Kate's tall vigorous figure emerged from the log cook-shack and her gusty calls quieted the dogs.

"Now ain't this a surprise?" Kate called delightedly. Her lumpy, weathered face beamed as Barbara dismounted. "I thought mebbe 'twas that Lockhart feller I tried to hire yesterday. Might 'a' knowed the son-of-a-gun wouldn't change his mind."

Laughing, Barbara said, "I met Alec Waggoman and he guessed you'd tried to hire Lockhart."

"With a foreman like Lockhart, I'd make Alec sweat balls of fire," Kate said with grim anticipation. Then her shrug put the thought aside. "I'll get some coffee from the big pot," Kate said sociably, "an' we'll have a real visit."

Elaborately casual, Barbara said, "I came to invite you to my wedding."

Kate was incredulous. "Who you marryin'?"

"Frank Darrah."

"Well!" exclaimed Kate weakly. Wordlessly she motioned Barbara into the house.

The front room they entered mirrored another aspect of Big Kate Canaday. Wine-red carpet lay soft and yielding on the floor. Tall brass andirons gleamed in the stone fireplace. A walnut organ stood against the wall. Rosewood sofa and comfortable chairs were covered with cheerful brocade. Window draperies were stately falls of starched white lace. They sat on the sofa side by side and Kate admired Frank's ring and volleyed questions about wedding plans and clothes.

Presently Kate broke off and heaved sheepishly to her feet. "I clean fergot the coffee."

Barbara looked up at her thoughtfully. "I don't think Jubal approves of Frank. Do you?"

Kate stood there, big and manlike in rough woolen shirt and skirt, her graying pompadour high and careless above the rough, amiable face, now puckering thoughtfully.

"Jubal," said Kate slowly, "ain't marryin' Darrah. I ain't, neither. You're real in love, ain't you?"

"Wouldn't I have to be?"

"Ain't a girl in the Territory'll get a better provider," Kate said. "Darrah's made money. He'll make more. Ain't bad lookin'. Healthy, too."

"And sound teeth," Barbara reminded, chuckling. Then, reluctantly she guessed, "You don't exactly approve, either, do you?"

"Didn't say so," Kate denied vigorously. "Can't help it if I run personal to he-men who'll keep a woman guessin' an' raise holy-how if she tries to tromp an' boss." Color was staining Barbara's face. Kate saw it. "The Lockhart kind stirs you warm, too, huh?"

"Ridiculous," Barbara denied.

Kate went for the coffee, leaving dryly over her shoulder, "I never heard it had to be reasonable."

Hours after Kate said that, Will Lockhart's tired roan gelding brought him through low hills to a smiling valley. The narrow road homed straight across the valley to tall cottonwoods and dusty streets and sun-baked plaza that were Roxton Springs. On a yellow bluff to the west, Fort Roxton's adobe structures and highflying flag overlooked the town. And between town and fort, a small sparkling stream fed smaller, wandering *acequias* which carried rippling water to cultivated fields and lush little town gardens.

From the Mogollon corrals, west of the plaza, Will walked to the near-by French's Hotel. A glance at the register was enough. He went on to the Riverside Hotel on the northwest corner of the plaza. Here he had stopped before. When he leaned the carbine against the desk counter and picked up the ink-crusted pen, the clerk remembered him with an admiring question.

"Ain't you the one who upset the Barb foreman in Coronado?"

Will's glance lifted from a name higher up on the register page: *F. L. Darrah*—

"There was a little trouble," Will said carelessly. He picked up the room key and the carbine and walked upstairs in mild annoyance. He was marked now for public notice it seemed. And, in a way, it confirmed the warning of Freall, the banker. Who touched Barb, touched trouble.

Will's room at the back of the upstairs hall was like the weathered clapboards outside, shabby and plain, scantily furnished with an ancient iron bed, a cane-seated rocker, lamp, washbowl, and pitcher. The westing sun glinted through pin-cracks in the stained window shade as Will stripped and washed. He left the carbine in the room when he went out again.

Darrah's key had been off the rack downstairs.

Will followed the worn brown carpet runner to the front cross hall. Darrah had room eleven, opening on the front second-story gallery and the open plaza. Darrah was probably asleep now, Will guessed, after the long night ride and business of the morning.

It should be easy to discover why the man had made a hurried, uncomfortable night ride from Coronado.

Inside room eleven Frank Darrah had slept soundly, and had awakened with an odd, heady sense of elation and triumph. He lay slackly, considering again the good fortune which ranked Barbara Kirby directly after Dave Waggoman as heir to Barb.

In two short weeks now, after the wedding, Frank Darrah, too, would be heir to everything Alec Waggoman owned. The thought was heady wine.

Frank idly listened to floor boards in the hall outside creak quietly under approaching footsteps. After a moment the footsteps turned back.

Lazily Frank got up and lighted a cigar. He opened the door to the front gallery outside and stared contentedly at the bare baked plaza. A tall striding figure caught his eye. The blue shirt, denim pants, and black hat worn with a slight rake were vaguely familiar. That was the tramp teamster Lockhart, just emerged from this hotel.

Frank recalled the footsteps halting near his door. That could have been Lockhart. Probably had been Lockhart. Which meant Lockhart's interest a few minutes ago had been directly on Frank Darrah.

Fear again belted Frank. Here was a stranger

watching him. Frank turned back into the room and caught his white cambric shirt off the bedpost. Short minutes later he hurried downstairs, driven by the suspicious, undermining fear.

Chapter Eleven

At the lobby desk, Frank almost fearfully scanned the register. Will Lockhart's boldly scrawled name seemed to dominate the smudged page. Lockhart had room three. That was in the rear corridor upstairs. So Lockhart had had no excuse to be in the front corridor.

Frank's lifted glance met the clerk's curious stare. He wondered irritably if the man suspected his agitation. "What brings Lockhart to town?" he bluntly queried.

He got a knowing smile. "A man in trouble with Barb'd sleep better here than in Coronado, wouldn't he?" The clerk remembered, "Lockhart asked who might have mules for sale. I told him Gil Caxton."

"Lockhart does need mules," Frank admitted grudgingly. Somewhat relieved he stepped from the lobby into the bar and put down a small whisky. But when he walked a block from the plaza and turned the corner there, the sight of freight wagons ahead brought back the uneasy foreboding.

Two massive, dust-whitened freight wagons were backed against the loading-platform of the thick-walled adobe warehouse Frank had under lease. Here freight for the Coronado store accumulated. Hides, grains, beans, wool, and other products bought outright or taken on account were often delivered to this more convenient warehouse.

Frank hurried up wooden steps to the end of the loading-platform. Stout wooden boxes were being unloaded. In the cool dim interior he found a growing pile of the boxes, each stenciled: *Bolt Goods, I. Perdoux, New Orleans.*

The warehouse clerk, a moonfaced, stolid, unimaginative man named Luther Hill, came over with a fistful of freight lists.

"This lot, Mr. Darrah, is fifty cases bolt goods. Want all of it sent on to Coronado?"

Frank said curtly, "Put the cases over there in the corner out of the way. Pile that sacked wool on top."

"Pepper," Hill droned from his lists. "Sugar—hardware—couple cases shoes—"

"Send all of that."

Frank eyed the New Orleans shipment with aversion as he turned away. Fifty cases. Each holding four new repeating rifles in factory grease. Only yesterday those battered, innocuous wooden boxes had represented immense profit with little risk. Now they threatened all the future.

Then Frank saw Chris Boldt slouched lazily in a wired wood armchair by the office door, smoking a stogie, watching the unloading, watching Frank's movements in narrow silence.

Anger boiled in Frank as he went to the man and demanded under his breath, "What the devil are *you* doing here?"

Chris Boldt got up effortlessly, a lithe man with a narrow mouth pinched at the corners and amber eyes bright with reckless slyness. His pants were slick-worn buckskin. Over his soiled calico shirt hung loosely a buckskin vest with hammered silver buttons. Boldt's grin had thin meaning as he pulled the dark twisted Pittsburg stogie from his mouth.

"Hill said you were in town. Saved me a trip to Coronado. Ain't that the stuff being unloaded?"

"*Quiet!*" Frank ordered savagely under his breath.

Insolence Frank had suspected other times became a resentful gleam in Chris Boldt's stare. A purple strawberry mark ran from the underside of Boldt's lean jaw to the leathery neck. Now the purple deepened angrily. But Boldt spoke coolly.

"You got the money in advance, like always. Climb off your high horse. Ain't that the stuff?"

Frank swallowed a groan. "We may be watched! Meet me in front of the hotel after dark!"

Boldt eyed him curiously. "Man, you're frightened. Who'd be watching?"

Frank tasted bitterness now, and a quick hot hatred of the unmistakable contempt in Boldt's tone. The man had been useful. This business of selling guns quietly had been Boldt's furtive suggestion in the first place. But now Boldt had nothing much to lose. Frank Darrah could be ruined.

"A man in New Orleans tried to trace this shipment," Frank warned malignantly under his breath. "It could be happening here, too!"

Boldt's thin smile doubted that. He pulled on the stogie and asked through the smoke, "You know a man named Charley Yuill?"

"No!"

Boldt spat a shred of tobacco off his lip and gave Frank a sardonic look. "Yuill's a breed. I stopped at his camp last night. Charley'd had moccasin visitors. I seen the sign when we pulled out this morning. Charley don't say much, but he pried about what I been doin' lately."

Frank said impatiently, "A half-breed you camped

with last night, isn't likely to have close connections
with New Orleans. Now get out. I'll see you after
dark."

Charley Yuill was a patient man. From a distance
Charley had watched Chris Bolt's movements, not
certain himself why he watched. Boldt was a rascal
in a stretch of country where rascals were selling
the tribesmen guns, was the way Charley instinctively summed it up.

When Chris Boldt had finally walked with lazy
purpose to Darrah's warehouse, Charley's nostrils
had twitched with satisfaction. Boldt's second trip
to the warehouse had found freight wagons unloading.

Watching from a distance, Charley saw Frank
Darrah enter the warehouse. When Chris Boldt
emerged a few minutes later, Charley faded toward the plaza, wishing Will Lockhart were not so
far away in Coronado. Starting now on his bareback mule, Charley calculated he might reach
Coronado around midnight.

Will Lockhart suspected none of that. He
guessed Charley Yuill now to be far out in the reservation country, and he leisurely walked the two
blocks to Caxton's Corrals, unkinking saddle-stiff
muscles and validating his excuse for being here in
Roxton Springs.

He found a big, circular mule corral at Caxton's
holding some twenty head. Mostly castoff packers
from the fort stables, Will's practiced glance
judged. He strolled to the adjoining feed corral and
quickly noticed there a powerful, mouse-colored
mule haltered at one of the feed boxes.

Effortlessly Will climbed to a seat on the top corral pole and gazed thoughtfully at the mule Charley Yuill had ridden from the salt lagoons, and not toward Roxton Springs.

A hostler in bib overalls was working inside the corral. Will called, "When did this mule come in?"

The answer he got was from someone else outside the corral, coming up behind him. "Mon, the beastie dinna been there long."

Only Charley Yuill, quarter-Zuni, quarter-Apache, and the rest of Charley's bizarre potpourri of bloods full Scot, could so blandly imitate his Scot father's burr.

Will swung around on the pole, grinning widely down at Charley's dark-skinned face and flaming red whisker stubble.

"You ran out of haggis," Will guessed.

Charley paused directly below Will, grinning, too, as he considered haggis, the Scottish dish of sheep's liver and heart, onions, and fat, mixed with oatmeal and boiled in the sheep's stomach.

"Mon, doff yer hat when ye speak of the noble haggis," Charley reproved. "Only me now," Charley confessed sheepishly, "I can't stand the oatmeal in it."

Will's shout of laughter followed as Charley climbed up beside him and hauled out tobacco sack and papers. "I met a cousin of my mother's aunt on her mother's side," Charley said. "The Apach' side."

"I won't try to unravel that one," Will decided.

Charley smiled faintly and flared a match on the rail under his hip. He drew smoke deep and spoke thoughtfully. "Wasn't no use going on. I heard enough. Apach' talk says any broncho who wants a new gun can pay old Taite, the medicine man in

Eagle Canyon, three hundred dollars Mex or American money, or melted-down gold or silver."

Will's astounded whistle was barely audible. "That's a fortune for a gun. A fortune for any wick-iup broncho to have."

"They don't raid for buttons," observed Charley. "A good man can accumulate. He pays old Taite an' waits. Finally Taite sends word his medicine says go to some spot an' the gun'll be hidden there. Many have paid and are angry now because the guns haven't come." Charley spat reflectively. "Cap'n, I'll guess a big raid is waitin' on them new guns."

Will nodded. "Who has their money now?"

Charley shrugged. "Old Taite is foxy. Never handles the guns. Everyone knows his big medicine is white men. But Taite won't admit it."

"What if the guns aren't delivered and Taite can't return the money?" Will wondered.

The thought made Charley chuckle. "Cap'n, there ain't enough medicine from the Chiricahuas to the Jicarillas to uncork old Taite from a mess like that. He'd get drunk on tulapai an' start his death song." Then Charley added, "I was startin' to Coronado to tell you about a man named Chris Boldt I sort of sided to town here."

Will listened closely as Charley outlined what he knew of Chris Boldt and the man's two visits to Darrah's warehouse.

"Darrah's clerk in Coronado sent a message," Will remembered. "It'll do for an excuse to visit the warehouse. See you at the hotel, Charley."

The freight wagons had departed. The heavy loading-doors were closed when Will reached the warehouse. He entered the small corner office and Hill, the paunchy round-faced clerk turned from a wall desk and recognized him from the stop Will's wagons had made here on the way to Coronado.

"I'm looking for Darrah," Will said casually, moving to the inner door.

Hill moved more nimbly. His paunchy bulk blocked the door. "Darrah ain't in there. No visitors. You, especially, Lockhart."

Will grinned at the man. "Why me, especially?"

Neither friendly nor unfriendly, Hill said stolidly, "Darrah said you were in town but not workin' for him now. Another fellow lookin' for him sat around in there. Darrah raised hell. I ain't askin' for more."

"Where," Will asked, "is Darrah?"

"Don't ask me."

"Tell Darrah I've a message from McGuire for him."

Hill shrugged, not really interested. "Where'll you be?"

Past the man's bulky shoulder, through the door glass, Will could see that the wide loading-doors of the warehouse were secured inside by heavy wooden bars dropped into strap-iron brackets. The back wall of the warehouse, he recalled, had no door at all. At night a man would have to come through the office here. Then the shielded light of a small candle would do to examine the warehouse contents. Will's grin covered thoughts which would have jolted Luther Hill out of his stolid disinterest and driven Frank Darrah to sweating apprehension.

"If Darrah wants the message," Will decided blandly, "he can look for me."

* * *

Frank Darrah was not thinking of Will Lockhart as Frank drove a single horse livery buggy toward Fort Roxton on the yellow bluff west of town. Chris Boldt had left Frank raging and worried. The guns had been paid for, Boldt had bluntly warned, and Boldt wanted them for delivery quickly. Frank licked dry lips and cut the buggy whip hard across the horse's flank. His business affairs were nicely solvent, Frank thought blackly, but always his expanding moves demanded more cash. It was impossible now to return the money quickly to Boldt.

Frank relieved helpless frustration by slashing the trotting horse into a sweating gallop. The sun was a molten ball beyond the high streaming flag of the fort when the blowing horse reached the sentry gate. Frank stated his business and was waved on in.

Roxton parade ground was a sweep of pounded dusty earth around which the low adobe structures of the fort ranged in drab simplicity.

A handful of troopers in blue garrison caps loafed in front of the long barracks line and stared silently as the sweating livery horse trotted clumsily past. Frank skirted the north end of the parade ground and eyed with critical interest several enlisted men's wives taking in wash from the festooned clotheslines behind tub row. He noted that the sutler's was filling up with end-of-the-day business, and decided to check such of the sutler's needs as he could supply.

Then, ahead, he saw a square-shouldered, solid figure emerge from the adjutant's building and start toward officer's row. "Captain Wyman!" Frank called.

Wyman swung about at the edge of the duck-boards, frowning at this prospect of more business at the fag end of a blistering day. Frank pulled up abreast and got out quickly, drawing on his best business cordiality for Wyman, the post quarter-master.

"Is it too late, Captain, to trouble you for some New York exchange?"

"How much, Mr. Darrah?"

"I've three thousand in greenbacks."

"I can use it," Captain Wyman admitted reluctantly.

Frank cynically reflected that Wyman would probably pursue him to the sentry gate for that much currency. The army always needed paper money for payrolls and local use. Merchants like himself, on the other hand, wished to avoid shipping cash money to the east in settlement of supply accounts. Quartermasters like Wyman were usually pleased to take the cash and issue mailable drafts against eastern points.

Wyman waved Frank ahead of him into the large front office of the adjutant's building where non-commissioned men still bent over paper work at tables and desks. In his office opening off the back of the room, Wyman unlocked his roll-top desk, indicated an adjoining chair, and turned to the iron safe.

Wyman's face was red and solid. His wheat-colored mustache was short and crisp with a hint of carefully tended vanity. Now that he was in for it, Wyman was cordial enough as he turned back to his desk with a pad of blank drafts.

He took up the thick wad of greenbacks Frank had placed on the desk. Rapidly, efficiently, Wyman ran through the count. "Three thousand," Wyman agreed. He reached for a pen and rapidly filled out the draft. He signed with a flourish, inspected the draft critically, and handed it to Frank.

"Thanks, Captain." Frank waved the slip of paper gently to dry the ink. "Isn't it about time for the army to invite bids on salt for the various forts?"

"Can't say. Handled from Santa Fe, you know."

"You frequently contact Santa Fe," Frank ventured pleasantly. "Could you mention I've leased the salt lagoons and now control about all the salt in this part of the Territory?"

Captain Wyman produced a plain white handkerchief and dried the ends of his mustache. His straw-colored eyebrows had lifted slightly. For a moment as he sat, handkerchief in hand, Wyman's slight smile had a disillusioned knowledge.

"The price of salt, I take it, Mr. Darrah, will advance somewhat," was Wyman's mildly ironic guess.

"Slightly. I'll be put to considerable expense."

Wyman's squint stopped the ghost of an admiring smile. "Not everyone would have thought of it," Wyman murmured. "Ordinary salt. But everyone must have it. The cattle and sheep men, miners, cooks—everyone. Even the Indians. And freighting it in is expensive. How high can a man squeeze the price?"

Frank's own slight smile was almost smug. Wyman, in his way, was a business man, too, appreciating a clever move. Inserting the draft into his black leather wallet, Frank suggested casually, "A sheep or cattle man trading with one of my competitors, might be glad to turn his trade to me when assured of plentiful salt at a reasonable price."

Softly Wyman said, "I'll be damned! Hadn't occurred to me. For nothing or an average profit, you club business your way."

Frank's correction was completely, smugly righteous. "Call it an inducement to trade with me."

Wyman's grim humor was not diverted. "You'll have your little joke, I see. But—try inducing too much trade, or whatever you call your salt squeeze, and I foresee ill will and perhaps violence. Which, no doubt, you are prepared to meet."

"I am," Frank said calmly.

Captain Wyman studied him with an odd, intent look and said thoughtfully, "Since you're leasing the salt lakes, what d'you know about a man named Lockhart who was digging salt there several days ago?"

Frank was startled. "Lockhart hauled some freight for me. Took his wagons to the lagoons and met trouble. Barb men, who controlled the lagoons until yesterday, shot Lockhart's mules and burned his wagons."

"But who is this Lockhart? Where's he from?" Wyman rubbed a stubby forefinger, under his crisp mustache, frowning over the finger at Frank. "Lieutenant Evans took a small patrol that way and saw the trouble. And Evans rode in today with an outlandish idea this man Lockhart is a Captain Lockhart, supposedly on duty on the upper Missouri."

Frank realized he had gone rigid against the straight back of the chair. The hot office had become unbearably oppressive. He tried to relax. It took an effort to force questions through the thickness in his throat.

"Why should an army captain from one of the northern forts be running his own tramp freight wagons around here? And be fighting on the street in Coronado like a saloon roughneck!"

Chapter Twelve

"Can't think of a reason," Captain Wyman agreed. "Someone in the bachelor's mess remembered this Captain Lockhart had a brother killed last year in the Dutch Canyon ambush. Evans has a fantastic idea this Lockhart at the salt lakes must be the surviving brother."

"Impossible, I'd say," Frank said tightly.

"Undoubtedly," Wyman agreed, his interest waning.

Frank desperately wanted to get away from the man's gossipy talk. He had to wait while Wyman relocked the desk, the safe, and leisurely accompanied him outside.

"Thank you, Captain."

"Not at all, Mr. Darrah."

Frank stepped into the buggy in a mist of sick fear. Forgetting any business with the sutler, he drove around the parade ground and out the sentry gate. The reins felt slippery in his sweating palms. Details of the Apache raid on the Fort Kilham supply train jostled in his thoughts. Even Chris Boldt had been worried about that raid.

Frank drove recklessly down the dusty, descending road of the bluff. Captain Wyman was a fool. This Lockhart must be the surviving brother. A gruesome, shaking thought intruded: It was like the dead walking again, searching even to far-off New Orleans and back to Coronado. Then here to Roxton Springs. Frank had no doubt now Lockhart had trailed him here. The end might be a bullet from Lockhart's gun. Or a legal hangrope—

Frank reached up and loosened the black string tie, easing pressure around his throat. *Must be an answer*—He was still Frank Darrah, a prospering merchant. Barbara Kirby was eagerly planning their wedding, and Alec Waggoman, half-blind, was running out his final days as lord of Barb. What could change all that? Only Chris Boldt knew about the past. Lockhart must be watching the future—those fifty cases of guns and who got them. But guns in Roxton Springs or Coronado weren't guilt if the past could not be proved.

Frank was calmer after that thought. His mind began to function in fresh clarity, coolly calculating, as he drove on toward town—toward Will Lockhart and Chris Boldt.

It was full night when Will Lockhart, tall and loosely striding, crossed the plaza, idly speculating on why Frank Darrah hadn't yet asked for McGuire's message. Oil lamps on tall poles glowed at the four plaza corners. Store windows and saloon fronts were illuminated. A starry night like this softened the harsh reality of a town, Will thought. Shabby buildings took on grace, and a kind of gallantry cloaked dimly seen figures. Will paused to let a buggy pass and smiled understandingly.

A young officer from the fort held the reins. The girl beside him sat discreetly over on her side of the seat. A town girl undoubtedly. Captain Will Lockhart had done exactly that on pleasant evenings in other garrison towns, and would again.

A slight nostalgia touched Will. He was an up-rooted shadow now, patiently stalking other shadows, and trouble was at his elbow if he strayed too far from the invisible rank still riding his shoulders by law and custom.

The Gem Café where he went for supper was a plain place with oilcloth on the tables. The counter stools were filled. Two men quitted a small table over against the wall and Will sat down there. A hurried waitress loaded the soiled dishes on a tray, swiped a damp towel over the white oilcloth, and took his order.

When the food came, Will ate thoughtfully, half his mind now on what was planned for the evening. Frank Darrah found him like that and dropped into the opposite chair, smiling ruefully.

"You're hard to find, Lockhart; hear you have a message for me."

Will ignored his dislike of this blond, assured young man and said calmly, "McGuire said to tell you the Half-Moon wagon got everything on the list. And on another list the driver brought."

He noted irritation in Darrah's glance. But the man's rueful smile came stronger. "More credit on the books. Kate Canaday has the devil's own way about her."

Will had to smile at that, even while he was wondering what Barbara Kirby found in this man worth love and marriage. One could see certain things about the man which might appeal to a woman. The narrow-brimmed townsman's hat in Darrah's hand had bared the close-cropped neatness of thick blond hair. The black string tie and white cambric shirt and blue broadcloth suit were all conservative and tasteful. And Darrah had the assurance of success.

That assurance was in Darrah's smiling comment now. "So you decided to pull out of Coronado?"

"Have to look for more wagons and mules."

"But you're not going back?"

"Why not?"

Darrah shrugged. "I've work for you then, after you get an outfit together. Steady hauling. I've leased the salt lakes."

"When?" Will asked quickly.

"Yesterday. From Alec Waggoman. You'll have no more trouble with Barb if you haul for me."

"I've been worried," Will said ironically.

There was a falseness about this talk, and in Darrah's smiling offer. "I might help you buy mules and wagons cheaper."

"I'll think it over," Will decided, and when Darrah left, Will ate thoughtfully, pondering the man.

When Will paid at the door and bought a cigar and stepped outside again, the tinny raucousness of the plaza saloons had increased. Three sun-blackened troopers swaggered by, their boot heels thumping the boardwalk.

Will smiled at their backs, guessing the trio knew every rascally trick in the barracks book. They were the kind who put starch and confidence in any grinding patrol.

Will was bringing the cigar to his mouth when he was bumped from the rear. The shock mashed the cigar end against his teeth, and Will turned irritably, finding a stranger in buckskins who weaved unsteadily and demanded, "Who you shovin'?"

Disgustedly Will pitched the ruined cigar to the gutter. "Never mind," he said briefly.

The next instant he was dodging a clumsy blow. Will slapped the arm down and shoved the man away. "Get going!"

But the man came back, lithe and not weaving at

all. The dark shadows were thick here and Will barely noted the stranger's hand sliding in behind his belt buckle. *Gun hidden there!* was Will's instant guess. *Cold sober, too!*

Will moved equally fast, jabbing his left fist at the man's head and pivoting a little as his right fist swung a completely vicious smash to the man's stomach.

A drunk would have collapsed over the sickening blow. This lithe stranger merely swayed back, grunting explosively. Will grabbed the reaching hand and heard the three troopers pounding joyously back to watch the fight.

It was more of a wild scuffle. The buckskins reeked of sweat, stale grease, and the rankness of old chip campfires. The stranger was silent. Will was struggling too furiously to speak. He felt the stranger's left hand trying to get past his guarding elbow, and remembered his own holstered gun on that hip.

Furious now, Will slapped his left hand to the man's concealed gun and snatched back to his holster. He got hold of his own gun and twisted the holster up enough to shoot through the bottom.

"Last chance!" Will panted against the stranger's sweating face.

Then he had proof it was all deliberate. The man slacked back to a weaving drunken state. His loud thick pleading reached the bystanders.

"Leggo, mister! Do' wan' trouble!"

Will got the gun from the pants top. Panting from the short wild struggle, he brought the hard gun steel up in a flat slamming blow to the side of the man's head. Then he stepped back and watched the slow, sodden collapse to the dusty walk boards.

Back in the shadows a voice jeered from the watching men who had gathered, "Hell on drunks, ain't you?"

"Who is he?" Will demanded malevolently.

No one seemed to know. Will threw the gun beside its owner and wheeled off the boardwalk, still panting as he ducked under the hitch-rail and headed across the plaza.

Half an hour later, walking toward the shadowy outskirts of town with Charley Yuill, Will said, more puzzled than angry now, "Charley, he was faking. He was sober and he meant to kill me."

"Had on buckskins?" Charley repeated Will's comment. "Did he have a red mark under the chin?"

"Yes. Who is he?"

"That was Chris Boldt. An' I never heard of Chris Boldt pullin' a shootin' drunk. He ain't the kind. Too foxy."

"Then Boldt must know who I am."

"Uh-huh."

"Which must mean the guns are here now." Charley's nod agreed, and an edge of grimness came into Will's decision. "We'll have that look inside Darrah's warehouse for sure now. In an hour or so if there's no one around."

They killed time by strolling on the fringe of town. Dogs barked at them. Horses snorted in small corrals they passed. The quiet night had the feel now, Will thought, of rising danger. He caught himself thinking in cold anger again of the sprawled dead of the Fort Kilham wagon train and isolated ranches flaming on dark nights like this.

Charley said musingly, "Three hun'red dollars a gun—Two hun'red guns— Lot of money, Cap'n."

Charley spat to the side. "Hell of a lot. Worth killin' you to keep it quiet." And then Charley wondered, "How'd Chris Boldt guess you were bad luck to him?"

"He's seen Darrah. And Darrah had something working on his mind tonight. Too friendly when he talked to me. Offered me steady hauling. Darrah's leased the salt lakes."

Charley's soft "Oh-oh!" drew Will's keen look. Charley said with a trace of sheepishness, "Old Grandmother Salt lives in them lakes. Couple thousan' years, anyway, the Indians think. Them lakes are sacred."

"Not too sacred," Will reminded. "The Apach' burned two wagons in sight of them the other day."

"Old Grandmother Salt ain't Apach'," said Charley, more seriously probably than he guessed. "But the Apach' needs salt, too. Even before guns. Cap'n, that Darrah'll find trouble if he meddles between the tribes an' their salt."

"Just now, it's Darrah and guns," Will reminded. "Suppose we meet at the warehouse in about an hour?"

The feeling of danger lingered as Will walked alone toward the plaza. Only now could he fully understand how close death had brushed in that wild scuffle with Chris Boldt. The feeling brought him alert, watchful, when two men angled across the street to his side and waited for him to pass.

One man was a trooper from the fort, staring hard as Will came abreast. The trooper murmured something and the other man said sharply, "Lockhart, the sheriff wants a talk with you."

Will made out the pale glint of a badge on the speaker's shirt, and halfway recognized the trooper as one of the trio that had doubled back joyously to watch the fight with Boldt.

"Why a talk with me?" Will countered.

"Johnson said to find you. We been looking all over town. Where you been?"

"Picking stars," Will said. The deputy's hand was hovering near his side-gun and Will asked sarcastically, "Expecting trouble?"

"I'll take your gun, Lockhart. Turn around."

"Want to try taking it?" Will invited calmly. "Or I'll walk with you like this."

Chapter Thirteen

Roxton courthouse was a squatty adobe structure built around a large, bare patio one could enter directly from the street. Sheriff Johnson's office was in the left back corner of the patio, and when Will stepped in ahead of his escort, the sheriff was tilted back in his desk chair waiting.

A competent man, was Will's swift judgment. Johnson looked him over keenly, too, as the rangy deputy and the trooper followed Will in. Johnson's drawl to his deputy was pointed.

"Ira, you going to learn the hard way about prisoners packing their guns in?"

Will said softly, "Prisoner?"

The trooper was grinning and Ira gave Will a sour look, and Will's caustic demand was to the sheriff. "Do you always take fights this seriously?"

"Nope," Johnson said politely. "You're the man, I take it, who slapped that drunken Boldt down with his own gun."

"He wasn't drunk."

Johnson glanced inquiringly at the trooper. "You saw it. Was he?"

"I'd say so for a civilian," was the grinning reply. "A good man from the fort now, he'd be down an' paralyzed before I'd give him the name."

Will chuckled and asked the sheriff, "How does the army get in on this?"

Johnson clasped hands behind his graying hair,

studying Will thoughtfully. "He saw the fight and could point you out. Where've you been?"

"Walking."

"You're the man who had trouble at the salt lakes and picked a hell of a fight with the Barb foreman in Coronado."

Will said dryly, "You get news fast."

"Where you from, Lockhart? What brought you to town here?"

"Mules. I've been freighting. I need more mules."

"Why'd you have trouble with Boldt?"

Johnson asked that in the same brief, direct way, and unclasped his hands from behind his head and leaned forward, listening carefully as Will told equally briefly what had happened.

Irony came then into Johnson's voice. "You're saying this Boldt—this stranger to you—went through all that foolishness of playing drunk before he tried to put a bullet in you?"

"It sounds foolish," Will admitted. "That's what happened."

"Not all that happened, Lockhart. Boldt's dead."

There was a shocking, believable simplicity in Johnson's statement. Sick regret caught Will. All he could say at the moment was a helpless, "I'd have sworn I didn't hit him that hard."

"Oh, that," said Johnson carelessly. "Hell, Boldt got up from that and walked away. It was later he was found under a wagon in a vacant lot, knifed four times in the back. And stabbed in the throat to make sure. He was a mess." Johnson stood up, a graying man almost as tall as Will. His manner was regretfully impersonal.

"You can see why I'm locking you up."

Will's tremendous relief flared into quick, angry

protest. "Hell, no, I don't see! You're making a wild guess now! Why would I stab a stranger I'd already left flat and helpless?"

Johnson kept the impersonal manner. "No one said you stabbed him. But you're a stranger, too. Trouble seems to boil up when you appear. You tell a cockeyed story about your trouble with Boldt. I want you around while we're looking into this." Johnson paused an instant and suggested mildly, "Now don't make Ira use that gun he's holding at your back."

Will's mind ran over the possibilities. He was boxed in here, and this was the law. In this austere office with whitewashed walls and a few pieces of plain furniture, Will fastened on a new and jabbing thought.

He'd been hunting a man coldly and patiently. But in some devious, sudden way, Will Lockhart himself seemed to have become the hunted one. He was the prisoner now. And Boldt's murder was still a mystery.

Behind Will, Ira sounded sourly satisfied as he plucked Will's gun from its holster.

"Right through that door there, Lockhart. We're kinda proud of our jail."

Will ignored Ira's small malice. "I want a lawyer," he told Johnson curtly. "The best lawyer in town. Now—tonight."

At the same time Will was wondering if Charley Yuill also was being hunted. Charley had a half-wild elusiveness. He might take care of himself— And certainly when Charley heard of Boldt's death, Charley would winnow the town, seeking the man who had knifed Boldt.

Johnson asked, "Got money to pay for a good lawyer?"

"I can get it."

Johnson stayed completely impersonal and almost regretful. "I'll get you a good lawyer if you're bound to waste the money. But it'll take a court order to get you out. And Judge Vandiger is out of town."

"Get the lawyer, anyway."

Disgusted now, and uneasy over what might happen while he was snarled in this legal red tape, Will moved toward the sheriff's cells ahead of Ira's satisfied malice.

In Coronado the next day, Barbara Kirby emerged from Hetty Smather's millinery and dressmaking shop and walked toward the near-by corner of Main with light, brisk steps. In her plain white linen suit, Barbara looked cool and fresh and young and purposeful. She was thinking wryly that the town males would be appalled—if not entirely surprised—at the industrious snipping of lives and secrets which went on in Hetty's quiet little shop.

For instance, one heard in Hetty's today that the tall, smiling stranger named Lockhart had paid his room rent at the hotel a week in advance. But on the Roxton road yesterday, with a bland smile, Will Lockhart had let Barbara assume he was leaving Coronado for good. Indignantly now, Barbara vowed to remember the man's bald evasion.

Also, today in Hetty's, there was gossip that McGuire, Frank Darrah's clerk, had paced his rented room at Mrs. Dillon's for half of last night. And what could be worrying that unmarried, frugal little man who lacked all questionable habits?

Barbara's smooth, tanned forehead knit over the

intriguing puzzle of McGuire's sleeplessness as she crossed the dusty width of Main and turned briskly along the boardwalk toward Frank's store to select some rickrack braid. In addition, today, the list of other things to buy and do was dismaying.

Everyone assumed that Barbara Kirby was wildly, excitedly happy. Actually, today, she was perplexed and harried by this rush into marriage. So much to do and think about—so little time— Naturally she was happy; but—

Barbara halted on that thought, smiling with quick pleasure as a loud, familiar voice called her name across the street. Kate Canaday crossed over with manlike strides, her broad, weathered face shining with haste and satisfaction.

"You seen Judge Andy Vandiger?" Kate demanded vigorously.

"Why, no," Barbara said, and Kate grumbled.

"He was in town this mornin'." Kate's knowing glance went back along the street to McGrath's big log saloon on the corner. "Bet you a rusty tin cup Andy Vandiger is wettin' his snoozle in McGrath's an' politickin' forty a lick."

Barbara smiled and her glance went casually to the big, black-bearded Barb foreman riding by in the street. When Vic Hansbro reined over to them, Kate's hoarse, far-carrying comment was bristling. "I'd swear a skunk was in town!"

Vic Hansbro slouched massively in the saddle, ignoring Kate. His bearded mouth, still slightly puffy from the fight with Will Lockhart, gave Barbara a quick, odd satisfaction. She had an unladylike wish she could have witnessed that bloody, savage brawl.

Hansbro's harsh politeness was directed at her.

"Ma'am, I hear you're marryin' Frank Darrah."

"Yes, Mr. Hansbro," Barbara said politely.

His stare rested on her for a long moment before he said briefly, "Darrah's gettin' a pretty wife." He rode on.

Kate said with the same bristle, " 'Twas a skunk! Wait'll I get that Lockhart man workin' for me! We'll run Hansbro an' Alec Waggoman back in their burrows."

Barbara's laugh came then. "Kate, do you really think you can hire Lockhart?"

"Watch me," promised Kate vigorously. "Why d'you think I want Andy Vandiger?" Then Kate smiled grimly at Barbara's puzzled look. "Ain't you heard Lockhart's jailed in Roxton Springs for killin' a man with a knife?"

"Why, Kate, I can't believe it!" slipped from Barbara instinctively and vehemently. Then at Kate's askance look, Barbara blushed.

Kate smiled grimly. "I don't figure Lockhart's the knifin' kind, either. But he's sure partial to trouble. An' this time it's real trouble. Wait'll I start coaxing through his jail bars with a writ from Andy Vandiger in my hand."

"But would Judge Vandiger—"

"For me, Andy Vandiger will," said Kate with amiable assurance. "Want to come along to Roxton an' watch me turn the screws on Lockhart?"

Barbara refused hastily, and stood there watching Kate stride toward McGrath's Bar. At the moment, Barbara was ready to believe Will Lockhart's smiling stubbornness would have small chance against Big Kate Canaday's vigorous determination.

Then as she turned to go on, Barbara saw that Vic Hansbro had left his roan horse at Frank Darrah's tie rail and had entered the store. To avoid further talk with the man, Barbara walked across the street to the post office. And there, from Aaron Sadler, the postmaster, Barbara heard the details of Lockhart's trouble in Roxton Springs, brought by a drummer not half an hour ago.

In Darrah's store, McGuire was politely regretful across the hardware counter to Vic Hansbro. "Mr. Darrah's not back yet."

This was Hansbro's third visit in two days, asking for Frank Darrah. McGuire stood thoughtfully as Hansbro stalked out.

Farther back in the same aisle, Jubal Kirby, leaning against the counter edge, asked mildly, "Why's Hansbro in a sweat to see Darrah?"

"Business, I suppose; we sell Barb a lot," McGuire answered carelessly. "Sell more, though, when Waggoman's away."

Jubal's head cocked slightly with interest. "Why more when Alec's away?"

"Hansbro runs the ranch then," said McGuire absently. "Seems like he'd rather trade here."

Three minutes later McGuire was thankful he hadn't said more to Jubal. Frank Darrah walked in from the back alley, looking dusty, tired, and short-tempered. He ignored McGuire and started into the office, and swung around frowning when McGuire called to him.

"Hansbro just left. He was in yesterday and this morning, too, wanting you."

"What does he want?" Frank snapped.

"Hansbro didn't say."

"Well, find him and tell him I'm here."

Frank shouldered on into the office, and closed the door and dropped tiredly into the desk chair.

For some moments he sat motionless, not bothering to remove his dusty, narrow-brimmed hat. Finally he yanked open a bottom drawer of the roll-top desk and lifted out a quart whisky bottle.

Frank looked at the bottle a moment before tilting it up and gulping from it straight. He put the uncorked bottle on the desk and sat feeling the raw whisky cut the edge of weariness. Finally a slow and satisfied smile touched the corners of Frank's mouth. There was always a way when a man was sure enough of himself. Frank Darrah had never killed a man before, but it had been surprisingly simple and quick, reaching an almost exalted satisfaction in knowing Chris Boldt had found Frank Darrah a coolly dangerous man to threaten. Dangerous—

Frank sat motionless, reflecting on the word. He had never considered himself a dangerous man— and he was dangerous. He was cool and keen, in the prime of life, and Barbara Kirby was lovely, and all the best years of life were opening ahead. Frank reached for the bottle again, and then turned his head, listening to heavy familiar steps scuffing back through the store to the office.

A final hasty swallow and Frank returned the bottle to the drawer. He was sitting in cool expectancy when Vic Hansbro stalked into the office.

"Shut the door," Frank directed. "What's on your mind, Vic?"

Chapter Fourteen

"Dave Waggoman's on my mind," Vic Hansbro growled. He dropped heavily to the chair beside the desk and worried the edge of his coarse, square-cut black beard with thick-fingers.

A smell of horses and corrals and sweat came off the man. Hansbro had a bearlike massiveness, almost animal-like, which Frank found faintly offensive now. There was a new kind of sullenness in the huge man's complaint.

"Alec raised hell over that trouble with Lockhart at the salt lakes."

"What about Dave?"

"He's turned on us," Hansbro said almost plaintively and more sullenly. "Told me in so many words he don't give a damn if Alec hears about them beeves you bought cheap for army contracts."

"Turned on me?" Frank said coldly. "How could he? I merely bought what Barb sold. Get that through your head, Hansbro. That's all I know."

"You paid cash an' understood it was on the quiet."

Frank glanced quickly at the closed office door. "Not so loud, you fool!"

"Let the damn' town hear if you're so lily-white, Darrah. You knew prime beef wouldn't go on the ranch books at that price. It'll all be Dave's money some day, so Dave took a little ahead of time for his own use."

"Then," advised Frank coldly, "let Dave explain it to his father. I merely bought what you offered."

"Dave'd get out of it. Dave'll still get Barb when Alec's gone, and he knows it. I handled the selling as a favor to Dave."

"Tell me what happened," Frank suggested.

It poured out of Hansbro bitterly. Alec Waggoman had warned Hansbro to control Dave's wild ways; Dave had defied Hansbro. And now, more clearly, Frank understood Alec Waggoman, Dave Waggoman, and Vic Hansbro. And the thought when it came was so subtle, so insidious that its bald, chill logic prickled along Frank's nerves.

Yesterday Frank Darrah would have turned hastily away from the tempting, almost dazzling idea. He would have been afraid. But this was to-day, after last night—after Chris Boldt—

Very carefully, very casually, smiling a little, Frank commented lightly, "Vic, it sounds as if you're damned if you do and damned if you don't. Too bad I'm not Alec Waggoman; we could get along. Have a drink."

"Wish you was Alec then," Hansbro growled, taking the bottle and tilting it to his mouth. When he lowered the bottle, Hansbro stared at it for a long moment before muttering absently, "Wouldn't your wife own Barb if anything happened to Dave?"

"I never thought of it that way; Barbara probably would," Frank agreed casually and then his long, slow breath came. Hansbro's ponderous mind had taken the oblique suggestion and built on it instinctively. And now Vic Hansbro would always believe his own sly and scheming thought had shaped what would logically follow.

"Alec won't live forever," Hansbro muttered

slowly. "Ain't anyone can tell what'll happen to Dave, the way he goes lookin' for trouble." Hansbro stared narrowly at Frank with new interest. "You sure might own Barb one day."

Frank laughed. "Then you'd be foreman for life, Vic. But Waggoman is healthy and Dave is young. Don't count on it."

Hansbro lifted the bottle and drank again, and ran his tongue slowly over his bruised lips. "Suppose Alec hears about them beeves you bought cheap and quiet?"

Frank shrugged. "If Alec Waggoman asks me, I'll tell him what I bought—what I paid. I can't afford to cover up for Dave's tricky schemes."

Vic Hansbro stood up slowly. He was, Frank thought distrustfully, a black-bearded brute of a man. He watched with a kind of hopeful fascination as Hansbro stood in scowling silence, thinking.

"You meant that?" Hansbro asked slowly.

"Meant what?"

"You'd have me run Barb for you?"

"I said so, didn't I? Who'd do it better, Vic? My present business affairs take all my time and attention." Frank leaned back in the chair. His chuckle put the idea in amusing perspective. "But, Vic—I don't own Barb. And there's mighty small chance I ever will. Don't start spending any salary you'll ever get from me."

Hansbro stared down at Frank, the beard hiding his expression. "I ain't counting on anything," Hansbro said finally. "But you made a promise I'll bring up if the time comes you can do it." Hansbro turned and stalked out, forgetting to close the door.

Frank sat motionless, staring at the empty doorway. A deep roil of new excitement and heady hope was stirring in him. Would it really happen? Would Hansbro's black thoughts goad him into making certain Frank Darrah would control Barb? Frank's new heady conviction had small doubt that it would happen quickly now. He sat speculating on whether it would be Alec Waggoman first, or Dave first—or both together.

Barbara Kirby's gay voice in the store brought Frank to his feet and out of the office. McGuire, smiling fatuously, was serving Barbara at the notions counter. Frank's own pulses quickened. In the simple white suit, Barbara had never looked more young and gay, more provocative and completely desirable.

Barbara's greeting was pleased. "Why, Frank! I didn't know you were back!"

"McGuire could have said so," was Frank's annoyed reminder to McGuire's bland glance.

Barbara studied the assortment of rickrack braid on the counter. "Ten yards of the narrow black," she decided. Her sobering interest returned to Frank. "Was that man Boldt drunk when he was murdered in Roxton Springs last night?"

"So they're talking about that here?" Frank tried to say indifferently. His throat had tightened and dried; he could feel the quickening thud of his heart. "I suppose he was drunk. Why?"

A small frown creased Barbara's smooth forehead. "I can't understand it. Did you see Lockhart after he was arrested?"

Frank stared. "So Lockhart did it?" he said after a moment. "I left Roxton before daybreak and hadn't heard."

"Do you think Lockhart is guilty?"

"The sheriff must think so," Frank said coolly

now. A kind of satisfied spite made him add, "Lockhart seems to make trouble everywhere he goes. This time it was bad—stabbing a man in the back and finishing him off in the throat after Boldt was on the ground."

"Did he do *that?*" was Barbara's shocked question.

McGuire, wrapping the black braid, reminded calmly, "Lockhart's fists were enough to stop Hansbro. He don't seem the throat-cutting kind."

Frank's anger at McGuire was completely unreasonable. He managed to hold it to a cold, "The trial will decide that."

Barbara started to say it mattered greatly whether Kate Canaday succeeded in hiring a cold-blooded killer as her foreman. But McGuire's calm conviction was oddly reassuring. Barbara took her small package and gave McGuire an innocently speculative look. "I'd guess you didn't sleep well last night, Mr. McGuire."

McGuire's stare was startled. Then his twinkling comprehension studied her. "Was Mrs. Dillon countin' snores on me?"

Barbara's chuckle admitted nothing. Frank went to the door with her, and when Frank turned back, he was curt with McGuire. "I'll be out until closing time." His dislike of McGuire was virulent now.

A new clerk would be hired as soon as possible, Frank decided. But at the moment a great bone-weariness from lack of rest all last night desperately needed a little sleep. And he could sleep peacefully now, Frank thought, with Lockhart safely jailed in Roxton Springs and Vic Hansbro riding back to Barb in a black, thoughtful mood. The future had never been brighter. Frank smiled leanly as he wondered what Lockhart's thoughts were now, in Roxton jail.

A lemon-yellow finger of the setting sun threaded the iron bars of Will Lockhart's cell window as the jail door creaked open.

Will heard Ira, the lank deputy, speak with surprising politeness. "This way, ma'am."

"You sure ain't keepin' a canary cage," was the vigorous, amiable voice Will heard next. Kate Canaday's broad, sun-reddened face advanced to the cell bars and peered through at him. "An' this ain't a canary," Kate decided. "It's got whiskers. If it was bald, I'd say it was a buzzard."

Will chuckled. This was the first breezy humor in a bleak night and day.

"Prisoner, ma'am, or visitor?" Will inquired.

"The sheriff may feel like lockin' me up before I leave. Half-Moon still needs a he-man foreman. Want it now, Lockhart?"

"No."

"Y' ain't the first one to bite a helping hand," said Kate amiably. She loomed there beyond the bars, a large, muscular, determined woman with a small black hat of battered straw trimmed with red cherries carelessly riding her iron-gray pompadour.

"One bite's all you git on me, young man," warned Kate cheerfully. She was hauling on a buckskin thong around her neck, bringing up a fat gold watch from her formidable bosom.

"A stranger who'd steal Barb salt, beat up a kindly man like Vic Hansbro, an' cut a throat here in Roxton Springs would try to duck honest work," Kate stated blandly. She was squinting at the watch, and she dropped it back into the capacious depths below her wind-burned throat. "In ten minutes, I'm headin' home, Lockhart. Maybe you ain't heard Judge Andy Vandiger'll be gone several weeks. This is your last chance to get out."

"Have you seen the judge?" Will inquired narrowly. He was thinking now of the scant hope offered by his lawyer. Two visits from Charley Yuill had brought small comfort. The final knife slash which had opened Chris Boldt's throat had offended even hardened Roxton Springs, Charley had pessimistically admitted.

"Yep," said Kate briskly. "Seen him in Coronado." From her sagging canvas brush jacket, Kate fished a folded document and held it up. "Ain't this a purty? Judge Andy signed it. Lets you out in my care until this knifin' is cleared up. Puts you back in if I say so." Kate beamed fondly at the document. "Be a cryin' shame to burn it. You got less'n eight minutes left."

Will smiled in wry exasperation. All the long, dragging day he had expected some officer from Fort Roxton to appear, checking on this Will Lockhart who was suspected of cold-blooded killing. Lieutenant Evans, Will had little doubt, would avidly investigate such a report. And Charley Yuill had brought disturbing news.

Last night a loaded freight wagon had rolled quietly away from Darrah's warehouse. Charley's guess matched Will's guess. The rifles from New Orleans had been in the warehouse, and had been hastily, furtively moved. But where? Charley was out of town now, searching.

"Five minutes, Lockhart."

Will asked narrowly, "Would you really burn that writ?"

"Wait an' see."

"You are," Will said calmly, "a hard-hearted, self-ish, scheming old woman."

"An' ugly, too," Kate Canaday reminded cheerfully. "I git nightmares thinkin' I'll be softhearted."

They eyed each other through the bars. Will's shrug, finally, was resigned. "All right—get me out of here."

Kate's chuckle came then.

"Y' had me sweatin', too. Now the Waggomans'll sweat. An' Vic Hansbro. Let's get home to Half-Moon."

She was, Will thought, as his trotting horse followed Kate Canaday's topless old buggy out of town, an amazing woman. He smiled faintly at remembrance of Sheriff Johnson's reluctant, irritated compliance with the writ.

Kate's buggy had carried him to the Mogollon Corrals for his horse. He had left a note for Charley Yuill at Charley's hotel. He knew now that Darrah had checked out of the Riverside Hotel about an hour after Darrah had been in the Gem Café.

All during that talk in the café, Darrah must have known a wagon was loading at his warehouse, known he was leaving town at once. Thinking of it, Will had a frustrating sense of failure. He had been neatly outmaneuvered while the rifles had been moved on, possibly toward the reservation country.

One small hope remained. If anyone could track the wagon, Charley could. Will was grateful now for Charley Yuill.

Night rolled purple, then moonless black over the wooded hills they were threading. Stars frosted the sky. Coyote clamor drifted on the wind and the lean, running hounds around Kate's buggy growled challenge. Will finally shook his horse to a faster trot and sided the buggy and lifted his voice in studied bluntness.

"Miss Canaday, I'm a stranger—not even a cattleman. I'm no good to you."

Her reply was amiable from the open buggy seat.

"You whipped Hansbro. You ain't kindly toward Barb. That'll do me."

"I've no quarrel with Barb. Waggoman paid me. And I've business of my own waiting."

"Nothin' to stop you ridin' off now."

"I promised to go to Half-Moon."

Kate's chuckle held grim satisfaction. "I told Judge Vandiger you'd keep a promise. Just between us, did you knife that feller?"

"No."

"Didn't think you did," said Kate genially. "This'll spoil your sleep: I outbluffed you. I'da got you out, anyway." Then Kate's shrewd guess came through the starlight. "You ain't a wagon freighter. Ain't got the hands or the talk. Your business concern Barb?"

"No."

"You workin' for Frank Darrah?"

"No. Does it matter?"

"Might. Darrah's sharp. He'd like to own Half-Moon if he can figure how to get it. He's already got Barb in his pocket."

Will's complete surprise made him blurt, "Got Barb? Darrah?"

"He's marryin' Barbara Kirby, ain't he? Her mother was Alec Waggoman's sister. If something happens to Dave, then Barbara gets Barb," came Kate's calm words through the dust-muffled trot of her team. "An' I wouldn't give a short two-bits for Dave's chance to grow gray hairs."

"Good God, no!" exclaimed Will.

Kate's quick retort jabbed back. "You seem certain about Dave dyin' young."

Will evaded. "He's a young hothead. How long can he back it up safely?"

"I been wondering," came Kate's ominous conviction. "That'll leave Barbara married to Darrah an' all Alec's holdings straight to them. I pinned diapers on that young lady. Her mother was my best friend. I ain't sure she oughta get married so hasty."

Will sensed much more behind the brief words. Kate Canaday's shadowy bulk on the open buggy seat was gazing toward him. He said nothing, and Kate's faintly grim voice went on.

"I ain't a fool old woman with a big hate on. Ain't a thought in Alec Waggoman's mind I can't guess. Alec's changed; his health ain't so good, although folks don't notice it. I know he's gettin' Barb ready for Dave. Alec took that chunk of my best winter graze the other day, so Dave'd have it. He told Barbara so. Alec never figured it'll only give Dave and Vic Hansbro ideas that they can snatch more of Half-Moon when they get control of Barb. And then finally we'll see Frank Darrah get it all. See what I'm tryin' to stop? My crew are good men. But they'll be a sight better under a foreman who's whipped Vic Hansbro with his fists."

It was a long speech. Will sensed a fierce, implacable determination behind the grim calmness of the big woman, silent now as she stared expectantly at him.

He told her soberly, "I've no doubt you're guessing correctly. But not about me. I can't help you against Barb. That's final."

"You'll go back to jail?" Kate asked incredulously.

"If I have to."

He heard then the first discouraged note in her assurance. "Y' fooled me. I'd still swear you ain't afraid."

"I've business of my own," Will reminded. His suggestion to her irresolution was cautiously oblique. "It might help me to be thought Half-Moon foreman, if I can move around— Might even help Miss Kirby."

He could see her sitting more erectly, peering alertly at him. "So that's how the bait cuts?" came her shrewd comment. "Y' mean that about Barbara?"

Will hesitated. "In confidence—"

"My loud mouth ain't a loose mouth," said Kate sharply. "Come on to Half-Moon then. They'll hear about it on Barb quick enough." Kate's laugh was short and grimly knowing. "It'll surprise a lot of folks who've thought Barb ruled the roost. Includin' Barb. You watch."

The swiftly spreading impact of what she had done would have pleased Kate Canaday immensely. Some of it would have surprised her. A little of it would have alarmed even Will Lockhart.

In Roxton Springs, indignation began to build over the release of the prisoner. Then details of Lockhart's wild fight with the Barb foreman began to circulate. There was growing, uneasy speculation as to what would happen now. In this region of vast, sun-washed distance and few settlers, all the gossip of a hundred distant miles was local property. All knew the Waggomans and Barb. All knew Kate Canaday and Half-Moon. And all recognized now the unmistakable promise of more trouble.

Lieutenant Evans heard the news from Sergeant Clancy, whose coldly critical eye was supervising muck-out of the long, low-roofed adobe stables at Fort Roxton. Lieutenant Evans fingered his sweeping tawny mustache and demanded with frowning formality, "Sergeant, are you completely certain of the facts?"

"That I am, sir," Clancy said with relish. "A Troop's McAllister heard it talked about in town las' night. Burdette, over there, seen the fight the night before. Same man that Barb burned out at the salt lakes." Clancy's lopsided grin considered the future. "This Lockhart'll be foreman of Half-Moon now, right next to Barb."

Evans's impatient shrug dismissed that. "You say Lockhart was arrested for murder? For knifing a man to death?"

"That he was." Clancy sounded envious. "Ain't every man has got a judge in his pocket to let him out after trouble like that."

Lieutenant Evans left the stables in frowning thought. He paused uncertainly at the corner of the quartermaster storehouse, came to a decision, and walked the echoing duckboards to the adjutant's building.

Ignoring the enlisted men at their endless paper

work in the big front room, Evans removed his garrison cap with crossed sabers above the visor and carefully knocked on the partly open door of Colonel Lake's office.

Chapter Fifteen

Lake's booming voice invited, "Well?"

"Lieutenant Evans, sir."

"Well, Evans, come in! Are you bashful?"

Flushing, Evans stepped in and with garrison cap formally under his left arm, saluted precisely. He was aware resentfully that the enlisted clerks had probably smirked at his back. Colonel Lake was a broad-shouldered man with fierce tufted eyebrows above pale-blue eyes, and his graying mustache was indifferently tended. Lake's blouse was unbuttoned at the neck. He lounged at the desk with a well-chewed cigar gone dead in his hand, and waited.

"Sir, I have a report which I should like to have quickly and quietly investigated. If the Colonel approves."

"Then close the door, Mister Evans, or there'll be nothing quiet about it."

Flushing again, Evans complied. Standing stiffly, cap under his arm, he formally explained the case of Lockhart.

Colonel Lake chewed slowly on the dead cigar and listened without expression. Colonel Mike Lake was, Evans knew, somewhat of a legend on the Indian frontier. And a complete disappointment when you reached his command. Lake was a loud man, carelessly indifferent to many of the niceties of regulations.

Lake's reply was colorlessly noncommittal. "Very

interesting, Mister Evans. I heard some of that after your patrol returned. You stood by, I understand, while a man's outfit was wantonly destroyed and his good mules slaughtered."

Red-faced, Evans reminded, "Sir, it was civilian business."

Lake took the cigar from his mouth. "Isn't the rest of your report civilian business also?"

"I believe, sir, the man is really Captain Lockhart. He has been arrested for suspected murder, a court-martial offense, entirely degrading to his army commission. There seems little doubt Lockhart is pursuing his feud with Barb Ranch. He will be in more trouble."

Lake's murmur was dry and neutral. "Quite a man. And how, Mister Evans, does all this concern you?"

"As an officer, sir, I feel that the man's identity should be established. This could result in a scandal of major proportion."

Lake's stare was thoughtful. "Possibly, if you should happen to be correct. I congratulate you, Mister Evans, on your devotion to regulations and—ah—the good name of the officers' corps." There was a bite in Lake's tone which carried into his question. "This man Lockhart has gone to Half-Moon Ranch as foreman?"

"Sergeant Clancy says so, sir."

"Very good, Mister Evans."

Saluting, wheeling precisely to leave, Evans had the uncomfortable, resentful feeling that an abrading sarcasm had backed the colonel's words. But with solid satisfaction, Evans felt the matter would not now be pigeonholed.

Colonel Lake watched the door close behind his

visitor. Slowly he swiped a match underneath the chair seat and got the chewed cigar going. He got to his feet and moved to the window, frowning. He stared out for some moments, and then shook his head and returned to the desk and scrawled a short message.

Request immediate and unofficial report on Captain William Lockhart. Where stationed. Present status. Present whereabouts. Repeat: confidential and unofficial. Michael Lake, Colonel, Commanding, Fort Roxton, Territory of New Mexico.

In Coronado late the same day, Jubal Kirby's dusty buckboard brought the mail again from Roxton Springs, and the astounding news that Will Lockhart, the stranger, was now foreman of Half-Moon. It aroused all the interest Jubal expected.

At home, Jubal found Barbara in the kitchen mixing a cake. Dusty, tired, and quizzically thoughtful, Jubal related what Kate Canaday had done. His expression grew reproachful as Barbara stood at the oilcloth-covered kitchen table and chuckled across the stoneware batter bowl.

"The poor man didn't have a chance," Barbara said in amusement. "Kate had her mind made up when she started to Roxton Springs after him."

"You knew Kate was up to that and didn't tell me?" Jubal accused. He shook his head and eyed his daughter dubiously. "If Kate wants trouble, she's got the makings now." Jubal ran fingers through his shock of Irish-black hair and considered his mirthful daughter warily. "Kate tell you what she's up to?"

Barbara lifted the spoon and critically watched

the creamy batter run off the end. "Barb and Alec Waggoman, naturally."

"Kate," said Jubal seriously, "had better keep her mind on Vic Hansbro and Dave. They're the powder. This man Lockhart is the match."

Barbara looked up, searching her father's face. "Is Lockhart that bad?"

"Kate oughtn't to put him that near Dave Waggoman and Hansbro," said Jubal absently. His glance had turned forlorn as it wandered around the kitchen. "Be mighty lonesome here after the wedding," Jubal admitted under his breath.

"You'll live with us."

Jubal made no comment, pretending not to notice the anxious look Barbara gave him. After a moment Barbara said slowly, "You don't want me to marry Frank, do you?"

Jubal's chuckle was rueful. "Only make you more stubborn if I said so, wouldn't it?" He studied her, and asked abruptly, "What does Kate Canaday think about it?"

"The same as you do, I think," Barbara admitted. "I don't know why."

"Kate knows there's not a man in these parts good enough for you."

"You're evading," Barbara said.

"A man with a spitfire daughter gets the habit," said Jubal largely. He ended their talk by going to his room to change his dusty driving clothes and shave and bathe.

Barbara poured the batter into three square cake pans in a sober mood. The youthful, chuckling lightheartedness seemed to have left Jubal. He was absent-minded and thoughtful much of the time. He had not, so far as Barbara knew, been in

McGrath's saloon since his tremendously successful evening at poker. He was not Jubal.

Tomorrow, Barbara decided, she would ride out to Half-Moon again and talk with Kate about Jubal— And talk again about Frank Darrah. Kate was the one person in the world who would bluntly, unselfishly give her shrewd advice. Barbara, suddenly and rather desperately, wanted advice.

In the same gathering dusk, Frank Darrah locked the front door of his store and began to empty the cash drawers. He was pleasantly, excitedly tired. Today he had dispatched more men and wagons to the salt lakes to join an advance crew he had sent from Roxton Springs. And all day with increasing expectancy his thoughts had been on Vic Hansbro, wondering what the man would do, and when it would happen. There was a mounting fever now in the hope that Barb—all of fabulous Barb—might suddenly come into Frank Darrah's control.

Frank stood motionless at the cash drawer under the canned goods counter, thinking of it, hardly noticing his clerk, McGuire, pausing in the aisle with broom and dustpan.

McGuire's casual "Kind of a surprise, Lockhart going to Half-Moon," brought Frank's glance up, frowning.

"The man's in jail," Frank said shortly.

"Was," McGuire corrected. "Miss Canaday got him out on a court order. Made him foreman."

Frank's stare was startled. Then he had the quick suspicion McGuire was covertly estimating his reaction. Then the full meaning of McGuire's statement hit hard. Lockhart was out— Lockhart was near Coronado again— Lockhart was close once more to Frank Darrah—

Sharply Frank ordered, "Get to your sweeping."

His mouth had dried out. His hand reaching for greenbacks in the cash drawer was unsteady. Frank stared helplessly at the hand and a vitriolic tide swept him.

Lockhart was taking on a creeping implacability. Frank had again the unreal sensation that dead hands were reaching from the Dutch Canyon massacre. His question to McGuire who had moved to the rear of the store had a thick forced sound.

"How d'you know all that about Lockhart?"

"Jubal Kirby brought the mail from Roxton an' told it." McGuire's guess was reflective. "No telling now what'll happen between Barb an' Half-Moon."

Frank stuffed greenbacks and coins into a canvas money sack and crossed to the other cash drawer. He paused there at the bolt goods counter thinking with rising fascination of Lockhart on Half-Moon, and Vic Hansbro, Alec Waggoman, and Dave close by on Barb. Trouble between those explosive men would be bitter and deadly. Men would die.

Frank's finger tips automatically fitted into the combination pulls of the cash drawer. He hardly heard the bell's thin tinkle warning as the drawer slid out. The trouble might easily be set off. Vic Hansbro could do it. Then a new, suggestive thought made Frank pause again.

Half-Moon might well be crippled financially if savage trouble broke out between the two big ranches. A keen trader might find an opening to take over control of Half-Moon quickly—

The thought held Frank fascinated as he emptied the day's cash onto his office desk for counting. If Vic Hansbro did not appear in town in the morning, Frank decided, a trip out to Barb might be immensely profitable. He would go.

George Freall heard the news in Kitty's Café. In frowning thought, Freall finished his coffee and retraced his steps to the bank he had just closed.

Freall liked to say the bank was successful because he understood the country and the people. Now with the bank's green window shades still down, Freall opened the safe and carried the small metal note case to his office desk.

He sat a long while considering certain notes and assignments bearing Kate Canaday's vigorous signature. His sober thoughts ranged over the possibilities if a feud exploded between Half-Moon and Barb. It had long been a possibility, Freall glumly admitted now. And this stranger Lockhart was the man to spark the feud off and make it totally dangerous.

Sighing, finally, Freall returned the note case to the safe. Uneasy premonitions, he knew, would plague his evening. He had known Alec Waggoman and Kate Canaday in the old days when the three of them were young. And this promised a tragic ending, George Freall thought apprehensively, to those still clear and cherished memories. And he had no idea of what he or the bank might do.

Not long before the post office closed, Tom Quigby, the deputy, got his mail, a lone letter from Sheriff Johnson at Roxton Springs.

On the boardwalk outside, Quigby read the sheriff's heavy scrawl casually, then intently.

> *Dear Tom: Maybe you've heard I arrested on suspicion of murder one Will Lockhart, who had the trouble with Barb at the salt lakes and fought the Barb foreman in Coronado. He had another fist fight after he got here. The other man was found knifed to death a little later. Man named Boldt. He'd been drunk. Lockhart claims he never saw Boldt before. So far I can't prove different. Can you?*
>
> *Anyway, Miss Canaday, of Half-Moon, turned up with an order signed by Judge Vandiger and took Lockhart to Half-Moon as foreman. I look for trouble now between Half-Moon and Barb. It'll put hell in your hip pocket if it breaks. Head it off if you can. Send me word if it starts.*

Quigby's soft oath was heartfelt as he shoved the letter into his pocket and moved on in frowning concentration. A lone stranger, Quigby reflected rather dismally, could cause enough trouble. But when the stranger was a lean, smiling, completely hard and dangerous man like Lockhart, already wronged by Barb, and backed now by someone like Kate Canaday and her Half-Moon crew, then the sheriff's fears were entirely justified.

The man named Boldt was not familiar to Quigby. He found a bartender presently in McGrath's saloon who recalled Boldt hazily, unfavorably, and none of it connected with Lockhart.

By then Quigby was aware of a mounting tension in the town, like a storm gathering on the peaks, barely muttering, but threatening devastation for the range. Everyone knew Barb and Kate Canaday, and the town had seen Lockhart in action.

A small rancher named Webb told Quigby apprehensively, "A shootin' feud'll draw cutthroats here from the Texas Llano to Tucson. With 'Paches at our backs now, a big range war'll bust us small outfits."

The man, Quigby knew, was right. And Tom Quigby was only one lone deputy on all this far-flung Coronado range. Not taken too seriously, either. Certainly not by Barb.

Then Quigby's Texan stubbornness and belligerency took command. Alec Waggoman and Lockhart were the key men. Each of them, Quigby decided, would have his warning in the morning. It might be possible to head off the trouble.

The next morning the steady road lope of Tom Quigby's horse was far from Coronado when Barbara Kirby saw Frank Darrah on the other side of Main Street and waved a greeting. Barbara halted, smiling, while Frank hurried across the street to her.

He looked as if he hadn't slept well, Barbara thought, as Frank stepped on the boardwalk beside her. Hat in hand, smiling, he referred to her divided riding-skirt. "Going somewhere?"

"Half-Moon," Barbara said lightly, and she wondered guiltily what Frank would say if he suspected her errand was a sober talk with Kate about Frank himself.

"I might," Frank said easily, "have to ride to Barb."

"I'll wait for you," offered Barbara impulsively.

Frank hesitated, then shook his head.

"Might be several hours. And I might not go." He took her hand, pressing tightly. "You're lovely this morning." A restrained huskiness filled Frank's admission, "Darling, it's hard to wait."

Later, riding out of town, Barbara caught her underlip absently between her teeth as she wondered why Frank's ardent confession had given her an uneasy sense of detachment and unreality this morning. The guilty feeling persisted as her roan gelding splashed into the ford of Chinaman Creek and dipped its muzzle into the cold, clear current. Then the gelding's head came up as a man riding bareback on a big mouse-colored mule emerged from the brush on the creek bank.

Barbara recognized the flaming red hair and beard bristle. He was Lockhart's man who had watered her horse at the salt lakes—Charley Yuill— and Yuill's grin behind the mule's long ears showed that he remembered her, too.

"Seems we meet at waterin'-places, ma'am."

Barbara laughed, while a cautious part of her mind reminded that he was Lockhart's man. She watched him shove the lop-brimmed black hat back on the startling red hair. He continued to grin while he asked a question.

"There's a stone building back in there. No windows in it. No one around. Got an iron door with a big lock, an' two extra padlocks. What is it?"

Chapter Sixteen

Barbara chuckled as her horse moved out of the water and halted beside the big placid mule. "That stone building," she told Charley Yuill, "is a powder house. Darrah's store in Coronado keeps a stock of powder there, where no damage will be done if the building blows up."

"Now whyn't I guess that?" he wondered.

"Are you still working for Lockhart?"

His bright black eyes regarded her with amusement. "What kind of work, ma'am, with him locked up in Roxton jail?"

"He's out, and foreman of Half-Moon now."

A startled look considered her. "Out? An' foreman of a ranch?"

Barbara nodded. His faint grin returned. "Well, now, he might have a job for me. How do I get to this Half-Moon?"

"I'm going there."

He wheeled the mule alongside her gelding. They were riding together before Barbara wondered why he had been back in the brush out of sight when she rode to the ford. "Were you," she asked casually, "in Roxton when Lockhart was arrested?"

He seemed to think that over before admitting, "I was."

"Did he really kill the man?"

The snort of denial was immediate. "Couldn't have. I was walkin' with Lockhart at the edge of town. The sheriff just wouldn't believe it."

An impulse made Barbara jab, "So you left Lockhart there in jail?"

"Uh-huh. Before the sheriff locked me up, too." His glance was quizzical. "How'd Lockhart get out an' light in a fine ranch job?"

"Half-Moon's owner, Miss Canaday, secured his release."

Charley Yuill seemed amused. "Might be I'll like ranchin', too—if Lockhart'll hire me."

Barbara's conviction crystallized that Lockhart would hire this man without question, and her vague distrust increased. Were more strangers coming to Half-Moon, to be hired by Lockhart? She glanced furtively at Charley Yuill. An impassive thoughtfulness had dropped on him. He rode now without looking at her. Completely uneasy, Barbara resolved on blunt talk with Kate Canaday about all this. And then with increasing apprehension she wondered what Alec Waggoman's reaction would be to Lockhart heading the Half-Moon crew.

At Barb this morning Alec Waggoman paced in slow restlessness through shafts of sunlight inside the east windows of the ranch office. The door stood open to the clean freshness of a new day. Waggoman stepped out on the porch, and the far-flung, blurred world before his failing eyes seemed almost in his grasp. But not quite. All that grandeur, all that beauty to the far horizon was clear and vivid only in memory. In aching memory.

He could smell the winy tang of the conifer forests on the high slopes back of the ranch headquarters. He could hear mountain jays calling raucously down the ranch road. A woodpecker was drumming on the tall dead tree beyond the horse corrals—

That much was left him, Waggoman thought with an odd, humble gratitude. His eyes would never see it again. But he could smell it. He could hear it.

The peckerwoods, he recalled, had come to that same tree for many years. With a faint smile, Waggoman wondered if the busy bird he could hear had been hatched in that tall, dead giant tree, and had come back this year to carry on its inheritance—like Dave would do with Barb—

Always, these days, his thoughts came back to Dave, Waggoman realized. His smile faded as he stood thinking about Dave. Then the steady beat of a loping horse on the ranch road intruded. Waggoman lifted his head, peering to see who was coming. Defeated, he turned back into the office, gripped by the growing ache of helplessness, of uselessness.

He heard the horse come directly to the short tie rail outside. He was sitting at the scarred old roll-top desk at the right of the office doorway, a lighted cigar between his fingers, when the rider dismounted. Purposeful steps came up on the porch and entered the office.

The man's greeting was serious and blunt. "Glad I caught you in, Mr. Waggoman."

Waggoman considered the faintly blurring, lanky figure. His question was mild. "Why, Quigby, are you glad I'm here?"

"Because that fellow Lockhart is foreman now at Half-Moon."

Waggoman sat very still. His first startled reaction was despair and anger. This he had feared. This he had hoped against. Now it had happened.

"So Kate hired the man?" he said without visible emotion.

"You hadn't heard?"

"Vic Hansbro came from town a couple of days ago and said Lockhart was in trouble at Roxton Springs. That's all."

Quigby dropped on the chair beside the desk without invitation. He was blunt. "Lockhart was being held on suspicion of murder. Miss Canaday got him out. That mean anything to you?"

"Why should it?"

With a kind of frustration, Quigby thought that this tall old man with the majestic sweep of white mustaches looked like the hard rock he was. No emotion at all on that bold-nosed, craggy face. No betraying flicker in the blank baffling stare.

"Lockhart had trouble with Barb. Miss Canaday don't like you. Looks like trouble now," Quigby said curtly.

"What kind of trouble?"

"Shooting."

"Not from Barb," said Waggoman in irritating mildness. "Go to Kate Canaday and Lockhart."

"I'm going to." Quigby thought the ghost of a smile touched Waggoman's mouth, lacking all humor, a little sad. He shook off the thought. Waggoman sad?

"Quigby, has there been much rustling this year?" came Waggoman's reflective question.

"No more than usual."

"I've been checking on our range tallies. They add up short."

"Beef roundup will probably straighten it out," Quigby hazarded.

"I doubt it," Waggoman said dryly. "I allowed for loose tallying. We had no winter drift. Indians haven't cut into us this year. Leaves rustling, doesn't it?"

Quigby's belligerence was instinctive. "Meaning rustlers have been operating under my nose and I don't know it?"

"Meaning nothing. I've been away. The small outfits can always use a little increase. You know it. I know it. Our men are out now, tallying down from the highest summer grass. If we find rustling sign, we'll look into it."

It was mild; it lacked threat, and Quigby had the awkward feeling his "Let me know," sounded equally awkward as he stood up. Yarns of the old days, of the scant mercy this tall old man had showed those who rustled Barb beef, came to Quigby now. He tried to read the old threat in Waggoman's manner, and failed. Yet Quigby had the annoyed feeling he'd been warned and dismissed.

In fact, came Quigby's irritable conviction, he hadn't accomplished much here. Alec Waggoman made him feel young and unneeded—made him seem unwanted, unnecessary. The best he could think to say was a grimly stubborn, "I'll get on over to Half-Moon."

"You do that," was Waggoman's mild suggestion. He was eyeing the cigar without expression when Quigby walked out, feeling a little foolish.

Alec Waggoman did not move until the beat of Quigby's departing horse faded. Then he stood up and walked heavily to the east windows and stared out at the soaring blur of the mountains.

He was thinking with restless foreboding of Dave again—Dave, riding the high country today with

Vic Hansbro and the rest of the crew. And when Waggoman thought of Lockhart, too, close now on Half-Moon, the despair came back in full tide.

Dave was almost entirely on his own now. And Dave was not ready. What was going to happen to Barb? And to Dave?

Vic Hansbro's heavy thoughts were pondering the same thing later in the day when Hansbro's horse kicked a small stone skittering off the narrow, steeply descending South Peak trail.

Hansbro's gaze left Dave's back just ahead and dipped to watch the small stone gathering speed down some fifty feet of steep slope under the trail edge. A feather of fine dust lingered as the stone arced out into space and fell from sight. It would strike, Hansbro knew, on jagged outcrops and would keep falling. Finally it would smash terribly on the talus rubble far below.

A horse—a rider—dropping off this high narrow trail would make the same great plunge through space. The two of them were here alone. No one but Vic Hansbro would know exactly what had happened.

The tempting, sweating knowledge had been in Hansbro's thoughts since he and Dave had started the short cut off the high grass meadows under South Peak's bald crown.

Vic Hansbro's gaze came back in nagging fascination to the bunching haunch muscles of Dave's long-backed gray gelding, lifted almost fearfully to Dave himself, braced unsuspectingly in the saddle.

Dave's horse was cautiously descending the treacherous footing, keeping over to the vertical rock on the inside of the trail. Dave's wiry body was braced back against the saddle cantle, feet strongly in the stirrups.

Vic Hansbro's half-hypnotized stare reached past Dave's shoulders and Dave's wide-brimmed gray hat to the trail's sharp turn to the right just ahead.

Below that elbow turn, vast and empty space dropped dizzily away.

Sweat came in a thin sheen to Hansbro's forehead and felt chill at the roots of his black, chopped-off beard. One sharp spur rake would drive his startled horse lunging between Dave's gray gelding and the inner rock of the cliff. Dave's horse would be shouldered to the trail edge and crowded off—

The rest of it fled through Hansbro's brain, vivid as the small stone he had watched fall. One screaming, kicking plunge over the edge; the helpless, scrambling slide—and then the great drop from sight. All over in a few brief seconds. One more accident in the mountains. No blame, no blame at all for Vic Hansbro.

Slowly, carefully, Hansbro worked his feet more solidly into the stirrups. His big fist tightened mechanically on the reins. Sweat slicked his palms. He glanced down at the hands, thinking they'd never perspired quite like this before. Then, gripping the reins tighter, Hansbro forced his gaze again to Dave's unsuspecting back.

Chapter Seventeen

It seemed to Hansbro that a tremendous effort of muscle and will was needed to spur his horse forward against Dave's horse. It had seemed easy, this quick, sure way for Vic Hansbro to dominate Barb in the years to come.

Now some great new unsuspected instinct was intruding with bewildering force. That was Dave's unsuspecting back which would plunge through dizzying space— *That was Dave—*

Then in a frightening way Dave seemed to sense his danger. Over a shoulder, Dave suddenly, sharply ordered, "Hold it, Vic!" Dave's haul on the reins stopped his horse.

In Hansbro, exploding reflexes made him savage his own horse to a halt. Then Hansbro sat stiffly while a great weakness seeped into his knees and his brain grappled with the flood of baffling emotion. He had shot men; he had beaten men bloody and helpless and had enjoyed both. But this was Dave, a part of Alec, a part of Barb itself.

In an oddly fearful way, it came to Vic Hansbro now that Dave was, somehow, a full part of his own life. Through the years he had tried to bind Dave close to Vic Hansbro, so that when Alec was dead, it would be Dave and Vic Hansbro and Barb. A flashing memory came of Dave, the small boy, riding trustfully, eagerly beside him—

All that, back through the years, seemed to have tied Vic Hansbro to Dave. Hansbro swallowed a bewildered groan and looked down fearfully at the great drop below the trail edge.

Dave was gazing intently into the valley below. "Hand me the glass," Dave ordered without looking around.

Hansbro fumbled for the leather-cased telescope tied behind his saddle. Reining carefully forward, he put the scuffed, powerful glass into Dave's back-reaching hand. Then, easing his horse clear, Hansbro sat in a bewildered slump, watching Dave focus the glass.

Here the upper slopes of South Peak dropped in naked cliffs to the lush green floor of the valley. The far side of the valley was easier, timbered slopes; and through the mottled greenery of the valley floor, Chinaman Creek writhed like a silver snake fleeing the peaks.

Barb steers down there looked sheep-size. Hansbro's question had a thick raspiness beyond his control. "What is it?"

"Shut up," said Dave carelessly, not moving the glass from his eye.

A year ago, was Hansbro's bitter thought, Dave wouldn't have used the careless, contemptuous tone. Nor six months ago. The change in Dave had begun with Alec's long trips away. Dave's natural arrogance had fed mightily on the lack of restraint. But the steers sold quietly to Frank Darrah had seemed to put a final contempt in Dave's manner.

That connivance with Dave had delivered Vic Hansbro completely into Dave's hands, Hansbro had realized in angry bitterness. He had hoped it would tie Dave closer, and it had undone all he'd tried to shape in Dave: the feeling that Vic Hansbro was Dave's needed friend. Now in gnawing indecisiveness, Hansbro watched Dave lower the glass and twist around in the saddle.

A quick, hot anger was thinning Dave's mouth. "Guess who's coming into the valley?"

"Who?"

"That Lockhart!"

"He was jailed at Roxton Springs!"

"Not now." Dave was smoldering. "He's heading into the valley, toward those steers. On Barb land again!"

A sullen caution moved in on Hansbro again. "Alec said to forget him."

Dave sneered. "Don't nursemaid me, Vic. If Lockhart's rustling, we'll take him." Then Dave's thin grin was taunting. "Maybe Lockhart rustled the steers Alec says are missing. The ones you peddled, Vic."

Stung, as Dave intended, Hansbro glowered. "I can show Alec there's been rustling."

"Who did it?" Dave taunted.

"Half-Moon."

"Vic, you fool! Not Half-Moon!"

"Alec'll believe it."

"How?"

"Never mind."

Dave's glance narrowed estimatingly. "Then you're better than I think," was Dave's grudging opinion. He leaned far back in the saddle, returning the glass. "Fitz and some of the men will be down the lower trail. We'll corral Lockhart."

Hansbro reminded thickly, "Alec said let him alone. You want Alec to fire me?"

Dave sneered again. "Who cares? Go back if you're afraid of Lockhart now." Dave rode on.

Hansbro held his horse from following. He

watched Dave pass from sight around the sharp bend in the trail, and then Hansbro began to curse helplessly. He'd been a fool, betrayed by some obscure weakness. And for what? Dave would fire him at the first whim of temper after Dave had Barb.

It wouldn't happen again, Hansbro promised himself wildly. But that tall old man back at the ranch office had given his final order about Lockhart, Hansbro knew in the bitterness which gripped him. And Alec was still boss. Hansbro short-reined his horse around on the narrow trail and started back toward the top.

Will Lockhart had made this day's ride into the high country while waiting for Charley Yuill to find the written instructions at Roxton Springs and follow to Half-Moon.

As he rode upward into lofty stands of Douglas fir and red spruce and white spruce, Will could see increasingly the far sweep of the lower country. Bleached sands of dry arroyos and the shadowy run of wide draws gashed patterns across the purpling distance.

Following the trails higher, Will found Half-Moon cattle increasingly in meadows, small parks, and grassy pockets of these upper slopes. When screaming winter gales piled vast drifts below the peaks, these half-wild steers and suspicious cows would be on the rich, sun-cured graze of the lower range. But Barb cattle would be on the huge Gallegos tract leased away from Half-Moon by Alec Waggoman. No wonder, Will reflected, Kate Canaday was disturbed, worried, belligerent. She would need that winter graze.

In this high country there were no line fences.

Will topped a great saddle of the mountain and found a park-like valley falling away before him, threaded by a sinuous, tumbling little stream. Naked yellow cliffs to the left soared high; the right side of this high, smiling valley was gentler forested slopes.

Scattered cattle grazed ahead, and Will presently sighted his first Barb steer. He reined over, studying the bold curved brand with its down-slashing barb at the tip. Near by a Half-Moon steer stared warily.

Along here, Will guessed, the two ranches came together without fence lines. He rode on down the pleasant valley, estimating the brands, for what interest Kate Canaday might have in the commingling with Barb. A little more and he'd turn back.

Will was wondering what chance there was of Charley Yuill being at Half-Moon when he returned when a snapping rifle shot slashed the valley quiet and bounced slamming echoes off the high cliff face.

Will's horse lunged, front legs buckling. Will's hand slapped instinctively to the saddle horn as he kicked the stirrups away. His instant furious thought was: *Barb again! Hansbro, probably! And no witnesses now to a killing!*

The horse fell heavily and Will barely launched clear. He struck the ground off balance on a skidding foot and fell hard, his handgun already out in his fist.

The horse's head heaved up convulsively as Will rolled to a prone position, searching for the hidden gun.

In the timeless past a great chunk of the high cliff had split off and fallen into a giants' rubble heap on the valley floor. From among those great rocks the shot had come. There now Will sighted a figure moving out from behind an immense, tilted chunk of the yellow sandstone—holding a rifle ready. Not Hansbro— This one lacked Hansbro's black, chopped-off beard. Will was already shooting through the dust haze around his horse.

He saw stone dust spurt beside the target and belated recognition came. That youthful, wiry figure with heavy silver on the sagging gunbelt was Dave Waggoman.

Will lowered the heavy, wooden-handled forty-four. He was remembering Alec Waggoman's curt order for Dave to stand back from the fight with Vic Hansbro in town. That tall old man with the bold-nosed, majestic face must be unaware of this.

Dave had dodged back out of sight. A second rifle shot drove its sharp report through the quivering valley. Dust fountained up an arm's length from Will's head. And this gun was behind him among the first trees on the lifting slope. He was boxed without cover, Will realized, glancing over his shoulder.

He weighed the chance of a dodging run toward the big rocks where Dave was hiding, and abandoned the idea as a second rifle shot back in the trees drove dirt spurting close again in pointed warning.

Will holstered the handgun and lifted an arm and sat up. His horse now lay inertly. He eyed the beast with somber anger and then watched six riders spur toward him from concealment among the trees.

Will got to his feet, retrieved his black hat, and knocked dirt from his denims as the running Barb horses drove sheets of spray from the small creek. The men reined up in a crescent beside him, and again Will was struck by the fine horses they rode, the competent, hard look of the men.

The short, sallow-faced rider at the end was Fitz, who had roped Will at the salt lagoons and held him while the mules were shot and four big freight wagons burned. Fitz dismounted, dropping the long reins, and stepped to Will and plucked out the holster gun.

"So Barb is killing horses this time," Will commented in cold disgust.

Fitz grinned as he examined Will's gun. "Mighta been you."

Fitz's head turned as one of the men muttered sharply, "Dave's hand! Now there'll be hell to pay!"

Dave was coming, rifle in his right hand and a blue bandanna wrapped around his left fist. Blood dripped from the bandanna cloth. One look at Dave's face and watchful, regretful calm settled on Will. Dave's features and full underlip which reminded Will vaguely of Barbara Kirby's mouth, were pale now in malignant anger.

"Get his gun!" Dave called in thin-voiced rage. He stepped around the dead horse's head. The bandanna on his left hand was sodden with blood. Dave's glare had a wild, pale fury.

Here, Will saw, tensing, was unbridled temper wildly out of control. He guessed shock and pain like this had never really happened to Dave before. Always there had been Barb; always Barb's power backed by the tough Barb crew. And behind that always the ruthless force of Alec Waggoman.

Dave's thin-voiced rage shook with the wild viciousness. "I should have killed you, Lockhart!"

The futility of arguing made Will shrug silently. Hansbro was evidently not with this bunch, and probably just as well, Will decided bleakly. Dave was bad enough now.

Dave shoved his rifle at Fitz. "Gimme his gun!" Dave's shaking voice ordered.

Silent unease had dropped on the Barb men. Fitz's sallow face had lost its grin as he surrendered Will's handgun.

"Y' ain't gonna kill him?" Fitz muttered.

"Shut up!" Dave was examining Will's gun. His hand was unsteady. He held up the left hand and watched the blood drip for a moment. "Hold his arms!" Dave ordered thinly.

Fitz caught Will's right arm. A brawnier Barb man gripped Will's other arm. Both men seemed uncertain, uneasy. Will saw the futility of trying to wrestle away and stood quietly.

Dave lifted his bleeding left hand again. "Look at it, damn you!" Dave choked, and Will stiffened against the blow Dave evidently meant to strike with Will's own gun. Then in pale rage, Dave shoved the gun muzzle at Will's left palm and pulled the trigger.

Will's unbelieving comprehension and great lunge to wrench the hand away were not enough. He felt the hands tighten convulsively on his arms as the shot crashed out.

Dave moved back from the swirl of black powder smoke, and Will stood with his own wild and helpless rage, head turned, staring at the mutilated hand. He felt no pain. That would come later. When the Barb men released the arm, it swung down against Will's leg and blood dripped off the fingers.

"Same hand, same gun!" Dave spat at him. "How d'you like it?"

Will had to swallow and breathe deep to keep his own wild outrage steady. "I don't like it!" he said thinly. "Tell your father there's a limit to what Barb can do! It's been passed!"

Dave sneered and spoke to the Barb men. "Shove him off our land and get back to work. I'll ride to Doc Seldon in town an' get this hand fixed. Fitz, get my horse."

Will was stripping off his own bandanna and wrapping the hand. There was, he saw with relief, no spurting arterial blood. More talk was useless. He watched Dave start down the valley, and then ran a coldly estimating gaze over the Barb men before wheeling away for the long punishing walk back to Half-Moon.

"Hold it, Lockhart!" It was the brawny man who had held Will's left arm. "We'll tie your saddle on my horse. This wasn't our doin'. It ain't the Old Man's way to have a man held while a bullet is pumped into him. Dave went crazy."

Most of Will's chill fury shifted from these hired hands. "Where's Hansbro?"

"Up higher."

"Is Alec Waggoman at the ranch?"

"Was this mornin'."

"I'll stop there on my way to the doctor," Will decided.

He got a flat "Dave'll be ahead of you. Ride to town on the Half-Moon side. See the Old Man later if you have to. Been enough trouble for today."

After a moment Will nodded, not certain he could trust himself if he did catch up with Dave. He waited for the saddle horse, and pain began to crawl up the arm, and the promise of great trouble ahead moved in with dark certainty.

Of those who rode this day from Coronado toward Barb and Half-Moon, Frank Darrah was the last. He had waited overly long for Vic Hansbro to appear in town. Finally, wishing he'd made the ride with Barbara, Frank had started for Barb.

Today he wore a revolver and shell belt under his coat and carried a carbine in the saddle scabbard, a thing he almost never bothered to do. There was insidious threat in the thought that Lockhart was close again, backed now by Kate Canaday's influential friendship. And she was influential. At times it seemed the big, loud, coarse-featured woman knew most people of importance in the Territory.

Alec Waggoman knew them also. Barb—Half-Moon—If those two big outfits warred openly, the destructive impact would be felt throughout the Territory. And it would be destructive, Frank mused. Only outsiders could possibly benefit. Someone like Frank Darrah, a cool, quick-thinking —yes, dangerous, too—young man, whose star was in an almost magical ascent. Everything fell right for a man who could grasp opportunity and turn it to his needs. And today Vic Hansbro might have the needed idea how Barb and Half-Moon could be set quickly at each other.

Hansbro might also have his own sullen wish to deal with Lockhart's presence on Half-Moon. Conning that idea closely, Frank made the turn off the Roxton road, and at the first wooded, sugar-loaf hills he rode onto Barb land.

The green oak thickets and grassy draws under

the low foothill ridges assumed today a new, grati-
fying significance. With a proprietary eye, Frank
reflected that all this, as far as one's gaze could
reach, might someday belong to Frank Darrah. In
an unbelievably short time, too, if Vic Hansbro
could be prodded in the right way.

The rough, narrow road cut up a shallow finger
canyon and debouched into a winding, grassy valley. The horse pricked ears inquiringly and Frank
had the quick, hopeful thought he might be meeting Vic Hansbro.

But the rider who came into sight was Dave Waggoman.

Frank halted his own horse with a disgruntled
yank of the reins. He could do without Dave; he had
little wish to see the arrogant young hothead today.
It was Vic Hansbro who was all-important now.

Chapter Eighteen

Dave's pale and set face lacked any friendliness. Then Frank saw the blood-crusted blue cloth around Dave's left hand and half-guilty fear struck him. Had Vic Hansbro made a try at Dave and failed? And then under pressure had Hansbro been forced to open his dark and greedy thoughts to the Waggomans?

It required an effort to ask as Dave reined up, "Your hand! What happened?"

Dave's glower and tight-lipped tension carried no particular enmity for Frank Darrah. "That fellow Lockhart shot me," Dave gritted. "Roll me a cigarette."

"Cigar?"

"Cigarette, dammit! Here, makin's in my pocket. I'm no good with one hand."

Frank inquired cautiously as he started the smoke, "How did it happen?"

"Caught him on Barb land again. God, this hand hurts!" Dave groaned; then viciously, "I hope his hand hurts worse!"

Quickly, hopefully, Frank asked, "Was Lockhart shot, too?"

Dave's satisfaction was white-lipped. "With the same damn' gun that shot my hand!" Dave pulled a wooden-handled forty-four from inside his wide, silver-buckled cartridge belt. "This one! I shoved it against his own damn' hand and pulled the trigger! Hope he loses the hand!" Dave sucked a breath of pain again, glowering at the bloody bandanna. "Doc Seldon in town?"

"He was this morning," Frank said, holding out the cigarette and a match. "What happened exactly, Dave?" Dave might have been killed. Frank breathed a little faster as all the possibilities raced through his mind. Here was the first violence between Barb and Half-Moon—between the Waggomans and Lockhart— The closest sort of a shave already for Dave.

Frank listened intently as Dave sucked smoke deep and jerkily related what had happened, with no capacity, Frank saw, for admitting that Dave Waggoman might have been wrong. Dave's natural arrogance was supreme; his belief in the ruthlessness of Barb overwhelming.

Thoughtfully Frank inquired, "Is Lockhart heading for Doc Seldon, too?"

"How the hell do I know?" Dave answered unpleasantly.

"You might run into Lockhart between here and town."

"Suits me."

"Going to send Lockhart's gun back?"

"I'll leave it in town."

Frank was unaware of the precise second the idea stirred full-blown and enticing in his brain. Suddenly his heart was pounding. The tension of it slid through nerves to tingling finger tips. He's passed no one, Frank recalled, since turning off the Roxton road.

Dave had come directly down from the high shoulders of South Peak, missing the Barb headquarters. All the Barb crew, Dave had just said, were in the high country today. And who had any idea that Frank Darrah had ridden this way? He hadn't mentioned it in town. And until the Barb crew returned at dusk, no one else would suspect that Dave was here in the foothills. Then it would be night—

"My business at the ranch," Frank decided, smiling, "wasn't very important. Mostly an excuse to get out from the store. I'll ride back to town with you." He was forcing the smile. His throat was tight; great slow thumps of his heart must surely be noticeable. In a lifetime—at least once—was Frank's rather desperate decision now, a gamble became so certain, the reward so great, that a man could not hesitate—

Dave was saying indifferently, "Suit yourself."

Dave lifted the reins with his good hand and rode on, and Frank wheeled his horse and rode with him, speaking lightly. "What will you do with Lockhart's gun?"

Dave passed over the heavy revolver. "Give it to Lockhart," was Dave's surly suggestion.

Frank held the weapon gingerly, fascinated. Dave put his horse into a slow lope and drew ahead. Frank gazed at Dave's unsuspecting back in growing fascination now, and rode that way, a little behind Dave, nerving himself.

At about the same time, a Half-Moon hound sighted Will Lockhart and barked, and the full yelping pack came streaming out of the ranch yard to investigate. A lean grin broke on Will's face as his greeting from the saddle made tails wag. Then as he rode into the ranch yard, Will sighted Kate Canaday's big figure in the back doorway of the spacious log ranch house.

"Had an idea 'twas you!" Kate called. "Anything

on the mountain worth the ride?" Below her gray-streaked pompadour, Kate's rough, weathered face was humorous. "Coffee an' a pretty girl waitin'," she stated jovially. Then Kate's movement out from the doorway was agile for so large a woman. "That's a Barb horse!" Kate stated sharply. And then more sharply, "What's wrong with your hand?"

Will dismounted and said tersely, "Bullet."

He got then a better measure of Kate Canaday. "Come in an' get patched up," Kate said calmly. She turned back into the kitchen. Will heard her brisk order reaching deeper into the house. "Barbara! We got a bullet hole to fix!"

Kate was pumping water at the iron sink inside the back kitchen windows when Barbara Kirby appeared. "Get clean towels an' that pint o' iodine on the medicine shelf," Kate directed vigorously. "An' the razor an' them little tweezers."

Barbara hurried out and Will smiled faintly. "A regimental surgeon wouldn't do better."

Turning from the sink, rolling up one sleeve, Kate demanded keenly, "How many army docs you seen in action, Lockhart?"

"I've heard of them," Will parried.

Kate gave him an oblique look and lifted the cast-iron lid of the range hot-water tank and tested the water with a finger. "Pop your hand in that pan of cold water in the sink an' soak the cloth loose," Kate ordered. She added with resignation as Will moved to the sink, "Seems all my life I been peckin' lead outa hard-luck Harrys."

Barbara came back with her hastily collected burden and Kate asked bluntly, "You got a weak stomach?"

"I don't think so," Barbara said uncertainly.

"This," said Kate briskly, "ain't an' won't be a purty. Fetch that whisky bottle from the pantry shelf. If Lockhart don't need it now, he will."

The cold water eased feverish throbbing in the hand and arm. Will stood in grateful relaxation, watching Barbara. Each time they met, she seemed slightly different, he decided. Today her divided riding-skirt was of cocoa-colored, soft-weave merino. Her small, square shoulders had the look of gay vigor he remembered so well. She caught her red underlip between white teeth as her greenish eyes soberly estimated him.

He knew her temper, her capacity for the unexpected. He knew she was going to marry Frank Darrah. A hardening disinterest possessed Will as he thought of that marriage and looked away.

Kate's brisk, "Well, let's get at it—" diverted his thoughts.

In the next moments he was wincing, clenching teeth while he marveled at the deftness of Kate's big, rough-looking hands. Barbara stood at Kate's elbow, doing quickly the things Kate demanded, and Will briefly told them what had happened.

Indignation burst from Barbara. "I wouldn't have thought even Dave would do such a thing!"

"Ain't Dave always done what he wanted?" Kate reminded shortly. She pumped water over the hand and bent with the small tweezers.

Will's comment was curt and bleak. "How did a man like Alec Waggoman have a son like Dave?"

Intent on her work, Kate muttered, "Alec married a pretty little fluff who knowed what she wanted an' got it. An' never fergot how pretty she was an' how rough her man was. Dave was mama's pet. He got anything he wanted. Alec was busy buildin' Barb. Time his wife died, the damage was done. Vic Hansbro did his share, helped Dave have his way. Dave was a swaggerin' little bully. He never changed." Kate's snort was disgusted. "Dave's mamma'd be proud of him, I reckon."

The bitter hostility in Kate's tone drew Will's thoughtful look. Barbara's calm voice changed the subject.

"A man named Charley Yuill is here. He rode up on the mountain on the chance he'd find you."

"I was expecting him," Will said, and he wondered why Barbara's glance sought his face in sober estimation.

Kate said briefly, "Quigby, the deputy, stopped by this mornin', lookin' for you."

"Do they want me back in jail?" Will asked, hardening.

"Quigby," said Kate dryly, "came to warn against any trouble with Barb. Said he'd already warned Alec. We'll see now what Quigby an' his law does about this."

Will was staring at his hand. "I'm going to ride to the doctor," he decided.

Kate nodded. "You better. Barbara can ride home with you."

Barbara's quick look was surprised. Will said soberly, "I'll probably need help." Then he grinned at Barbara's askance look.

Later with the hand bound massively in strips torn off a sheet, Will sat at the kitchen table and ate a meat sandwich Barbara had made for him. He heard the dogs give cry once more. Barbara glanced out a back window.

"Your redheaded friend."

Will pushed back his chair. "This won't take long; then we can start."

Charley Yuill's friendly grin had never been more welcome as Charley slipped nimbly off the bareback mule. "Ridin' the grub line, lookin' for work," Charley drawled. "What's the matter with your hand?"

Will told it as they walked toward the horse corral, Charley leading the mule. Charley's dark face took on Indian impassiveness. "What do we do, Cap'n?" Charley's dark eyes had a dangerous glow.

"Nothing now, Charley. Remember that, if you meet any Barb men. What luck did you have?"

They halted by the poles of the horse corral. Charley dropped the mule's reins and took tobacco sack and papers from his shirt pocket. They were alone here.

"That wagon from Darrah's warehouse in Roxton Springs was hard to track," Charley said thoughtfully. "Four-horse wagon. Horses shod. The off-wheeler stomped his off-front shoe a mite harder than the others."

Charley twisted the cigarette end and handed the smoke to Will, and struck a match on his flat heavy belt buckle. Will inhaled gratefully. Charley, he realized now, was that rare individual, one who read trail with the sensitivity of the half wild. Charley was starting his own smoke, frowning thoughtfully at the thin brown paper and dry golden grains of tobacco.

"Lost the sign in town," Charley said reflectively. "So I moved out a few miles on the Coronado road. No luck. I cut 'cross country to the Caxton road. No luck. Tried the El Paso road. No luck."

Will could visualize the solitary figure on the bareback mule searching patiently in a great circle around Roxton Springs. He listened intently to Charley's soft tone.

"Finally picked up that dug-in toe mark on the piece of trail that leads to the salt lakes. Last place I'd have figured. But it made sense. I'd heard in town that Darrah had sent men to dig salt."

Charley flared another match on his belt buckle and inhaled deeply, too. "Looked like that shipment of rifles was headed for Apach' country," said Charley slowly. "But about ten miles out a saddle horse had caught up with the wagon. Couple cigarette ends an' a cigar butt on the ground there. The saddle hoss had turned back to town. A few miles farther on, the wagon had cut across open country." Charley shrugged. "Too dark by then to trail. I cut back west to the salt lakes for water."

"Had Darrah been at the lakes?"

"Nope. Just the five men he'd sent from Roxton. They said more men was comin' from Coronado to get all the salt possible in before harvest time ends."

"Harvest time for salt?" Will asked, smiling. "Like fruit?"

"Sort of," Charley agreed mildly. "Low water makes the brine stronger. The salt settles out on the bottom an' along the shore. Then the rains thin the water down an' there ain't no more salt until next dry season."

Charley stood silent for a moment, frowning at the cigarette between his fingers. "Darrah gave orders to keep everyone away from the salt. Even Indians. The men had already run off some Zuni salt gatherers. Put rifle shots close to show there was no foolin'."

Alertly Will asked, "Does that mean trouble with the Zunis?"

"You can bet the moccasin telegraph got busy quick," said Charley softly. "It's let the Acomas know, an' the Lagunas, the Santa Annas, the Jemez, and the Santo Domingo people. It's reached the Navajos an' the Apaches. No salt for their meat; no salt for their skins this winter. Old Grandmother Salt's held by the guns of the white men."

Charley turned his head and spat thoughtfully, and looked at Will seriously. "Cap'n, the Navajos are tough. The 'Paches are plain hell!"

"I know," Will murmured.

"Darrah's a fool. He just ain't got any idea," Charley said in a smoldering tone.

"He's greedy," Will mused. "That's always a weakness, Charley. Where did the wagon go?"

"I tracked it next mornin'," Charley continued. "'Cross country to the Coronado road. Then almost to Chinaman Creek, near Coronado. Back off the road a half mile or so, the wagon had been unloaded at a stone building with an iron door. Miss Kirby says it's a powder house Darrah owns."

"Are you certain the guns couldn't have been unloaded along the way?"

"No sign of it."

"Then we know where the guns are," Will said with some satisfaction. "Darrah must have been worried. He wouldn't have moved them at night in that roundabout way if he wasn't afraid."

Charley's eye corners crinkled at a thought. "I seen a man in Roxton who was headin' toward the reservation country. I told him to tell the first Apach' he seen to tell old Taite, the medicine man in Eagle Canyon, that Chris Boldt was dead."

Charley's slight grin was relishing. "Might be Taite knows the guns came through Darrah." Charley pointed with his chin, Indian-fashion, at the bandage on Will's hand. "What about that?"

"I'm riding to the doctor," Will said soberly. "Wait here until morning, Charley, and then take some grub and watch that powder house. I'll have the same room at the hotel. If I start back to Half-Moon, I'll see you. Don't let Darrah slip those rifles away again. They might vanish."

Charley's grin doubted that. There would be a trail to follow. Then Charley's look sobered also as it returned to the bandaged hand. Will knew what Charley was thinking; it was in his own mind. He might lose the hand. His army career would end. The future would be bleak indeed for Will Lockhart.

And a little later when Will started the ride to Coronado, he saw the same concern on Kate Canaday's broad face. He was on a Half-Moon horse now, and Kate stood by the stirrup and advised with some concern, "You get to Doc Seldon quick as you can."

She would have been more concerned if she had guessed the increasing pain in the arm. As the ranch buildings dropped behind, Barbara Kirby's glance studied Will's face.

"It hurts, doesn't it?" Barbara guessed quietly.

"A little."

"Your face shows it," Barbara murmured. She rode beside him, erect and light in the saddle, the westing sun golden on her smooth features and red lips. Under the edge of her small, jaunty red hat, coppery-gold glints moved again in her hair.

She belonged to another man. She belonged to

Frank Darrah. And someday she might own all of Barb—and Darrah no doubt was aware of it—

"You are looking at me queerly," Barbara said suddenly.

Will smiled and did not deny it. He was wondering what lay ahead for her. None of it was good that he could see. He remembered Kate's disapproval of this girl marrying Darrah, and he wondered what had been in Kate's mind when she urged on Barbara this ride with him. He saw Barbara studying him from the corner of her eye, and he wondered what she was thinking.

They rode in silence now, aware of each other, and it was oddly pleasant, intriguing. It was antidote for the pounding pain in his hand and arm.

Alec Waggoman heard the story when Vic Hansbro rode in ahead of the main crew, bringing Fitz, who had witnessed Dave's folly.

Waggoman had heard the run of their approaching horses and had walked out into the yard, tall and bareheaded. Wind off the pine slopes riffled his hair and white mustaches as he stood there in the open, listening impassively to Hansbro's harsh, chopped account of the trouble. Fitz's slight, uneasy figure stood by, and their froth-flecked horses blew hard in the background.

On Hansbro's harsh tones, Waggoman's close attention riveted. More and more, he was aware, he leaned to senses other than his failing eyes.

Vic's sweating, was his thought now. *Afraid he'll be blamed.*

Hansbro's harsh voice was almost pleading out of the short black beard.

"I wasn't there, Alec. Probably couldn't have stopped it, anyway. Ask Fitz."

Fitz said bleakly, "Dave thought Lockhart had busted outa jail, or was slippin' around up there on some kind of trouble. Dave didn't speak of shootin' Lockhart's horse. Then it all happened quicklike."

Waggoman knew his voice had a cold remoteness. He felt that way. "And you helped hold Lockhart while Dave tried to blow his hand off?"

Chapter Nineteen

"Before God!" Fitz swore earnestly. "Wasn't a way to tell what Dave meant to do! He was boss!"

They waited. They were apprehensive. Hansbro, because this might mean the end of his long stay on Barb. Fitz, because he dimly sensed the full gravity of what had happened.

"Tell me again. Everything," Waggoman ordered evenly.

He listened, knowing every rock of that high valley of Chinaman Creek under South Peak. In full clarity he could visualize Dave's folly. And to Waggoman while he listened, the despair came again. What he had feared had now happened. This was not an ending; this was a beginning.

Dave's insane recklessness had started a feud to the death with that tall, sun-blackened stranger, who was now backed by Half-Moon. There could be no illusions. Cripple a man like Lockhart, as Dave had done, and there would be an accounting.

"Dave rode alone to town?" Waggoman asked.

Fitz's rusty spur chains jingled slightly as he moved uneasily. His "Yes" had furtive uncertainty.

"Lockhart headed back toward Half-Moon?"

"Yes, sir."

"You men did well to put Lockhart on a horse," Waggoman conceded coldly. "Now get fresh horses. Ride to town, both of you. Dave will probably try to get drunk after his hand is fixed. Stop him, Vic. Tie him up if you have to."

Hansbro muttered, "Alec, he won't like anything like that."

Then Fitz stared, his mouth going agape, as he heard a kind of terrible, held-in anger lash at Hansbro.

"Vic, damn you, never tell me again what Dave likes! If Dave doesn't start back sober and peaceful from Seldon's office, bring him back tied on his horse or in a wagon bed! You hear, Vic?"

The thick, worried mumble from Vic Hansbro was new to Fitz also. "I'll do it, Alec."

"You'd better!" was the cold warning.

Fitz was still gaping as the tall old man walked from them. Hansbro's hoarse "Get the horses!" snapped Fitz into action.

Later Alec Waggoman sat on the office porch in an old barrel chair covered with scarred bullhide. His vacant gaze watched the sun's blazing dip to the western horizon. He had paced the office; he had stood at the windows lost in his thoughts. Now he gazed into the blurred distance, considering a ride to Half-Moon, and he put the idea aside.

What could a man say of Dave's folly? What could Alec Waggoman say to the ancient bitterness of Kate Canaday's sharp tongue? Or say to Lockhart's chill and justified fury?

The crew rode in more quietly than usual. Correctly Waggoman guessed they were speculating uncertainly on the violence which would surely follow Dave's deed. He heard the remuda being hazed toward the horse pasture, the men washing up outside the bunkhouse. He knew they were furtively watching his silent figure on the office porch. The cook beat summons to supper, and Alec Waggoman held a dead cigar forgotten between his fingers and sat with the vacant, despairing sense of helplessness about the future.

Dave could not hold Barb. Now Waggoman knew it. Soon even Alec Waggoman could not hold Barb. Then what?

The futility of the rough, ruthless, tireless years it had taken to build Barb moved in on Waggoman. What had been the use of it all? He asked it in quiet bitterness. What had the years meant? Then the increasing keenness of his hearing as sight failed picked up the far, furious beat of a horse ridden at full gallop—the kind of run which would kill a horse on the rising grades from the lower range.

Waggoman stood up, alerting with the tingling chill which always came with great danger. No man would ride a horse like that today with good news.

He was on the bottom step, the cigar still forgotten in his fingers, when the furious slashing run came straight to the short hitchrack in front of the office. It became a foaming horse with whistling, red-flaring nostrils, staggering as it was hauled up and the rider launched off.

The man was Fitz, jerking out his report.

"Dave never got to town! Doctor ain't seen him! Ain't a sign of him along the road! Hansbro stayed in town lookin'!"

Waggoman asked carefully, "Did Dave say what way he was taking to town?"

"No! He headed down the mountain to cut the road somewhere," was all Fitz could say.

"And you're sure Lockhart didn't follow him?"

"Lockhart headed for Half-Moon." Fitz swallowed. "But he sure coulda circled an' tracked Dave."

"He could have," Waggoman agreed calmly. "I would have. Hitch up the buckboard. Tell the men to saddle fresh horses. We'll do what we can before dark."

"Yes, sir." Fitz headed toward the cookshack in a stiff-legged run and with confused thoughts.

That tall old man with the bold nose and rock-like face completely lacked emotion, Fitz now believed in a kind of fearful unease. Alec Waggoman was like his face; he was rock inside. All the tales about him were true. He was Waggoman of Barb, hard, ruthless, unfeeling.

God help Lockhart an' Half-Moon if anything's happened to Dave! was Fitz's conviction now.

In the same deepening dusk, in, Coronado, a nickel-based lamp glowed in the side room office of Doctor Matt Seldon's modest frame house on Main Street.

Outside the house, gray-purple twilight was deepening into new night. In a small hallway Barbara Kirby sat quietly gazing through the open doorway at Will Lockhart's arm on the doctor's oilcloth-covered table. The same table held the lamp, basins of water, and a litter of gleaming steel instruments. The house was very quiet. Now and then Barbara swallowed silently and closed her eyes.

Will had liked Seldon at first glance. The man's eyes were a deep, smiling blue with puckered threads at the corners. Seldon's hair and Van Dyke were streaked with gray. His smile was warm and quizzical. About him was an air of keen thoughtfulness.

Bluntly Seldon had warned, "This will hurt. Will you have chloroform?"

Will was standing then. His "No" was emphatic. But finally he had had to sit down, sweating, shaken, as Seldon, shirt sleeves rolled up, hands reeking of raw alcohol, worked on the hand with swift intentness which bordered on callousness.

It was not callousness, Will knew. Seldon was a man of skill, doing what had to be done. When Seldon began to bandage the hand again, Will saw that the doctor was perspiring, too. Relief filled Seldon's brief comment.

"You'll have a hand, I think. The bones had me worried." Seldon fitted a thin wood splint along the palm and bound it in. "Where are you staying tonight?"

"The hotel." Teeth marks were blue in Will's lips.

Barbara spoke from the doorway where she had stepped, unnoticed. "He had better stay at our house tonight."

"I think so," Seldon agreed.

"Wouldn't think of it," Will objected quickly. He forced a smile, glancing at her. "Appreciated, Miss Kirby. But no need to trouble you and your father."

Seldon chuckled as he reached for scissors and snipped the bandage. "Doctor's order," Seldon said. "You'll need attention tonight. Stay with the Kirbys."

Later, propped against bed pillows in Jubal Kirby's small, neat bedroom, Will had a sense of the fantastic about all this. Jubal had taken his horse to the feed corral, had brought Will's canvas duffel bag from the hotel, had helped Will wash, shave, and pull on a clean shirt. Barbara, in a gay flowered gingham apron had brought a tray of supper. Now Jubal was laying a folded blanket across Will's legs on the bed.

"Penny ante, my boy, will beat Seldon's pills," Jubal promised drolly. Under the rumpled, Irish-black hair, Jubal's eyes were bright with anticipation.

Will grinned, liking already this small, clean-shaven man whose run of raffish anecdotes seemed inexhaustible. Jubal was a man who entertained and did not pry.

In the kitchen Barbara heard their voices and paused, listening, smiling faintly. Frank Darrah had never been like this with Jubal, came regretfully to her memory. An instinctive camaraderie was audible in Jubal's bedroom. Will Lockhart's bursts of laughter were full-throated. Then again his easy chuckling voice roused Jubal to mirth.

Presently, the dishes washed, Barbara hung her apron behind the door and left the lamp in the kitchen. In the living-room shadows she sat in a comfortable rocker where she could see through the open bedroom doorway.

The bedside lamp in there glowed cheerfully on Lockhart's broad shoulders propped against the pillows. So different now, Barbara mused, from the filthy, salt-crusted stranger she had met at the salt lagoons. In the lamplight now, his young, sun-blackened features had a smiling, vastly human warmth. He was obviously sincere when he shouted with laughter; he was human when pain and somber thought etched briefly into his lean dark face.

A thought touched Barbara's gratitude into full awareness. This man, this stranger with depths of experience and self-assurance; this Will Lockhart, lean and hard and competent, was finding qualities in Jubal Kirby to like, to admire, and even to respect—qualities which Barbara passionately knew were there, even when she was most vexed with Jubal's flamboyant, irresponsible ways.

She was smiling a little as she watched unnoticed from the living-room shadows. The creaking hinges of the front gate broke into her thoughts. Regretfully Barbara went quickly out on the front porch. She closed the front door behind her, suspecting who was calling.

Frank Darrah came lightly up the porch steps and confidently took her in his arms. Frank's hungry lips found her mouth and lingered. Then Frank asked, "Nice day?" Deep urges were husky in his voice.

"The ride to Half-Moon was nice," Barbara said in truthful evasion. She felt oddly detached, uncomfortable as she sat in one of the cane rockers on the porch.

Frank pulled another rocker close, and glanced over his shoulder as laughter lifted inside the house. "Company?" Frank asked, dropping into the rocker.

"Doctor Matt wanted Lockhart to stay here tonight where he can have attention," Barbara said. "He has an injured hand."

Frank's quick protest was vehement. "Why should a bullet wound in the hand bring a stranger like that into your house? Lockhart managed to ride from South Peak, didn't he?"

"Doctor Matt ordered it, Frank."

Almost unreasonably furious, Frank snapped, "Seldon's a fool! What does he mean, asking you to take in a killer?"

"I don't think many people believe that story," Barbara said defensively.

It infuriated Frank more. "What do you know

about him, Barbara? A wagon tramp! A stranger! Jailed in Roxton! Why, right now he's a desperado working for Half-Moon!"

"Kate is our friend."

"But Lockhart will have trouble now with Barb!" Frank said hotly. "Barbara! We're to be married in a few days! This will make talk!"

"He's father's guest," Barbara said calmly. "Frank, you're upset about nothing. Stop it."

Frank glowered helplessly, aware of a baffling, infuriating stubbornness in this small, gay girl. His temper resolved that after they were married there would be no opposition to his wishes.

Barbara said mildly, "They are playing cards. Don't you want to join them?"

"I do not! And I don't want to sit here and listen to them!"

"That," said Barbara quietly, "is your privilege, Frank."

Reason intruded into Frank's fury. Barbara was not yet married to him. Her infuriating stubborn side could well enough decide not to be married at this time. And they must be married now; they must. Frank reached for Barbara's hand. His laugh was rueful, sheepish.

"Can you blame me, darling? The way I feel about you? Let's walk. I want to be alone with you."

Barbara pressed his hand understandingly. Yet these flashes of a total stranger which issued from Frank vaguely troubled her. And as they walked from the house together, idle curiosity prompted a question.

"Frank, how do you know so much about Lockhart's hand? Where it happened and all that?"

For a moment Frank did not answer. Then his

voice was oddly strained. "Let's don't talk about the man."

"It was about you, Frank; can't I be curious?" Barbara was smiling.

"Well, Lockhart went to Seldon, didn't he?" Frank said after another sulky moment. "And I've seen Seldon. Now let's talk about ourselves."

"Let's," Barbara agreed, and she was ruefully aware of thinking even now about the card game and bursts of laughter in Jubal's bedroom.

Frank's mood quickly turned to a kind of exhilaration. He began to talk of the future, ranging widely, expansively over all they would do. The future seemed to intoxicate Frank tonight, giving his fancies heated and at times almost incoherent assurance.

Laughing finally, Barbara begged, "Come back to earth."

Frank laughed, too, sheepishly. They were strolling in deep shadows under tall shade trees. His arm brought her close.

"How," Frank asked gaily, "can I be serious when I think of all that's ahead for us?" Then a dark mood descended on him again. "I won't sleep tonight, thinking of that fellow in your house! You waiting on him!"

Barbara's chuckle dismissed it. Her reminder, "If he needs attention, then I'll be awake, too. We'll both be sleepy tomorrow, won't we?" gave Frank small comfort.

Almost malevolently now, Frank thought of Lockhart. Close now, even into Barbara's home— Frank writhed inside at the thought, knowing he was helpless against Barbara's smiling stubbornness.

A new fear lurked with him, too. What a fool to

blurt in startled anger his knowledge of Lockhart's trouble with Dave—knowledge that only Lockhart, Doctor Seldon, and Barbara should possess tonight. And Jubal Kirby, of course.

Frank had seen Vic Hansbro down the street before dark and had turned into a doorway, not wishing to face Hansbro's black-browed, boring stare. He had guessed why Hansbro was in town, and he had waited. And now he had talked in loose fury to Barbara. But she was a gay, lightheaded, pretty little thing, easily satisfied that he'd heard the details from Doc Seldon.

Barbara would not think of it again. Obviously she would not ask Seldon if he had talked with Frank Darrah. Why should she? Barbara was in love; she was going to be married; in the morning her head would be full of the future.

In the morning, Barbara's question from the bedroom doorway was smiling. "Breakfast in bed or in the kitchen?"

From the bed pillows, Will told her firmly, "I'll walk to the café."

"The kitchen—in fifteen minutes—since you're able to walk so far," Barbara informed him, and Will hesitated and assented meekly, "Yes, ma'am."

This morning he knew her better. It had been a night of fitful sleep, of pain, and Barbara's soothing visits in a plain blue wrapper with hair braids over her small shoulders. A night of compresses on his arm and hand, and gingerly snipped bandages which eased angry swollen flesh.

He would never, Will thought as he went to the kitchen, forget the faint, comforting fragrance of her nearness in the quiet night hours.

Eggs and ham and clear tart grape jelly; rich, strong coffee, stewed dried peaches— A red-checked cloth on the kitchen table, and Barbara fresh-looking, gay as the sunshine outside. The range heat pinked her cheeks as she moved between range and table with light, quick steps.

Using his one good hand, Will buttered a hot biscuit and reflected that this was but one morning out of a lifetime that he would sit at her table like this. The rest of the mornings—all the rest—belonged to Frank Darrah.

He put it into words, lightly and smiling. "Darrah is a lucky man."

Jubal had eaten earlier and gone out. They were alone. Barbara's quick look seemed to suspect irony. Finding none, she countered, "You do know how to please the cook."

She took his knife and fork and cut his ham bite-size, and she buttered two biscuits for him, completely without coquetry, Will noticed. Since their meeting at the salt lakes, she had never tried to impress him. Close now, her faint scent of Cologne water and femininity recalled the night hours.

Then midway of the meal they heard a vigorous voice out front halting horses. A pleased exclamation came from Barbara. "There's Kate!" She hurried out.

Big Kate came into the kitchen like an invigorating gust, demanding, "How's that fist?" She pulled out the chair opposite Will and sat down heavily. "I et before I started," she told Barbara. "Coffee'll do." Kate's keen look sought Will's face. "You two ain't heard the news?"

Will put down his fork. "What news?"

"Dave Waggoman never got to town yesterday.

The Barb men have been huntin' him all night."
Kate shook her head, obviously troubled. "You
know anything about it, Lockhart?"

"No."

"I didn't think so," Kate said, sounding grim
now. She dipped sugar into the black coffee Barbara put before her, and she drank half the cup at a
gulp. It was, Will guessed, a measure of the big
woman's inner agitation.

Barbara's question was plainly worried. "What
could have happened to Dave?"

"Dunno," Kate muttered. "Cinch mighta broke;
his hoss mighta throwed him. You ridin' in with
Lockhart takes care of that."

She might have had that in mind, Will guessed
now, when she urged Barbara to ride with him.
Barbara had made a perfect witness to any chance
of trouble. "What," Will asked thoughtfully, "takes
care of the time I rode to Half-Moon?"

"Dave didn't head down your side of the mountain," Kate said absently. Her blunt fingers still
held the cup handle. Her gaze was unseeing on the
red-checked tablecloth. "Alec must be worried,"
Kate said under her breath. The stiff black-straw
hat bobbed on her hair as her head shook regretfully. "Dave ain't much to worry about—but he's
all Alec's got."

Kate finished her coffee and addressed Will's
thoughtfulness briskly. "I stopped at Doc Seldon's
house. He says you're bringing the hand to him for
more fixin'. I'll take you there soon as you're ready.
Then you can go back to the ranch."

Will made a blunt guess. "Before there's a
chance of more trouble with Barb over Dave?"

"You guessed it," Kate told him frankly. "I got a

feeling this is bad. You ain't in shape to handle trouble with one hand."

She was shrewdly correct, Will conceded in his own sobered and rather grim thoughts. Barbara could not hide her worry. Much of Will's appetite had vanished. The three of them had little to talk about now. They were thinking of Dave Waggoman.

A little later Will heaved his duffel bag into the back of Kate's old topless buggy. Before he stepped up to the buggy seat, he thanked Barbara gravely for his night's care, and as the buggy pulled away, he saw Barbara's faint smile give way again to gravity.

"There's a girl now," Kate's comment broke into his thoughts. "Like her?"

"Any man would," Will admitted. The buggy and its escort of trotting hound dogs turned into Palace and he immediately noted that more people than usual were abroad this morning.

There was a tenseness about the small groups loitering on the broadwalks, a furtive, close interest in the glances turned on Kate's buggy.

It was visible; it was in the air. These Coronado people, Will sensed, had lived with Barb and Half-Moon, and they were apprehensive now. Kate called amiable greetings to friends, and in the block beyond the stores she pulled up before Doctor Seldon's modest frame house.

She accompanied Will into the small hallway which served as waiting-room. There, bluntly, Kate demanded of Seldon, "This ain't a time for double talk. What about his hand?"

"Sit down, Kate, out of the way," Seldon ordered with his own calm bluntness. "How do I know so soon?"

Once more Will sat by the oilcloth-covered table. This time Seldon worked slower, easier. His small grunt of satisfaction as he studied the hand was more heartening than talk. When Seldon began to bandage the hand again, he said dryly, "No gangrene or corruption. You're lucky, young man. Lucky."

The bandaging was almost finished when Will's ears caught a faint sound, an ominous sound. Seldon heard it a moment later and his hands paused.

In any cattle town one heard sounds like this—but not on a quiet morning like this—not in Coronado like this—the low, slow, muted strike of many shod hoofs in the muffling street dust.

There were many horses. They were walking slowly, coming into town. And the slow, measured beat of their approach filled the street with unmistakable foreboding.

Kate Canaday heard it, too. Her chair scraped in the hallway as Kate stood up. Never had Will heard her voice sound like this, quiet, too, and heavy with knowledge.

"They've found Dave!" Kate stepped to the door and went out.

Chapter Twenty

Barb was coming into Coronado. Will stood at Seldon's elbow, looking over the white half-curtain of the office window, and the sight was ominous.

All the Barb crew and others who had searched for Dave Waggoman were coming into town. The lanky figure of Tom Quigby, the deputy, was among them. Townspeople were gathering on the walks, watching the slow cavalcade in apprehensive silence.

They filled the street, those slow-riding, grim men on tired horses. And catching the eye, catching the emotions, was the tall old man who close-reined a gray stallion beside a weathered buckboard.

The long, canvas-wrapped burden on the buckboard gave its mute story. For the last time Alec Waggoman was bringing Dave to town.

He sat erect in the saddle, that tall old man with the hard, calm look of power. His gaze was ahead, oblivious to those on the walks, ignoring the buckboard he sided so closely.

Will heard Seldon exclaim softly, "Don't do it, Kate!"

At the edge of the boardwalk now, Kate Canaday was an arresting figure in canvas jacket and coarse wool skirt; and as the buckboard and its accompanying rider came abreast, Kate stepped out into the street.

"Alec!"

For a moment Will thought she was being ignored. Then Waggoman reined the big gray horse facing her, and the buckboard halted and the street full of riders pulled up.

A tight quiet dropped on the street. Bit chains clinked softly. A restless horse or two snorted. The abrupt quiet made Kate's voice sound louder.

"I'm sorry, Alec."

He eyed her while a man might count ten. The craggy face behind the long white mustaches had never, Will thought, looked more like stone. Not an emotion showed. Then coldly, Waggoman's countering demand asked Kate, "*Are* you sorry?"

"Yes, Alec."

"He was shot in the back. He never had a chance."

Kate's work-roughened hand lifted and dropped in a helpless gesture. "Don't think wrong, Alec. Barbara rode to town with Lockhart and went to the doctor with him. She took Lockhart to Jubal's house for the night."

Will stepped away from the window and Doctor Seldon's quick, sharp advice followed him. "Man, don't go out there!"

"I'll tell him myself."

As Will's deliberate figure descended the doctor's steps, a startled awareness caught the horsemen in the street. Will noted them shifting alertly in saddles and turning tense, expectant stares to Alec Waggoman's reaction.

At the walk edge Will halted and spoke to the tall old man who was ignoring him.

"Waggoman! You'll not believe I'm sorry. But I'll tell you this wasn't my doing. I might have gone after him later. But it would have been to his face."

Kate had turned uncertainly. Waggoman's head

came up, peering intently. A great straining tension drew out, thinning dangerously.

Waggoman broke it evenly.

"If you'd killed him fair, Lockhart, I'd not have blamed you, even when I killed you for it. But no one has accused you of this. You haven't seemed to be the kind who'd shoot at the back. Or," the cold tone added, "knife a man in the back like they say you did at Roxton Springs."

The hooded gaze went back to Kate Canaday and a queer certainty touched Will.

The present, he guessed, was not now between that craggy old man and the rough, weathered woman who faced him in the street dust. Their eyes were locking now across the past, the long past turbulent years seeded with dislike, ancient enmities and suspicions.

Slowly, coldly, Waggoman broke the silence again.

"It's done; he's gone." And a new, rough tone drove at Kate and filled the street. "Someone did it and I'll find him!"

That was all. Will knew death, and this was death as Alec Waggoman rode on. The slow, dust-muffled cadence of the Barb riders followed, with Quigby's narrow gaze estimating Will.

Kate stared after the buckboard and Will's glance followed the hard, bitter straightness of Alec Waggoman's back. Will's conviction was complete.

He'll never stop until he finds the man who did it. And kills him.

Slowly Kate turned and stepped up on the boardwalk. Her comment was quiet. "Now Frank Darrah gets Barb."

Will nodded. Kate started to speak again, and then only shook her head in silent disapproval.

The wild and helpless bitterness which churned in Alec Waggoman through these empty hours found no help in the past, no hope in the future. With Dave gone, there was no future. Somehow the long day passed. Doctor Seldon headed a brief inquest in the afternoon. Testimony was brief. Dave's saddled horse had been found. Backtracking had located Dave's body in thick brush beside the lower ranch road. New tracks covered the road, blotting out all sign. The inquest verdict was a cruelly uncertain, "Death by party or parties unknown."

The funeral next day was immense, and Dave rested finally beside his mother in the small, tree-shaded town cemetery. The minister spoke well of Dave. Waggoman answered the endless condolences courteously, with an empty sense of moving in a bitter void around which the blurring hours swirled without purpose.

Finally he could climb stiffly on his horse and ride erect, dry-eyed through the empty miles to the empty vastness of Barb. Alone in the fortlike stone house he faced the empty future.

He had whisky, and that was not the answer, Waggoman knew as he paced the silent rooms. A hard inner core rejected self-pity, aimless grief.

Slowly the chaos in his brain became stern order and he dropped on his bed and slept. At dawn he was up energetically, bathing, shaving. When the iron triangle outside the cookshack clanged loudly for breakfast, he left the house with a new, purposeful stride.

The crew at the long plank table were subdued,

uncertain. Curious glances watched Waggoman eating calmly at the table head with a healthy appetite. Midway of the meal, Waggoman broke the custom of years. He spoke of the day's business to Vic Hansbro, silently bolting food at the other end of the long table.

"Vic, I'm satisfied the beef count is short." A startled quiet dropped along the table. Vic Hansbro discarded knife and fork and swiped a huge hand over his bearded mouth, and Waggoman continued calmly. "A short tally means rustling. We'll cure that like we used to. And we'll bear in mind that rustlers may have shot Dave."

Hansbro gulped his mouthful of food and mumbled, "They sure could of."

"We'll hunt the missing beef," Waggoman said briefly. "Five hundred dollars to any man who finds Barb beef that seems to have been rustled. Five thousand dollars if Dave's killer is turned up."

A startled moment of incredulous silence broke in excited talk. Waggoman let it run unchecked. His blurred sight marked a man or two sitting in narrowing thought. Cynical logic already had suggested that some knowledge of rustling, even of Dave's death, might lurk here among the crew. Lavish use of money was the one swift way to root it out, Waggoman knew.

He had the money, was Waggoman's sad thought as he left the cookshack. Money and power at least were left. He had buckled on his old shell belt with its holster worn low and slanting forward. The gun's familiar weight against his leg rolled back the years as he walked to the corrals and watched horses roped and saddled.

A noisy, jubilant eagerness in the activity

reached into shuttered nooks of memory. A thin, grim smile of remembrance shaped under Waggoman's white mustache. Long ago each morning had started this way, and Alec Waggoman had been the loudest of his fighting crew. The memories put back his shoulders a little. He swung lightly on his own big gray horse and watched the rush and buck of mounts unkinking as the men rode off in pairs and singles.

When the last man was gone, Waggoman rode his own way alone into the morning which blurred relentlessly in front of his eyes. Before night, he knew, word of all this would have spread far over the range. It would raise consternation, soul-searching, and apprehension. That much, Waggoman thought coldly, was left him. He had wanted peace and he had lost Dave. Soon now all his sight would be gone. When that was upon him, he meant to have no regrets about Dave.

In that unyielding thought was escape from grief. The new, gnawing loneliness could be cheated by driving body and mind as he had in the younger years. So he had decided before sleeping last night.

When the day ended, not all the men had returned from the far circles they were riding. Tired himself, Waggoman slept soundly. The next day he rode out once more, and at sunset he sat loosely, wearily in the old bullhide chair on the office porch and watched the crew straggle in once more on tired horses.

One man had ridden far north to Turkey Creek, and had found a Barb yearling brush-penned in a small pocket canyon near a homesteader's meager adobe which swarmed with children.

Waggoman listened in silence to the man's hopeful report. His comment lacked rancor.

"Probably been cooking our meat since they settled there. Let the young'uns eat this steer, too. They probably need it." And to his man's crestfallen look, Waggoman dryly added, "It'll be the first five-hundred-dollar steer that hungry sod-man ever butchered."

Elation brightened the man's face. Waggoman's faintly cynical gaze watched him swagger toward the bunkhouse. This would fire the rest of the crew to stiffer search.

Vic Hansbro was not back for supper. Waggoman ate leisurely and sat on the top office step afterward, smoking a cigar, thinking of how he'd almost fired Vic. And now the big foreman's bullying ruthlessness was an asset, as it had been long ago.

Blue-black shadows and the first thin night chill were deepening when Hansbro finally rode in and dismounted at the steps.

"Any luck?" Waggoman inquired perfunctorily. And when Hansbro growled, "Looks so," Waggoman came instantly attentive.

"Rustling—or about Dave?"

"Both, I reckon."

Waggoman got to his feet on the steps and tossed the cigar away. It bounced red sparks on the ground and the steps creaked as he came down, tall and coldly demanding in front of Hansbro.

"Let's have it, Vic."

Hansbro stood big and massive and almost sullenly defiant behind the black beard. "You won't like it, Alec."

"I'll judge that."

"Well, I had a hunch. An' I was right. It's Half-Moon, Alec. No tellin' how long they been at our young stuff. Makes it pretty plain, too, don't it, that they got Dave?"

Hard disappointment sharpened Waggoman's rejection of the idea.

"You're trying too hard, Vic. Kate Canaday never rustled from anyone, let alone Barb. And she'd never have had Dave harmed."

Hansbro's wide shoulders hunched stubbornly. "I c'n prove it, Alec. Fire me if I'm wrong. I'll take you to the rustled stuff an' show you."

Mechanically Waggoman groped in his coat pocket for another cigar. Vic, dead certain like this, was usually right. And even grudging admission of that fact was enough to send derision howling and mocking through the long corridors of memory. Kate's enmity had never abated; she had always made that plain. But to strike finally at Dave—*at Dave*—

Waggoman's voice sounded thin to his own ears. "Well then, Vic, prove it in the morning. And I'll want Quigby along. Send a man for him tonight."

"That damn' dep'ty won't do much," Hansbro grumbled.

"Get him!" Waggoman ordered in abruptly furious harshness. "I'll decide what will be done!"

For two days now reports had reached Half-Moon that armed Barb riders were ranging wide and arrogantly. Last night Will Lockhart had dropped off to sleep pondering Alec Waggoman's intentions.

Now, after breakfast this morning, with his bandaged hand cradled in a black-cloth neck sling, Will walked thoughtfully from the Half-Moon bunkhouse toward the saddle shed, and Waggoman and Barb were still on his mind.

The armed Barb crew had not yet invaded Half-Moon land. Last night Kate Canaday had said bluntly, "There ain't a way to guess what Alec's up to. But I know the old bull; he's throwin' dust an' spoilin' for trouble. We'd best sit tight an' watch."

Will came to an interested halt now as the sun-drenched ranch yard echoed with the bell-toned challenge of Old Roy, the gaunt, wise red-bone hound who dominated Kate's other dogs. A premonition of trouble caught Will as he watched the other hounds follow clamoring out of the yard.

This was an early hour for visitors. The blazing sunrise only now was probing cottony night mists clotting the great folds and canyons below South Peak. The after-breakfast clatter of pans and dishes still came from the squat log cookshack. Part of the crew had ridden off scant minutes ago. Will gazed after the dogs and thought of Charley Yuill.

Yesterday Charley had ridden in to report that Frank Darrah apparently had dropped all interest in the stone powder house which possibly held the rifle shipment from New Orleans. And Charley's warning had been blunt.

"Watch yourself, Cap'n. They're sayin' in Coronado you might have shot young Waggoman after all. You had the reason."

That, too, Will thought darkly now, was part of the increasing frustration over Frank Darrah. The coldly patient search for a man or men who had sold guns to the Apaches had seemed rewarded in Roxton Springs. But now, by locking the rifle shipment in his powder house and doing nothing, Darrah was quite safe.

Also, Darrah's swiftly nearing marriage to Barbara Kirby probably occupied his time. Will found dismal comfort in the thought. There was a kind of obscene mockery in the knowledge that Darrah would someday control all of fabulous Barb, and have all of Barbara Kirby, too.

Will bent his head, listening. He could hear faintly now the distant, hammering roll of bunched horses in full run. In moments they came into sight on the ranch road, lifting dust. And the leader, tall and erect on a gray horse, was all Will's sense of trouble had expected.

He stood with tightening wariness as the headlong rush thundered into the ranch yard. Barb men on fine Barb horses. Every man heavily armed. And none of them more menacing than the tall, white-mustached old man who led them.

Alec Waggoman's coat was tied behind his saddle. Black hatbrim had an arrogant up-tilt in front. And in some subtle way the man had changed.

That thought struck Will with foreboding. In Coronado, Alec Waggoman had been a deliberate man, slow-moving. In this crisp sunrise today, Waggoman led his armed crew with a driving belligerency. He sat the galloping gray horse with the grim *élan* of a younger man.

Kate Canaday emerged hurriedly from the long ranch house of thick logs, and Will wondered if Kate, too, would see this change in Waggoman.

The running gray horse was hard-reined to a stamping halt in front of Kate. The thundering rush of the other riders brought up sharply and quieted as Will's long strides headed to Kate. He heard her vigorous challenge.

"You ain't welcome here, Alec! An' twice that fer

the whiskered bully-boy you keep as foreman. Get that bunch of hard-cases off Half-Moon land!"

Vic Hansbro had reined up behind Waggoman. He ignored Kate. Waggoman pulled off his black hat. His voice was clipped and thrusting.

"Kate, I'm told your Half-Moon iron has been run on Barb sleepers, longears, and mavericks."

Sleepers were calves which rustlers had ear-marked and would brand after weaning. Longears were unbranded calves ready to wean. Mavericks had weaned themselves and were still unbranded after calf roundup. The curtly blunt accusation made Will's temper stir.

And he had never seen Kate swell like this, seeming to grow bigger, taller under her upsweep of graying pompadour. Kate's brown dress was plain, her broad, weathered face even plainer. But one forgot all that, Will thought admiringly, before the big woman's swelling, wrathful dignity. And her booming reply.

"It's a low-down lie, ye white-horned old scrim-shank, an' well you know it!"

"Tom Quigby's here to see," was the curt retort. "Come along, if you're interested."

Kate's formidable bosom swelled mightily as she breathed deeply. Scarlet outrage was flooding her broad face. Blazing dignity choked in her reply.

"I ain't sure what you're schemin', you snake-natured old mossy-horn stuffed with bile an' con-ceit! But you never was righter, Alec, me boy! I'm comin'! We're all comin'! Wait'll we get saddled!"

Chapter Twenty-one

Kate stalked back into the house, and Alec Waggoman lounged powerfully in the saddle, estimating Will. His comment was brusk. "Lockhart, I'm wondering about you, too."

"And I'm wondering," Will said evenly, "about you. A man who can't tell a lady from a cow thief must be blind." He was mildly startled by the quick fury which blazed on the craggy face, and as quickly receded under iron control.

Waggoman reined away and Will headed toward the horse corrals, reflecting soberly on that blazing surge of emotion. In Waggoman, deep and hidden, must lurk the genesis of Dave's wild temper. Waggoman, too, Will guessed, was capable of destructive rages.

Kate had hastily donned a divided riding-skirt of gray wool. Will watched with new approval as the big woman's muscular bulk stepped capably into the saddle. Under a man's broad gray hat, Kate's face was grim as she rode to Waggoman.

"Now, ye misguided old gas-bag, show me rustlin'."

The Half-Moon crew rode together, six of them, twice outnumbered and more by the Barb crew. Vic Hansbro galloped ahead. Quigby, the lanky deputy, reined over to Will and they trailed the others.

Quigby's remark was laconic. "What about it?" Will shrugged, and Quigby's glance was sharp. "A lot of folks, Lockhart, are uncertain about you."

"Are you?"

"It adds up." Quigby's tone was dry. "You were jailed over a killing in Roxton Springs, had a feud with Barb an' Hansbro, had a reason to shoot Dave Waggoman— And your gun, not Dave's, was missing from the body." Quigby spat and pushed up his hat. "Can you blame folks for thinkin' you might have circled fast, killed Dave, an' then quirted hard enough to reach Half-Moon when Miss Kirby said you did?"

"So?"

"If you'd run for it, I'd have been after you. But you didn't run." Quigby rode thoughtfully for a moment. 'My idea, Lockhart, is you're too cagey to have lifted just your gun off of Dave."

In dry irony Will said, "Thanks."

"But somebody did," Quigby reminded. "That'n won't be safe from Alec Waggoman until Dave's murder is hung on someone."

"Me, for instance?"

"Who else?"

"I've been wondering," Will admitted. He rode his thoughtful moment, too, before saying, "I'm new to Half-Moon—but I assume I know a lady. What's behind this bluff about rustling?"

Quigby was not comfortable about it. "Waggoman sent for me. I've never heard he'd bluff about rustlin'."

"We'll see," was all Will could say.

Vic Hansbro was guiding them through the lower shin oak and cedar toward the high shoulders of South Peak. They reached the tall, murmuring pines where deep needle duff muffled their passing. They ascended a small, twisting canyon with forested sides and a lean run of clear water tumbling between bottom rocks coated with green moss and blotches of silver-gray lichen.

In a small valley still higher, the sheer side rocks were banded in colorful yellows and reds. Another climbing trail carried them up through tall, silent spruce, and here Will noted how the strung-out riders had gone silent, also.

The same restraint leaned Quigby's leathery face. Every man, Will decided, was increasingly aware that this might be the explosive climax between Barb and Half-Moon—between Kate Canaday and Alec Waggoman.

They rode out of the shadowy spruce into a wide belt of mountain meadow, golden with sunlight, dotted with grazing cattle. Ahead and higher was the great bald hogback over which Will had ridden into the upper valley of Chinaman Creek.

Memory of that meeting with Dave Waggoman ran tight along Will's nerves. His aching hand in the neck sling warned increasingly now that Barb—all of Barb—was dangerous.

The riders were bunching up again. Will rode ahead, near Kate Canaday and Alec Waggoman. Vic Hansbro, out in front, was sharply scanning the Half-Moon cattle. Hansbro's abruptly lifted arm and halted horse stopped everyone.

"Fitz!" Hansbro called back, and when Fitz spurred out from the Barb crew, Hansbro pointed ahead and down the meadow slope a little, where seven or eight Half-Moon steers warily watched this intrusion.

"Couple of long yearlin's in that bunch have got left ears cropped just a mite," Hansbro said bruskly. "Rope me one."

Grinning now, a short thin man remarkably

dexterous with his loop, as Will well knew, Fitz shook out his coiled rope and rode leisurely down the slope below the uncertain steers. Slowly Fitz circled, angling upslope beyond the gradually alarming steers.

Hansbro gave another order. "Charley! If he busts 'em this way, get that other crop-ear."

The steers started a nervous walk downslope, and Fitz spurred at them. The steers bunched and swerved back toward the waiting riders. The spurred run of Charley's black horse put danger there and the steers scattered in panic.

Fitz's loop snaked out low, heeling his victim by a hind leg and dropping it heavily. As Fitz slipped nimbly from the saddle and ran along his taut rope, Charley's loop circled the neck of a second steer and jerked it into a slamming fall.

Fitz's horse was braced against the taut rope and Fitz was sitting on the helpless steer's head, grinning broadly, when Hansbro, Waggoman, and Kate rode to the spot and dismounted. All the other men rode close in an intent semicircle.

Hansbro drew a glinting knife blade from a leather sheath on his hip. The steer was clearly branded Half-Moon on the left hip. Even now a close look was needed to see the slightly cropped tip of the left ear. The beast's right ear was boldly mutilated with Half-Moon's full half-crop and underslit. And not even Kate, by the perplexed look on her broad face, could see anything amiss here. Her gusty indignation demanded, "What's wrong with that critter?"

Hansbro drew the knife blade across the callused heel of his palm. He looked confident, he sounded confident and relishing as he spoke to Waggoman.

"Last year I had an idea our range tally was short some. I couldn't find out why, so I baited some of the calf crop."

Will saw Kate's lips press hard together. Every eye was watching Hansbro kneel beside the steer's head. The man's big left hand worked down the loose skin under the neck. His satisfied grunt was audible. With the knife's sharp edge, Hansbro expertly cut a fold of the loose skin. His thick, blunt forefinger worked inside the opening and slid out a small metallic object. Hansbro stood up, rubbed the object against his leg, and held it out.

"When I banked this two-bits in the neck here, this was an unbranded Barb calf," Hansbro growled. "Looks like a Half-Moon yearlin' now."

Kate had a stunned look. She started to speak, then glanced at Will. Her blue, shrewd eyes were dark with a kind of pain and puzzlement. Kate turned and called to her men, gazing blankly from their horses, "Any of you know about this?"

They did not, and to Alec Waggoman Kate said with an obvious effort, "Alec, I ain't got any idea."

Waggoman had taken the coin in silence. He looked tall and frigidly aloof as he handed it to Kate. His order to Hansbro was colorless. "Show me another."

It's there, Will guessed as he moved with the others to the steer Charley had downed. Quigby stepped close to Hansbro and intently watched each movement of the huge man's hands. And in these wire-taut moments, a warning sense struck Will that something else was happening. Old habits of army training swung his attention from Hansbro to the semicircle of mounted men. And he saw the reason for his vague unease.

Casually, unnoticed, the Barb crew had been reining among the Half-Moon riders. Hansbro's satisfied growl said, "Here's another two-bits," and Will lifted his voice in sharp warning.

"Half-Moon! Keep together!"

Barb men now bracketed each Half-Moon man. Hansbro's quick shout, "*Now,* Barb!" followed Will's warning. The startled Half-Moon men found themselves covered by drawn guns.

Will moved swiftly to one side despite a Colt's sighted on him by the nearest rider. Charley, still sitting on the rope steer's head, was covering Quigby with a long-barreled forty-five.

Quigby glared at the weapon and bit out with confident authority of his law badge, "Put that up! I'm taking charge here!"

Alec Waggoman dropped the second coin in his coat pocket. He turned slowly and looked directly into Kate's distressed face, and Will held his breath.

Even in Coronado, escorting his son's body, that tall old man had not looked like this. The brief *élan* of youth had passed. He looked old. The hooded stare resting on Kate held detestation. He spoke slowly, bitterly.

"Hating all these years— Spiteful— And now thieving—"

Quigby's anger broke in roughly. "Waggoman! Hold your men!"

Waggoman replied without turning his head. "Your gun will be shot out of your hand, Quigby." A great anger deep in the man worked visibly against iron control. His voice shook slightly as he spoke again to Kate. "Maybe Dave, too— This is the end, Kate." And a terrible, repressed, matter-of-factness filled the order to Hansbro. "Take their guns." He walked to his horse and hauled heavily into the saddle.

Kate had a white, drawn look as she spoke to her men. "Don't fight 'em, boys."

The Half-Moon men were being disarmed as Will walked to Waggoman's gray horse. He was not aware his lean, sun-blackened indolence was wire-hard with challenge. But inside he felt that way as he looked up at Waggoman.

"The last time Barb took my gun," Will reminded thinly, "I was held and my hand almost shot off." Will moved back, facing all the Barb men. Left hand in the cloth sling, right hand loose near his belt, Will promised, "Not this time— Not again—"

This, he knew, was folly. They could riddle him. He watched the tall, white-mustached old man who peered down at him without expression. And when Waggoman said, "Keep your gun," it was anticlimax, leaving Waggoman somehow supreme and unruffled.

"All right, Vic," Waggoman said. He wheeled the gray horse, and as his men drew together and followed, he put his horse into a lope back the way they had come.

Will's saddle gun had been taken. Kate looked at her disarmed crew, at the tight anger on Quigby's face. She turned and looked after the two young steers which had bolted away.

"So we're rustlers," Kate said, half to herself. A tired note entered her comment to Will. "He ain't through. We'd best go home an' think about it."

Kate rode to one side, alone, her head bowed in thought. She, too, looked older now, Will thought, and still a little dazed. Quigby's anger was almost incoherent as the deputy rode briefly beside Will.

"The man's a fool! These aren't the old days!"

"Seems to be," Will reminded mildly.

They had reached the slopes above the ranch when Will sighted the first climbing swirls of greasy smoke. His sharp "Look!" brought Kate from her bemused state.

Kate looked, and used her braided quirt then, riding like a man in a reckless gallop down the slopes covered with shin oak and brush. And even Will felt a little sick when they burst out of the last trees into the open, and the full sight lay below them.

All was burning—haystacks and bunkhouse, sheds and cookshack—

Chapter Twenty-two

Smoke and flames were spurting from broken windows of the big house. Fire was bursting through the dry shake roof. As Will's racing horse drew near, he saw the house roof mushroom into a scarlet wall of fire gushing high.

The wide yard was ringed by burning structures spewing smoke, flames, and whorls of red embers. All that Kate had built in a lifetime was vanishing in wanton destruction. Barb men were even slashing the dried rawhide lashings of corral poles and hurling the poles on blazing heaps of other poles. In the veils of hot drifting smoke, the moving figures had a busy, evil look.

The forlorn cook stood helplessly near his burning cookshack. Barb horses were bunched outside the fire-ringed yard, guarded by two men with carbines ready. The threatening guns waved the Half-Moon rush to a stop.

Will made out Vic Hansbro striding about the smoke-filled yard, black hat shoved back as Hansbro bawled orders. Alec Waggoman sat his uneasy gray horse near the burning cookshack, a silent, solitary figure, watching impassively.

Kate ignored the two warning carbines and forced her horse on into the flame-ringed yard. Her shoulders sagged now in a defeated look.

Will, driven by helpless anger, put his own frightened horse through showering sparks and acrid smoke to Alec Waggoman. Boxes of cartridges in the bunkhouse and the big house were exploding in ragged bursts as Will reached the tall old man who peered at him without expression.

In cold anger, Will said, "You've done this now, like your son worked on me. You can't undo this. But I've seen you try to be fair, mister. Didn't you even take time to wonder whether a thief couldn't have branded Barb calves, and then waited to see Kate Canaday accused?"

New lines had graved into Waggoman's face. His reply was a colorless, "Why should a thief bother?"

And Will had to admit, "I don't know; I only know Kate Canaday— And you should know her even better."

Then Will watched some great stirring of emotion move in the man, deep and held in. A sadness such as Will had never seen spread on the lined face.

"If I ever thought that," came from Waggoman slowly, "I'd come crawling on hands and knees, begging forgiveness."

Then Will had the feeling he drifted out of the man's thoughts. Waggoman spurred his horse on by and his harsh order reached through the smoke to Hansbro.

"Get the men!"

Every structure was a mass of flame; little now could be salvaged, Will saw, as the Barb crew piled into saddles and the lot of them rode off on the ranch road, taking the guns of the Half-Moon men.

Quigby had already left. Kate had dismounted in the flame-ringed yard. She was holding the reins, looking around when Will stepped down beside her. They watched the Half-Moon crew gather with them.

Kate shook her head. Some of her stunned help-lessness was lifting. She sounded more like herself.

"Ain't much we can do now." And to her long-faced, indecisive men, Kate said, "Boys, you still got your britches. Get to work. I'll send to town for bedrolls. We're burnt out but we ain't run out."

And then Will knew he would always admire this big, indomitable woman.

As the Barb men rode away, Vic Hansbro looked back at the geysering smoke and flames. The chopped-off black beard hid his sly satisfaction. Now Alec Waggoman would be satisfied about the missing cattle. And Alec would always believe he had acted righteously.

The thought worked pleasantly in Hansbro's brain. He could handle Alec; and the Kirby girl and Frank Darrah could be handled, too. Hansbro looked at his tough Barb crew stringing out ahead, talking, laughing. His narrowing gaze went to Waggoman, riding at his right, chin sunk on chest. The old man had aged, Hansbro thought critically. Alec's craggy face had a haggard look; he rode slumped and withdrawn, with a lonely, solitary look. Hansbro waited with covertly sneering patience when Waggoman glanced at him and asked a quiet, musing question.

"Vic, why wasn't I told our calves had been marked this way?"

Hansbro had long planned the reply to this inevitable question. "You were off on a trip, Alec. It kinda slipped my mind later."

"I see. How many two-bits did you plant?"

"Forty-fifty."

"And no one missed that many unbranded calves?"

A faint unease dug at Hansbro. When Alec quietly pursued some thought like this, he was dangerous. Hansbro's hasty thoughts floundered and brought out a lame, "I kep' it quiet, Alec. Did it all alone; kep' it to myself."

Waggoman was peering oddly at him. The old man's musing voice said, "Lockhart suggested someone else could have put Kate's brand on our calves."

"Meanin' me?" Hansbro flared.

After a moment Hansbro got back only a slow, "Not particularly, Vic. Lockhart could have meant me." The old man rode silently before saying mildly, "But I didn't, Vic. And why you?"

"No reason," Hansbro growled sulkily.

"I can't think of a reason, Vic." Waggoman looked, sounded, old and tired. A little later he gathered the reins. His shoulders went back. "I'm going up on Chinaman Creek. Keep the men around the bunkhouse until I get back."

He reined off the road without saying more. A driving brute like Hansbro would not understand, Waggoman knew sadly. Who could understand that close under the high peaks a lonely man could gaze in anguish and vivid memory on his own life moving through the grandeur which rolled toward those now-blurred horizons?

Alone up there a man could relive for an hour the hot triumphs, the great mistakes. He could taste again the exultations, the brooding, the grief. He could admit the mistakes.

In growing anguish, Waggoman's thoughts ran on the tall young stranger of great perception whose cold condemnation had bared truth Waggoman had always known deep inside. Never would Kate Canaday have rustled from Barb—or anyone else. Waggoman struck his clenched fist to the brass saddle horn helplessly.

And behind him now out of sight Vic Hansbro was riding for a sweating mile. There would be more questions. Alec was that way when mystified. In sudden decision, Hansbro rode to the lead of the strung-out men and halted them. He forced booming joviality.

"Alec's cuttin' back to look over more of Half-Moon. I'm riding to town for him. You men stay around the bunkhouse. Alec's orders. He said to get some whisky outa the house pantry. Everyone gets a big blowout on the boss."

The quick grins and no questions asked were what Hansbro had expected. He listened, satisfied, to the yell which lifted. "Last man stays sober!" Spurs raked, quirts flailed—

Hansbro watched them out of sight, and then rode up the mountain. He was afraid. But he would go, Hansbro knew now, to those high headwaters of Chinaman Creek. That tall and sometimes terrible old man had become suspicious and dangerous. Vic Hansbro's future on Barb was safe now only with Barbara Kirby and Frank Darrah. That pair could be handled. And with all of Half-Moon in a killing mood toward Alec Waggoman now, this was the day to gamble greatly.

At Half-Moon the fires had burned down to ashes and rubble, and Will Lockhart, working with the others, pondered this calamity for Kate, and the reasons for it.

Kate Canaday was an honest woman. Alec Waggoman had his fairness. But behind those two, in the background, Vic Hansbro loomed malignantly.

Will's thoughts kept coming back to the huge, bearded foreman. What could Hansbro have gained by all this? And as sunset neared, Will decided to ride to Barb tonight and question Waggoman bluntly.

He had thought all afternoon that Barbara Kirby would come quickly when she heard. He sighted her finally riding through the blazing sunset, and he called to Kate and watched.

Like all the rest, Will was grimed with wood ashes and black char. But he became less tired as he watched Barbara leave her froth-flecked sorrel horse and reach comforting arms to Kate. Barbara was loyal; she was kind.

Then Will stood motionless, caught by his thoughts again. In a way now, Barbara was the great Barb ranch, too. And after she owned Barb, who else would profit? Frank Darrah would— But what of Hansbro?

Frowning over this new thought, Will walked to the two women and heard Kate telling Barbara ruefully, "Child, you made a long ride for a skimpy supper."

Barbara was gazing around at the gray smoke wisps and rubble heaps which had been Kate's home and life. In a low, scathing voice, Barbara said, "I thought Uncle Alec was decent and fair. But this—" Barbara swallowed. "Tonight I'll tell him—"

Kate's grimy hand pushed graying hair off her smudged forehead. Her advice was tolerant. "Don't waste good temper, child. I'm tougher'n that old scalawag'll ever be. Forget him."

Some secretive look of women passed between them, and Barbara's face softened. She looked small and young in the denim skirt and jacket Will had seen before. A small gray felt hat with chin cord of braided leather rode carelessly back on her wind-blown hair. Anger had put a silken bloom on her face. The stubborn outthrust of her red lower lip was provocative, and the stubbornness edged her reply to Kate.

"He's mentioned my owning Barb. Tonight he'll hear what I think of Barb and of him."

"It's a long ride after dark." Kate's speculative glance touched Will.

His eyebrow cocked in faint amusement at Kate's unspoken wish. To Barbara, Will said gravely, "I'm riding to Barb as soon as we eat. Can't I tell your uncle for you?"

"I'll tell him," said Barbara coolly.

A little later, washing awkwardly with one hand in the windmill trough, made from a huge hollowed log, Will had the dismal feeling that this first graying twilight made the destruction look far more grim and complete.

Wreckage had been cleared away from the cook's iron range. Pans and pots, tinware and cutlery had been raked from the hot ashes. An old roundup wagon had been backed close to the range, its tailboard forming a worktable. A vealer calf had been butchered.

Now smoke gushed from an upright length of stove pipe on the back of the range. The forlorn cook was frying steaks and tossing bits of meat to Kate's disconsolate hounds. For two hours the huge coffeepot had been filled with rank, fire-charred coffee.

In a way, recovery from hopelessness had started,

Will reflected as he used the black neck sling for an indifferent towel. But what good all this effort if disaster could strike again? But presently, sitting on the ground beside Barbara, relishing good steak and fried doughballs made from the center flour of a charred barrel, Will felt more cheerful.

As she had done in her own kitchen, Barbara cut his meat into bite-sized bits. In repose, her face was still provocative with anger. And as Will ate, he wondered what the unkind fates held for this girl who would one day own all of great Barb. Any possible answer was disturbing.

Shortly they were riding toward Barb, and in the first mile Barbara asked the question Will was expecting.

"Why are you going to Barb tonight?"

"I never miss a chance to ride anywhere with a pretty girl," Will said gravely. He watched her flush, and his grin came.

"And now why?" Barbara asked again.

"Hansbro seems to be back of all this," Will said, sobering. "Your uncle may know why."

"I've never liked Vic Hansbro," was Barbara's troubled admission. "But why should he hurt Kate?"

Will said slowly, "A man like Hansbro isn't complex. Self-interest or hatred will motivate most of his actions."

"You don't," said Barbara coolly, "talk like a mule skinner."

Will laughed softly. "You mean a mule skinner doesn't talk like me. Is Hansbro in your uncle's will?"

Barbara's quick look was startled. She said slowly, "Uncle Alec will know," and she lapsed into silence.

A smell of dust and cedar spiced the night. The

sky in these early hours before moonrise became smooth jet splashed with stars. Their saddles creaked softly, and Will fell to musing on the intimate night hours this warmhearted girl had nursed him in her home. And now all her nights would be Frank Darrah's. He put the thought away almost violently.

Finally Barbara said they were nearing Barb headquarters. Minutes later they reined up suddenly as distant gunshots bounced echoes through the night ahead. Yells and snatches of song came faintly.

Will judged dryly, "They're celebrating."

Barbara was indignant as they rode on. "Uncle Alec *couldn't* be celebrating Kate's loss. And he's always been strict about whisky around the bunkhouse."

"They're not full of pump water," Will murmured, listening to the ribald sounds.

They sighted red fire glow against the sky. A final bend in the road and they saw a great pile of dead wood blazing in the ranch yard. Crimson glare and dark shadows wavered on the fortlike stone house and outbuildings. Dark figures were moving around the fire.

They were sighted. The towering figure of Vic Hansbro strode from the fire to meet them. Will rode ahead, watching Hansbro halt in startled recognition. Barbara moved up beside Will and as they reached the man, Hansbro snatched off his black hat.

"Comp'ny wasn't expected, ma'am," he greeted Barbara with heavy sheepishness.

Curtly Will asked, "Where's Waggoman?"

The scowl he got switched to an uncertain grin

at Barbara. Will watched the white teeth showing in the black beard and made a cynical guess. *He's not forgetting she'll be boss one day.* He listened to Hansbro tell Barbara genially, "I'm sorry, miss. Your uncle ain't back yet."

And suddenly the drunk and ribald crew around the fire was understandable. And more— Something was wrong here. Greatly wrong—

The men were straggling to them, some staggering a little, many grinning, others owlishly curious. A taunting question was called. "You wan' them Half-Moon guns?"

Hansbro called an angry order. "All of you get to the bunkhouse an' keep quiet!" And to Barbara, he was hurriedly apologetic. "They likkered up while I was gone to town, miss."

A loosely grinning puncher whooped, "Ol' Alec said to git the whisky an' we sure did!"

Hansbro reached the man in a striding lunge. His fist smashed the loose grin. Will had been hit by that great fist; he winced from memory and watched the man stagger back and fall and huddle on his side motionless.

The crimson fire glare played on Barbara's pallor as she watched the men back away from Hansbro's rage. Her uncertain question barely reached Will.

"What shall we do?"

"Wait in the house."

They rode to the back steps and dismounted before Hansbro got there. "Go in," Will told Barbara. He followed her up the steps and turned in the doorway as Hansbro reached the bottom step. "We'll wait alone," Will said curtly when the big man started up. "Where's Waggoman?"

He knew Hansbro's malevolent score against

him; yet surprisingly the man backed off the step and explained genially, "I rode to town. Alec turned back to scout Half-Moon land. He oughta be home now."

"We'll wait," Will said again and stepped in the kitchen and closed the door.

A glass lamp with white opaque shade was glowing on the worn pine kitchen table. And on the same table in the middle of the room, a litter of soiled tumblers and empty quart whisky bottles stood in a slop of spilled whiskey and water. Men had spat on the floor and tossed down cigarette ends. The kitchen reeked of stale tobacco smoke, stale whisky, stale sweat.

Barbara's pallor was greater as she looked around. Her low voice asked, "Did he say Uncle Alec rode back on Kate's ranch alone?"

"Yes," Will said absently. He was turning to a back window. Out there in the wide yard, Hansbro's tall figure loomed by the crackling fire. He was rolling a cigarette and eyeing the house. Will turned back and considered the table. He said slowly, "So Waggoman told them to do this—"

"I don't believe it," Barbara said under her breath. "If you knew how he's always been— This isn't like him—" The house was very quiet. Strain tightened Barbara's voice. "Why should he ride back alone on Kate's land?"

"Waggoman went one way. Hansbro another. The crew came here and started drinking—" Will glanced down at his bandaged hand. His gray hard glance came up to Barbara.

"The other day I went one way. Dave Waggoman went another. And that night Dave didn't return, either."

"Not Uncle Alec, too." This was fear, Barbara thought helplessly—this chill feeling as she watched Lockhart's chin indicate the table, listened to Lockhart's new, cold-eyed intentness.

"Waggoman knows the way home. Would this mess be here if the foreman expected him back any minute?"

Then Barbara shivered.

She watched Lockhart prowl the kitchen. All his easy indolence and smiling irony had vanished. His dark, weather-scoured face looked hard and harsh. He looked, Barbara thought with new awareness of him, older now and dominating. A man used to commanding. She obeyed without question when he lifted the lamp from the table and said briefly, "Show me your uncle's bedroom."

In the plain quiet bedroom, he put the lamp on a walnut bureau and from the foot post of the brass bed lifted a soiled blue shirt. He rolled it tightly and rammed it in a hip pocket.

"Why that?" Barbara had to ask as he picked up the lamp again.

"An idea," was Lockhart's vague explanation. In the kitchen as he put the lamp down, he said, "I think it's useless to wait. But if you care to—"

Barbara looked out the same back window. Vic Hansbro was waiting alone by the fire. He looked huge, formidable. "What will happen if we try to leave?" Barbara murmured. When she turned, Lockhart's smile was ironic again.

"Nothing will happen while you're along," he said with the same irony. "You'll be needed to inherit Barb."

Barbara had the disturbed feeling he meant more than the surface words. It could wait; she wanted now only to get away from this brooding, filthy kitchen. Lockhart followed her down the back steps and gave her a quick, easy lift to the saddle with his good hand while Hansbro was striding to them.

Grinning again and affable, Hansbro spoke to her. "Ma'am, you ain't waitin' long."

Barbara said "No" evenly, and Will Lockhart's clipped voice said, "Tell Waggoman we were here. It's important he talk with Miss Kirby."

"Sure will," Hansbro promised genially.

Barbara did not look back. She had the tight feeling Hansbro was scowling after them. She felt like shivering again. Something monstrous, darkly evil seemed to be prowling all of Barb.

Miles away they pulled down to a walk and Barbara spoke her miserable thought. "It might take days to find him. Tom Quigby came to Coronado and started immediately to Roxton Springs for the sheriff. He won't be back until tomorrow."

Lockhart's voice was thoughtful in the starlight. "Kate Canaday has been bragging how her dogs can hold any trail, especially Old Roy, the leader. Waggoman was on a horse—but there might be a chance—"

"So you brought that shirt?"

Lockhart's chuckle sounded dry. "A nice dirty shirt full of Waggoman's scent, if Kate cares to try her dogs."

Without hesitation, Barbara said, "Kate will try."

Chapter Twenty-three

A light spring wagon loaded with tarps, blankets, and supplies had reached Half-Moon after dark. The crew were sleeping in bedrolls near where their bunkhouse had stood.

The solitary figure of Kate Canaday, wrapped in a gaudy new blanket, Indian-style, was slowly pacing near the debris of her home when Will and Barbara rode in.

Kate listened intently to Will's terse account. She did not hesitate. "I got three dogs that might track Alec." In the pallid light of a rising moon—a half-moon, Will suddenly noticed—Kate bulked big and shadowy inside the green-and-purple blanket. Behind her the red, fitful glow of scattered embers pinpointed the black rubble of her home as Kate said quietly, "Just like Dave went, ain't it? We better get started."

"You sleep," Will urged. "I'll take the dogs and a man or so."

Kate's gaze lacked any expression that he could see. But her decision had blunt finality. "I'm goin', mister."

Will shook three men awake.

Herb Palmas, a chunky man of grinning humor, stood up yawning, groaning disgustedly. "The damn' old wolf got my guns an' burnt my bed. Now I got to hunt him."

Brodie Keenan and Long Joe were no happier. But they went to saddle horses. Near midnight the search started, and Barbara was stubbornly accompanying Kate.

A half mile out, Kate, with the gaudy blanket still over her shoulders, dismounted in the ranch road and held Waggoman's shirt to the three dogs. A moment later, whining eagerly, the dogs began casting for scent.

Will was hoping Waggoman had turned off this road and had touched brush with his body, leaving scent that would hover stronger tonight. They advanced slowly, the dogs weaving over the road and out through the brush.

A long time later, it seemed to Will's impatience, one dog bayed loudly in brush off to the right. The other dogs raced there, and the excited clamor surged away.

Kate spurred off the road after them. Will followed, bucking brush up a rising slope. The clamoring dogs were heading toward higher country. Kate was recklessly following.

Will burst through the brush after her, branches slapping his body, raking his face. He heard Barbara and the men thrashing behind, and he knew this upgrade gallop would have to ease off.

When Kate pulled her winded horse to a walk, she had lost her broad-brimmed gray hat. The blanket was across her saddle and knees now, and Kate was breathing hard.

"They're headin' for the Yellow Rocks," Kate panted, listening.

Will took the lead here at a slower pace. The dogs, he suspected, were running on hot scent of cougar or bear—running hard, baying, yelping, up into the dark pine stands—and on higher, where the wan moon flooded open meadows with ghostly light—

And always far ahead the bugling clamor echoed and faded off higher cliffs and forest and sky.

And then long after midnight they lost the dogs. "Should have roped 'em," Kate grumbled.

They advanced blindly now into higher country, pausing often to listen. And finally they heard far, faint barking.

"Sounds above Chinaman Creek, on Barb land," Kate decided.

In the first graying of false dawn they were crossing high meadows under South Peak. Here the faint echoing yelps were plainly ahead. Kate said, "We should have gone over Saddleback. The trail down to Chinaman Creek ain't a purty."

And the trail was all Kate promised, a narrow, treacherous pitch down the sheer side of a canyon wall, crumbling outer edges hanging over shadow-clotted depths. Will advanced first, slowly, listening to the frustrated barking of the dogs funnel and echo up the narrow canyon below.

A turn of the trail finally revealed the parklike valley of Chinaman Creek into which they were descending. The creek water gleamed down there in the moonlight.

Will's carefully advancing horse rounded another sharp bend and halted. The dogs were just ahead, barking vigorously. Bald rock backed them. Empty space dropped away from the trail's edge. And here Will was finally convinced that Alec Waggoman must have come this way—this far—

Over a shoulder, Will called, "It ends here." And behind him, Kate's reply was strained and tired. "We can ride to the bottom an' turn back in the canyon an' see what it was."

The dogs trotted quietly ahead now. Dawn was

steel gray in the east when they entered the narrow canyon, and presently found Alec Waggoman.

Horse and man had plunged off the trail and fallen to an old talus slope matted with brush. The horse had rolled to the bottom. Waggoman lay higher in a thick tangle of the brush.

Kate, gasping for breath, reached the body seconds after Will. Alec Waggoman lay crumpled and hatless, white hair disheveled and his face bent away from the creeping dawn. Barbara and the three men, breathing hard, reached the spot as Kate bent over Waggoman's face.

Kate's murmur barely reached Will.

"It was yellow then, an' flying in the wind—" Her rough hand was smoothing the white hair off Waggoman's temple. Under her breath, absently, Kate recalled, "Always laughing—"

Will's glance at the men turned them awkwardly back. Barbara turned, too, and as Will stepped to help her down the rough slope, he saw that Kate's hand had closed on Waggoman's slack fingers.

"So it was that way?" Will muttered, wonderingly.

They halted at the bottom. Barbara looked back, and her mouth softened. Her faint smile was understanding, tender, a little sad.

"Jubal says they were young and big and shouting with laughter," Barbara said under her breath. "They did everything together. They rode, danced, played together. She helped him work his first few cattle. They talked and planned of the great ranch they'd build together."

Barbara's thoughts held her, smiling faintly.

"One can see how it must have been," Will said quietly.

"Jubal says she wasn't pretty, even then," Barbara remembered. "But she was big and laughing and vital—And she loved him like storm in the sunshine—"

Watching Barbara's face, Will mused, "Riches for any man."

Barbara's look touched him and sobered. "Or any woman," said Barbara slowly, and her silence was pensive.

"And then?" Will asked.

Barbara turned up small palms in a gesture of futility. "A pampered little beauty ended it. She came visiting from Chicago with trunks of the latest French clothes. She had traveled on the Continent. She was exquisite and flirtatious. She was everything Kate was not. And she had never met a man like Alec Waggoman. Or he a woman like her. Before anyone suspected what was happening, he carried her suddenly to Roxton Springs and married her."

"And they lived happily?"

"Miserably," Barbara said slowly. "She disliked the frontier. Soon she resented Alec. She nagged, complained, and after Dave was born she lived to pamper him. Alec drew into a shell and lost himself in building Barb. He never spoke unkindly of her, never complained. Too proud, Jubal used to tell me, to admit he'd made a mistake."

"And Kate lived near them, hurting and hating," mused Will.

Barbara glanced up the brush-choked, talus slope again. "Is that hate?" her quiet voice asked.

"No," Will admitted. He hesitated. "Now you own Barb. You, at least, will be happily married."

He had not meant to speak this edged, hard irony which drew Barbara's quick look.

They stared at one another. A great, startled uncertainty pooled darkly in Barbara's greenish-blue eyes—and then Kate's great shaken cry came between them.

"Alec ain't dead!"

At Barb ranch, the cook beat his iron triangle for breakfast, as usual. A little later from the head of the long crowded table in the cookshack, Vic Hansbro surveyed the bloodshot eyes and glum hangovers of the crew. His promise was sarcastic.

"You had the whisky last night. Now you'll sweat it out lookin' for the Old Man. He didn't come in." No one spoke and Hansbro said, "He headed back on Half-Moon. No tellin' what happened."

That stirred their lethargy, and Hansbro gave brusque orders. "Charley, you ride to town an' look. The rest of you scatter over Half-Moon. Watch for buzzards. Alec might've got what Dave did."

"If they shot the Old Man, what'll they do to us?" was Fitz's sarcastic question.

Hansbro growled, "That'll help you sweat. Don't start trouble. All we want is Alec. I'll wait here for him."

When the men had ridden off, Hansbro carried a quart of whisky from the house pantry to Waggoman's office. He grunted with satisfaction as his bulk settled in Waggoman's creaking swivel chair. He was grinning with relish as he lighted a cigar from Waggoman's box in the scarred old roll-top desk.

Two hours later Hansbro corked the half-empty

bottle with a swat of a broad palm. He was not drunk as he stood up and wandered outside. In a contented mellow glow, he continued to relish the great satisfying thought that Vic Hansbro was now boss.

The Kirby girl might not like it. But Frank Darrah would rule that roost. Hansbro grinned at the thought and strolled to the cookshack for a tin cup of black coffee.

He carried the cup to the office steps where Alec Waggoman had often sat gazing into the immensity of distance that was all Barb. Now, in a way, it was all Vic Hansbro's. He was hunched on the top step musing contentedly when Fitz rode a foaming horse into the ranch yard and swung off.

"Half-Moon found him at daybreak!" Fitz called.

A sweep of Hansbro's big hand tumbled the empty tin cup off the step. He came to his feet with believable anger. "I knew damn' well they probably killed him!"

Fitz canted his head, gazing up with a thin grin. "He ain't dead. Doc Seldon is tendin' him at Half-Moon. Folks are headin' there from town to see what we burned, an' how the Old Man is. I met Jubal Kirby drivin' there. He told me."

Hansbro asked stupidly, "Alec ain't dead?"

"Nope."

"He's at Half-Moon, talkin' with folks from town?"

"Yep."

"Get the men back here!" Hansbro ordered thickly. Fitz was staring curiously and Hansbro yelled, "Get 'em, dammit!"

Fitz turned to his horse. Hansbro hesitated and wheeled back into the office. His hand was shaking as he grabbed the bottle off the desk. Alec hadn't died in that plunge off the Chinaman Creek trail. And now Alec was telling what had happened— Hansbro shuddered as a great gulp of whisky burned down his throat. What would happen now, Hansbro knew despairingly, would be brutal, ruthless, and merciless—

This was the morning also that Colonel Lake, at Fort Roxton, bent his tufted, graying brows above a message just laid on his desk.

> *Confidential, unofficial: Captain William Lockhart stationed Fort Laramie. Now on extended furlough. Whereabouts not known.*

Lake swore softly. That stiff young prig, Lieutenant Evans, might have been right after all. The Lockhart arrested in Roxton Springs could be Lockhart of Laramie. An unofficial visit to Coronado and Half-Moon was in order, Lake decided. He was grim about it. Officers, furloughed or not, did not knife men where Michael Lake commanded.

Herb Palmas had made the wild ride from Chinaman Creek to the doctor in Coronado.

Long Joe had quirted his horse down dangerous short cuts to Half-Moon.

Four lunging horses—with saddle ropes helping when needed—had snaked the light spring wagon recklessly to that high valley of Chinaman Creek. On open bedrolls piled in the wagon bed, they had brought Alec Waggoman down to Half-Moon a little before Doctor Matt Seldon's hard-whipped buggy team raced in.

Beneath a tarp stretched from the wagon side-
boards to supporting poles, Seldon worked on
Alec Waggoman's broken ribs and fractured arm.
There was concussion.

Finally Seldon stepped out into the sunlight,
turning down his sleeves. The crew were uncertain
in the background. Will had been watching, waiting while Kate and Barbara helped Seldon when
they could.

It was Kate's silent question that Seldon answered. "I can't say. That concussion—"

"He won't die," Kate muttered, as if dogged
stubbornness could prevail. And now Will could
understand why Seldon's reply was wondrously
gentle to the big, tired, weatherbeaten woman.
"Something is helping him, Kate."

Will glanced to the piled bedrolls under the
shading tarp. Alec Waggoman lay quietly, eyes
closed. A kind of majestic serenity had settled on
the craggy face, as if this border of life where Waggoman paused now held its own new peace.

Will pushed finger tips through the over-night
stubble on his dark face. The thought that had been
nagging him came out. "Waggoman's horse hadn't
been shot. Or Waggoman himself. How did he
happen to go off that trail?"

"I think I should speak of it now," Seldon decided reluctantly. "Alec has been losing his sight.
Cataracts. He was half blind."

Dryly Will asked, "Did the horse have cataracts,
too? The horse was carrying him."

Seldon's blue, puckered eyes studied Will.
"What are you suggesting, Lockhart?"

"Hansbro says he went to town yesterday, after

Waggoman turned back alone. Did you see Hansbro in town?"

Seldon shook his head. "But that doesn't indicate Hansbro wasn't there."

Barbara had been standing quietly at Will's right, listening. All the way down the mountain she had withdrawn into her thoughts. Barbara's pallor now was noticeable as she spoke to Seldon.

"After you dressed Will Lockhart's hand the other evening, Doctor Matt, whom did you discuss it with?"

Seldon was surprised. "No one, Barbara. I never talk about patients."

"Are you certain? Not a word to—to anyone?"

"Not a word," Seldon said firmly.

The slight quaver in Barbara's voice betrayed a quick misery behind her pallor. Questions that were crowding Will's own mind stayed unspoken as he looked at her.

And it was Kate Canaday, blunt and shrewd, who asked the one question Will had to know.

"That evening, Barbara, did anyone speak to you about Lockhart's trouble with Dave Waggoman?"

Barbara's swallow moved the tanned smoothness of her throat. Her head shook silently, denying or refusing, and she turned away, walking slowly toward the stripped posts of the corrals.

Will gazed at her back. The jauntiness of Barbara's small, square shoulders was listless now. Her eyes were on the ground. Her one visitor at home that evening, Will remembered well, had been Frank Darrah. Was it possible Darrah had mentioned Dave's rage on Chinaman Creek and use of a gun?

Kate broke the moment of uncomfortable silence.

She sounded portentous, grim. She said the things Will was thinking.

"Someone mentioned that trouble to Barbara that evening. Nothing else would have made her ask Matt such a question. And Dave Waggoman was the only other person near town who could have let it out that quick. No one's admitted meeting Dave before he was killed. But if someone did meet Dave, and let slip to Barbara later that he knew about the trouble—ain't we close now to the man who musta killed Dave?"

Will warned, "You're only guessing."

"It fits," said Kate stubbornly. "And this ain't the first ideas I've had that way, either. Dave's death put Barbara closer to inheriting Barb. Alec's death would have given her Barb almost as soon as she was married. Who'd like that to happen?"

"Kate," Seldon warned quietly, "you're talking too much."

"Someone better start talkin'. Where was Frank Darrah when Dave was killed? Where was he when Alec was hurt?"

"Would Darrah," Will asked, "have been able to brand those Barb calves in your iron?"

"The devil," said Kate flatly, "ain't one-armed. If his right hand didn't do it, maybe his left hand did. Go ask Barbara what she knows."

"Barbara will decide what she knows."

"Ain't you interested?"

Will shrugged, and saw with faint amusement that it baffled Kate, exasperated her. The uncertain waiting which followed was hardest, Will presently decided. That tall old man lay ominously still under the shading tarp, and only he could tell what had happened.

Kate sat quietly beside the pallet of bedrolls on an upended box, deceptively calm. Will had the odd suspicion that fierce emotion deep in the big, rough-featured woman was beating through the mists where Waggoman lingered, and was holding him, calling him.

Barbara had walked out of sight. A buggy arrived from Coronado with friends of Kate. More visitors began to arrive, and Will remained in the background. Only when Jubal Kirby's weathered buckboard appeared did Will's long strides cross the yard.

Jubal stopped under a great cottonwood at the edge of the yard and stepped down and asked his sober questions. "'Tis bad," was Jubal's quiet opinion.

"Is Darrah coming?"

Jubal's oblique glance was probing. "Later. Two of his crew at the salt lakes came in. Smoke signals had them worried about an Indian raid." Jubal's gaze was searching the yard. "Where's Barbara?"

Will indicated the first slopes beyond the stripped corral posts, and Jubal walked that way.

Then, finally, from halfway across the yard, Will saw Doctor Seldon go to his knees beside the pallet and bend low over Waggoman's face. Seldon got to his feet, saw Will coming, and hurried to meet him.

Chapter Twenty-four

Anger had molded an aggressive bristle behind Seldon's graying Van Dyke. But the man's first words were professionally routine.

"I think Alec is better. His mind seems to be functioning. He mumbled a few words just then."

Alert now, Will demanded, "Can he help us?"

"He has helped," Seldon said in tight-lipped anger, emphatically. "I will take oath in court that Alec mumbled, *'Vic, you're crowding me off the trail!'*"

Will stared. "That simple a trick," he said softly. "Caught up with him and waited, and crowded him off the trail. An accident that couldn't be helped, no doubt, so long as Waggoman couldn't refute it."

Seldon's contemptuous snort answered the idea of an accident. Will put his own contempt into words. "Hansbro is as stupid as he is treacherous. He should have gone on down into the canyon and made certain."

"Tom Quigby, the deputy, should be notified," Seldon urged.

"I'll send a man," Will said, and when Seldon turned back to his patient, Will went for Brodie Keenan. He told Keenan to saddle two horses. When that was done, Kate was at Waggoman's side again, and Barbara and her father had not returned.

Will's final order to Brodie Keenan was terse. "Don't talk to anyone about Waggoman. If Quigby isn't in Coronado, ride to Roxton Springs after him."

He watched Keenan ride off, and then hauled up on the second horse and skirted the yard and burned buildings at an unobtrusive walk. On the ranch road, Will eased the horse through a trot into a hard run toward Barb. The misery on Barbara's face had promised there would be more to learn from Vic Hansbro.

In Coronado this was another day of clear sunshine. A bracing day, with the promise of more good fortune, was Frank Darrah's pleasant thought as he walked toward Kitty's Café. His furtive glance slanted complacently at his reflection in the window of Nordoff's Harness Shop as he passed. The morning razor had smoothed his pinkish face to a healthy glow. In the neat salt-and-pepper suit, he looked precisely what he was, a solid, prosperous young man of business, liked and respected, Frank saw with satisfaction.

Business returned to his thoughts. Yesterday Alec Waggoman had burned Kate Canaday's ranch buildings. The town and range were abuzz with the news. Frank's reflective smile lingered. With that old feud finally erupting, it might be possible now to pick up control of Half-Moon at a bargain.

And then, a few minutes later in Kitty's place, Frank heard of Alec Waggoman's serious accident.

Shaken, Frank forgot food. He partially gulped a mug of black coffee and hurried out. His thoughts were in a wild roil as he walked aimlessly toward the lower end of town. At this moment, Alec Waggoman might be dead—

Frank realized his strides were pounding faster on the walk planks. His face had flushed. He was breathing harder. Natural caution took command.

His pace slowed. Now, if ever, he needed to be sober, regretful.

Calm now, Frank walked back to his store and let the day's routine take over. When two men from the salt lakes came in for their pay, Frank was sarcastic at their ideas that smoke signals meant an Indian raid on the salt crew.

When Jubal Kirby appeared and said he was driving to Half-Moon, Frank said a little impatiently he would have to follow later. He wanted to be alone with his thoughts. And, speculating on Vic Hansbro's possible part in Waggoman's injury, Frank decided righteously to discharge Hansbro as soon as possible. One could never trust that huge, ruthless brute.

Finally, giving McGuire curt instructions for the day, Frank walked to the Sierra Corrals. He rode out of town with the exciting thought that even now he might be the nominal owner of Barb. And recalling his arrival in this ratty frontier town, and what he had accomplished in a few short years, Frank marveled.

At the brawling Chinaman Creek ford, he thought of the rifle shipment from New Orleans, cached near by in the powder house. That profitable trade with the Apaches was finished. But Frank had the uneasy feeling he would worry until the stranger Lockhart moved on. His face darkened at the thought of Lockhart.

On the narrow ranch road to Barb and Half-Moon, Frank studied the piling mountains ahead. On that high summer graze, Barb cattle were thick—and even now he might own the cattle and all the range, too. The heady excitement came back.

The narrow road was twisting through the

foothills where green junipers and taller piñon pines covered the slopes. Silver-gray chamisa bushes massed along the road, and Frank was mildly startled when, without warning, a gray horse carrying Hansbro moved out of the chamisa into the road ahead.

"You surprised me," Frank said shortly when he reached the man. He was annoyed by Hansbro's stare. Anger came with a rush when Hansbro said, "You're the man I want. I need five thousand, quick."

"If I had five thousand, you'd not get it!" Frank snapped.

"Ain't a loan. They've found Alec Waggoman." A kind of muddy malice darkened Hansbro's stare. "I crowded Alec off that trail, an' like a fool didn't make sure. Now Alec's talking. And I'm leaving while there's a chance. I'm broke. I need money."

"So you tried to kill Waggoman?" A shaking frustration put harshness into Frank's sneering threat. "You'd better get going fast. You'll get no help from me. I should send word to the sheriff."

Hansbro's spurred horse jumped close before Frank realized what was intended. Hansbro's thick-fingered hand grabbed out and caught Frank's neck. A yank dragged Frank off balance. The powerful hand shook him by the throat.

Frank gasped and began to gag helplessly. The great calloused fingers were shutting off his wind—

Dizzily he heard Hansbro cursing him. In frantic fear he clawed at the hand and thick wrist. And then the unbelievable happened. Hansbro's other hand swung in great brutal slaps which stung, hurt, and beat Frank's head back and forth.

"I'll swear you paid me to kill Alec!" Hansbro

promised viciously. "I'll tell about those cattle you bought on the side. An' the kickbacks I got for paying you high prices when Alec was away. Your clerk McGuire ain't a fool. He's guessed how you squeezed Barb on prices an' kicked back to me."

A contemptuous shove put Frank upright again, and Hansbro's promise was malevolent. "That'll fix you on marryin' the Kirby girl! And Alec'll make damn' sure your crooked fists don't get into any part of Barb."

Frank was gasping and near tears of pain and humiliation as he straightened his hat. He was dizzy from the terrible palm clouts. He could taste the hot, metallic parch of fear in his aching throat. In one terrible crescendo of fright, he'd thought this bearded brute would snap his neck.

He choked, "All right—five thousand."

"And another six-gun an' belt an' cartridges," Hansbro growled. "How quick can you get back?"

"I'll have to borrow at the bank."

"Make it fast. And don't forget five thousand is cheap to make sure you get Barb."

Pain surged in Frank's bruised head. Helplessness clogged his aching throat. He was stripped of dignity; he was despised by even this ignorant brute, and he tried wildly to think.

"Another thousand," he gasped thickly, "if I hear Lockhart is dead."

Hansbro cursed him again. "Do your own dirt! I'm gettin' out!"

Frank wrenched his horse around and lashed wildly with the rein ends. Not until he was back at the Chinaman Creek ford did he ease the furiously whipped gallop. The wild frustration, the sick fear and humiliation still gripped him. But he was thinking again. Five thousand was cheap enough to buy Hansbro's silence. But there must be a way to block the bearded brute. In venomous concentration, Frank rode on to Coronado.

At about the same time, Will Lockhart sat his sweating horse near the Barb bunkhouse and listened to Fitz's bland statement. Six more of the crew were gathering, and their hostility had dwindled, Will saw as his hard gaze searched their faces.

"When Hansbro heard the Old Man had been found," Fitz was saying, "he said call off the search. When we got back, Hansbro was gone. How's the Old Man?"

"Talking," said Will curtly. "Hansbro crowded him off that trail. Left him for dead." By their astounded, bewildered expressions, he saw they knew nothing of this. "Where would Hansbro be apt to ride if he thought Waggoman had started you men after him?" Will asked.

Fitz's grin grew relishing. "Straight up, if he could make it."

A drawling man back of Fitz said, "Joie, the cook, says Hansbro rode to the cookshack door an' said something about going to Half-Moon."

"They'd like to see him at Half-Moon," said Will dryly. He told these men, "You know about Hansbro now. He's worth five hundred to me personally. Alive."

Fitz made an impudent guess.

"He'll be worth a damn' sight more dead when the Old Man lays a bounty on him." Then incomprehension laid a puzzled look on Fitz's thin, sallow face. "Why'n hell did Hansbro try to kill Waggoman?"

"Ask Hansbro," Will advised.

He rode across the yard to the cookshack. Here where horses rarely came, shod marks were visible on the hard-packed earth. Will followed the tracks back across the yard, wishing keenly for that master tracker, Charley Yuill, who was still watching Darrah's powder house near the Chinaman Creek ford.

When the hoofprints lengthened out and drove deeper into the road dirt, the story was plain. Hansbro had spurred to a gallop, and not toward Half-Moon—

The wire-taut tension of the hunt built in Will as he followed. It crossed his mind that this time he had all the proof needed. And if he sighted Hansbro, one of them would surely die. Perhaps both of them.

At Half-Moon, they had said Will Lockhart had gone to Coronado with Brodie Keenan, after the sheriff. Barbara's panicky thought had been otherwise. Lockhart must have gone after Frank Darrah—

Already Barbara had decided she must see Frank. Jubal, kindly and understanding father, had agreed, had seemed relieved at her decision, had offered to drive her in the buckboard. Barbara rode her horse, and the insidious nightmare of Frank Darrah went with her.

Frank had known how Dave Waggoman had crippled Will Lockhart's hand. And Doctor Matt hadn't told Frank.

Barbara was unaware she passed the narrowed scrutiny of Vic Hansbro, waiting in cover near the road. She was surprised when two men in sky-blue cavalry uniforms appeared ahead of her. They pulled their horses to a halt. When Barbara checked her blowing horse by them, dusty black field hats with gold cord came off gallantly.

Barbara's surprise increased as she recognized the older man's fierce tufted eyebrows and careless, graying mustache. He was Colonel Lake, of Fort Roxton, and his question was polite.

"Is this the road to Half-Moon Ranch?"

"It is," Barbara said. "Have you seen the sheriff or his deputy?"

"I spoke with them in Roxton Springs, on my way out," the colonel informed her. "Sheriff Johnson is having trouble gathering a posse to beard Alec Waggoman and his Barb crew."

"That trouble is settled," Barbara said. "Only one man now needs to be arrested."

"Waggoman?"

"His foreman," Barbara said. "Vic Hansbro tried to kill Alec Waggoman."

"Indeed?" said the colonel with diminishing interest. He asked no questions about the incident. His question was thoughtful. "Will we find a young man on Half-Moon named Lockhart?"

Caution caught at Barbara. "I hadn't heard that Will Lockhart had connections with the fort," she said vaguely.

The colonel's gaze lighted with a hint of reserved humor. He said politely, "I'm Colonel Lake, from the fort, young lady. This is Lieutenant Braswell."

"I'm Barbara Kirby."

"A pleasure, Miss Kirby." The dryness came back into Colonel Lake's tone. "It has been suggested that this Lockhart, at Half-Moon, is a Captain Lockhart, of whom I am somewhat acquainted."

All that Barbara knew of Will Lockhart came

vividly into her startled thoughts—his way of assuming cool, instinctive command—the mystery of his background— *Of course*, Barbara thought with a flare of perverse indignation. *From the first he was deceitful. Captain Will Lockhart, pretending to be a wagon freighter!* Barbara was unable to resist the question she tried to ask indifferently. "Is your Captain Lockhart married?"

Stronger humor entered Lake's gaze. "I haven't heard so, Miss Kirby. But one never knows. These young rascals skirmish like fiends, and then cave to the first pretty face." The colonel's counterquestion was dryly quizzical. "Is your Will Lockhart married?"

"He is not 'my Lockhart,' " Barbara said emphatically. The flush she felt was vexing. "A wife," she said aloofly, "hasn't been mentioned."

Lake's grave humor was appraising her denim riding-outfit, her gray hat with leather chin cord back on gleaming chestnut hair. *Pretty and flustered,* passed through Lake's mind with new interest and mild amusement. A girl like this would brighten the grinding routine of any officers' row. Casually Lake tried again.

"Could it be possible this man is my Captain Lockhart?"

Barbara was remembering Will Lockhart's arrest in Roxton Springs and his savage fight with Vic Hansbro in Coronado. And this was the commanding colonel at Fort Roxton questioning her—

"I can't tell you," Barbara said with more vagueness.

The colonel's "Indeed?" suggested dry understanding of her evasion. "Will we find the man at Half-Moon, Miss Kirby?"

"He was there this morning." Barbara smiled at the two officers. A flick of her braided leather quirt sent her horse on.

Lieutenant Braswell's admiring gaze followed her, and swung hastily, deferentially to Lake's curt order.

"You will not mention this, Mister Braswell." Lake's gaze also was following Barbara, and he mused, "Possibly we've not wasted the day." Lake pointed his tall black gelding toward Half-Moon again and his remark was resigned. "Quite possibly, also, Lockhart isn't at the ranch now. And if not, I suspect our charming young lady knows it."

In the Coronado bank, George Freall had been slightly reluctant and plainly curious as he made the quick cash loan. The canvas money sack holding good double eagles and greenbacks was not conspicuous as Frank Darrah carried it across the street to his store. His head still ached. The frustrating rage still churned. But in the plan he had made, Frank found a vicious, comforting satisfaction.

He stopped at the gun counter in his store and selected a black-leather holster belt and two boxes of cartridges. Alone at his office desk he hastily thumbed cartridges into the belt's leather loops.

Then from the tall iron safe Frank took out a revolver wrapped in newspaper. He held the gun in momentary fascination, hearing again the loud, echoing reports at Dave Waggoman's back. Frank moistened his lips and swallowed; memory was vivid of Dave sagging off his horse. Then satisfaction over his foresight in keeping this gun wiped out the momentary unpleasantness.

The crude *L*, for Lockhart, burned into the

smooth cedar grip, was widely known now as men looked for this gun. It had last been seen in Dave's possession. If found on Vic Hansbro's body, who would doubt that Hansbro had killed Dave? No one, Frank thought malevolently. And Hansbro had forced this.

Frank shoved the gun into the belt holster and stepped out into the store again.

McGuire was occupied with a customer at the front, but Frank had the feeling the small, prying clerk was covertly watching him. McGuire had been openly curious at the unexpected return. Scowling as he thought of McGuire, Frank took a small two-barrel derringer of large caliber, and shells to load it, from the gun case.

It was a deadly little weapon, Frank thought with satisfaction as he returned to the office and loaded both barrels. Opening the money sack, he nested the little gun among the greenbacks.

Then he reached in and grasped the derringer and aimed the stubby muzzle through the concealing canvas. He repeated the move many times, until his hand went in smoothly and surely, ready to shoot.

When he finally closed the sack, Frank stood in a blank moment of indecision. The sick fear was beginning to knot again inside. If he missed, then Vic Hansbro would surely kill him quickly, ruthlessly—

Frank almost jumped as the office door opened. He saw it was Barbara's small, straight figure entering, and he swept the money sack and gunbelt back in the desk and pulled down the lid. He tried to sound eager.

"Darling, I thought you were at Half-Moon."

Barbara looked tired. Her mouth with its full red lower lip was not smiling. "I'm not," Barbara said, and when Frank moved to take her in his arms, her cool "Don't, Frank," stopped him. Barbara's greenish eyes were appraising his face. "Has Lockhart been here?"

"He has not," said Frank shortly, and it was galling to see the relief on Barbara's face. Her next remark was strangely cool. "You said Doctor Matt told you Dave shot Lockhart's hand."

Frank shrugged. He remembered. He hadn't thought Barbara would think of it again.

Barbara's cool voice said, "Doctor Matt didn't tell you, Frank. You lied to me."

Pettishly Frank exploded, "Is that a way to talk? I must have been mistaken. Vic Hansbro was in town that evening, looking for Dave. He probably told me."

Barbara looked at him a long moment. Her eyes were big and distant. She was like a stranger as her head shook slightly. "Not Hansbro, either, Frank. You would have told me. Here—"

Barbara's hand came from the pocket of her denim jacket. Frank stared at the diamond ring in her small palm, extended to him. "Barbara, I don't understand. Aren't you being unreasonable?"

He thought a kind of sadness touched Barbara's small dusty face. "Perhaps, Frank. But I've decided. Here is your ring."

"No!"

Barbara dropped the ring. It bounced on the floor and stopped near Frank's shoe. He stared down at it, reddening, and a furious suspicion burst out thickly. "Has that fellow Lockhart been feeding you lies about me?"

Barbara denied it with a shake of her head. "Not Will Lockhart, Frank." She was reaching for the doorknob.

"Barbara—please—"

Barbara closed the door behind her. Frank listened to her light rapid steps receding toward the front door. Then the full blow came down on him. No chance now of ever owning Barb. He groaned and stooped for the whisky bottle in the bottom desk drawer.

Moments later he decided this angry impulse of Barbara's could be changed. No girl could turn so finally, so abruptly from her wedding, on such a slim excuse.

Then the immediate danger hammered feverishly in Frank's brain. Vic Hansbro must be handled quickly now. He pushed up the desk lid and reached for the money sack and gunbelt.

Smashing the future had been easier than Barbara had thought, and harder, too. Frank had looked ghastly. Blindly Barbara crossed the street to the post office. In the bare, dusty little room, she found Aaron Sadler's shrewd wrinkled face peering at her through his wicket. They were alone, and Aaron said tartly, "Ain't no love letters. You're the same as an old married woman now."

"Am I?" said Barbara. She had to draw a deep breath before telling Aaron. "I've just returned Frank's ring. We're not going to be married."

Aaron blinked, and then said dryly, "Looks like you've finally growed into sense."

"I'll be," said Barbara dismally, "a vinegary old maid."

"Vinegary, mebbe," Aaron assented. He was peering over his steel-framed spectacles, and his lean mouth twitched. "But an old maid?" Aaron commented. "You?" Aaron's knowing chuckle followed.

Barbara gave him a jaundiced look and walked out. Before night, Aaron would inform the town. That had been her purpose in telling Aaron at once.

The rest of it was not hers to decide, Barbara knew miserably. Frank's fate rested with Frank now. Through the post office window she had seen Frank mount his horse and ride down the street. Barbara felt tired, drained out as she crossed the street to Frank's hitchrack, where her horse was tied. Then a final thought sent her back into Frank's store.

McGuire came forward to meet her. He was smiling. Barbara liked this small, stocky, droll clerk, and now she made her request confidently.

"If Will Lockhart comes in, will you send him to our house?"

"That I will," assented McGuire readily. He was regarding her oddly. His question was odd. "Would Darrah be going to meet Lockhart now?"

"I'm sure not." Barbara hesitated, and then told McGuire, also. "Frank and I are not going to be married. He didn't tell me what his plans are today."

The smile which lighted McGuire's face became real and friendly and reflective. "So—" said McGuire slowly. "All over, eh?" And when Barbara nodded, McGuire mused slowly, "That might be explaining why Darrah left in a rage, ready for trouble."

"Trouble?"

Watching her, McGuire said, "Sure now, the man

never before slipped a derringer out of stock, and bullets to load it. And added the gunbelt and gun I seen under his coat when he left."

"But Frank never goes armed."

McGuire shrugged. He had the look of knowing more. Barbara walked slowly out to the hitchrack. She was on her horse before the full enormity of it crystallized, and on quick, panicky impulse she reined her horse the way Frank had gone.

At the Chinaman Creek ford, a dark-featured, familiar figure with flaming red whisker bristle moved out of the brush and stood grinning as her horse splashed through the water to him.

"Seems we always meet here," Charley Yuill greeted.

"Have you seen Will Lockhart?" Barbara asked. A shake of his head denied it, and she asked, "Has Frank Darrah passed?"

"He's got the habit," Charley drawled. "He passed out from town—passed back to town fast— an' passed out again fast a short while ago." Charley grinned again. "You only went to town an' came back."

"Have you been watching this ford?"

Charley's grin in the bristly red whisker brush did not deny it. A thought caught at Barbara. "Are you Captain Lockhart's friend?" she inquired offhandedly.

His skin was chocolate hue over wide cheekbones of Indian blood, and now an Indianlike impassiveness dropped on Charley Yuill's dark face. His drawled question was silken.

"Did Darrah tell you to ask about Cap'n Lockhart?"

Barbara said, "No," and then worriedly, "Frank Darrah is carrying a revolver and a derringer, and he might meet Will Lockhart—"

"Has somethin' happened?" Charley broke in keenly.

Barbara told briefly of the finding of Alec Waggoman, the guilt of Vic Hansbro—and a dangerous glow began to smolder in Charley's look. His curt "Wait!" interrupted her.

He vanished soundlessly back into the brush. Moments later, with almost no noise, he returned astride the same big bareback, mouse-colored mule, a carbine clutched in his left hand.

"Tell me the rest," Charley said, and he brought a vast reassurance and relief as his long-eared mule broke into a trot beside her horse.

From the wooded crest of the steep-sided foothill where he waited, Vic Hansbro could see the ranch road for several miles in either direction. He sat comfortably against the rough trunk of a large piñon pine, rolling and smoking brown-paper cigarettes. Now and then he restlessly cursed this enforced wait for Frank Darrah.

He had just rolled another cigarette when he sighted a horse and rider on the farthest reach of road toward Barb and Half-Moon. Hansbro stood up, the cigarette forgotten in his fingers.

Intently he watched the horse and rider vanish as the road swung out of sight, and when they appeared again, closer, Hansbro muttered profanely. Now he could make out the rider's left hand cradled awkwardly in a cloth neck sling.

Hansbro dropped the unlighted cigarette and

caught his carbine off the matted pine needles. His horse was tied out of sight beyond the crest of the hill, and he let the horse stay there.

Treading lithely for all his bulk, stooping to keep out of sight, Hansbro moved down the hill nearer the road where Will Lockhart would pass.

Chapter Twenty-five

The hoofmarks of Vic Hansbro's horse had been easy to follow. But when the sign veered abruptly left into the tall roadside chamisa brush, Will reined up and gazed warily around.

The road here was threading foothills covered with piñon and juniper and smaller brush. The hot midday quiet was peaceful. But Will's unshaven face drew taut as he followed the tracks into the chamisa. He had no doubt that Hansbro would kill.

The dry brush crackled softly. Back up the road a jay called. Overhead a dove's fluting whisper passed, and faded. Beyond the chamisa, Hansbro's trail went up the hillside a short distance, and then angled back down into the brush and back into the road.

Here the sign said a second horse had come from the direction of Coronado. It had trampled dirt beside Hansbro's horse, and then had turned back to town. Then Hansbro's trail led up the opposite hillside into screening trees.

Too far away to shoot, Vic Hansbro swore softly as he watched Will Lockhart's deliberate advance. A growing uneasiness made Hansbro consider retreating to rougher country. But that would miss Frank Darrah. And Lockhart was alone, with only one hand he could use—

Stooping behind cover, Hansbro stealthily headed back to higher ground where Will Lockhart would come through the tree growth.

The long sleepless night dragged a yawn from Will as he halted among the trees and tried to think like Hansbro.

The man had met someone on the road. After that, Hansbro had leisurely detoured to this higher ground, and turned his horse parallel to the road atop this long, ridgelike hill. Now why? Had Hansbro changed his destination?

Cautiously Will followed the sign through shade and bright splotches of sunlight. The quiet seemed now to have a brooding quality. The sense of lurking danger was increasing.

Even his horse, Will noted, seemed to be affected. The horse's nervously twitching ears were testing the quiet ahead. And then, without warning, the horse nickered, and a second horse nickered back, ahead and to the right.

Will instinctively reined hard to the right, and as his horse lunged ahead, the flat blurt of a rifle shot tore the peace.

The bullet keened close and ripped away through the growth. Will ducked under a low tree limb and heard another shrilling bullet miss. He braced in the stirrups as his bolting horse cleared a fallen tree trunk, and he had not yet sighted Hansbro.

The other horse had sounded over the brow of the hill, on the back slope. Will gambled on being an uncertain target and drove his horse faster, and heard Hansbro shooting wildly and missing.

Bent low, Will reached the back slope of the hill at full gallop and swung along that slope, and his guess had been right. A gray horse was tied to a thick juniper branch.

Will hauled up, flung off, yanked carbine from the saddle scabbard, and pounded up the slope to an outcrop of weathered rock. Kneeling there behind cover, he dropped the carbine and drew the Colt's revolver he had borrowed from Kate Canaday.

He heard Hansbro running noisily and then stop. And wrath at the man's skulking trap put a cold taunt into Will's call.

"Barb and Half-Moon men are coming for you, Hansbro! Want your horse now?"

Two fast shots replied. The bullets glanced in screaming ricochet off the rock. Kneeling, panting, Will was remembering his fist fight with the big man. Hansbro angered easily. His thoughts were ponderous. To the unexpected, Hansbro reacted with blind fury and force.

Now Hansbro's stealthy ambush had failed. He was cut off from his horse. His own guilt would be anticipating quick pursuit by the Barb and Half-Moon men.

Will's laugh was jeering.

"Hansbro, they mean to hang you!" He heard the big man swearing at him. Jeering again, Will reminded, "You're cornered now! You're finished, Hansbro! This will please Alec Waggoman!"

The shots Hansbro fired rapidly struck chips from the rock and spewed up dirt close beside Will. There was a wild viciousness in the fusillade which suggested Hansbro's temper was close to cracking.

Will remembered his own reason for wanting to corner this man.

"Who asked you to kill Waggoman?" he called, and got no reply. Hansbro might be creeping closer. Will goaded the man with another jeer. "You're not crowding an old man off the trail now! They're bringing a rope for that thick neck!"

Hansbro hadn't moved. His savage promise came from the same spot. "Before they get here, I'll kill you an' be gone!"

Will's horse had moved uneasily down the slope, dragging the reins. Hansbro's gray horse was still tied to the juniper branch. Hansbro could see it. The man must be baffled, raging. Will laughed again.

"I can wait, Hansbro! You can't!"

And in the hot, silent moments which followed, a brace of spaced gun reports echoed across the top of the hill from some near-by point on the road.

Will was startled. It might be help for Hansbro. He tried again to goad the man's slow-thinking brain. "They're coming, Hansbro! You'll hang quick now!"

Hansbro's gun breached the quiet once more— and a second time, sounding closer. Will cocked the revolver; and when Hansbro's third shot was unmistakably nearer, Will stood up. He was braced for what he saw, and yet Vic Hansbro was a formidable sight.

Black hat yanked low, black beard abristle, Hansbro was running down the brush-dotted slope with great plunging strides, levering shells into his carbine and shooting as he ran.

Will fired at the shifting target and missed. Hansbro's answering shot missed, too, and Hansbro hurled his carbine aside and yanked the revolver from his side holster. His rush was closing fast as Will dropped to a knee and steadied the revolver barrel across his raised left arm.

A bullet from Hansbro's revolver whisked through the crown of Will's hat before the front gunsight steadied. Slowly Will squeezed the trigger, and he saw Hansbro flinch.

Carefully, coldly, Will sighted and fired again. He was sighting once more through the spew of muzzle vapor when Hansbro wobbled half around. The long legs crossed, and the great charging bulk hurtled forward in a slamming fall which skidded and rolled down the slope to a stop, face down.

Hansbro had lost hat and gun. He was breathing harshly, moving slowly, when Will reached him and caught a shoulder and rolled him face up. Wounded in chest and stomach, Hansbro already was blowing bits of flecked froth across the bearded lips.

"I don't think you'll make it," was Will's sober decision.

His mouth open, panting, Hansbro glared back. And when a voice hailed up in the trees, Hansbro's head tilted fearfully that way. Will drew the Colt's gun again before he hailed back. And then startled wariness caught Will as two strangers in sky-blue cavalry uniform rode into view, and down the brushy slope to them.

Slowly Will holstered the gun. His dark, unshaven face tightened as he took in the older man's broad shoulders, bristling eyebrows, and careless graying mustache—and the rank of colonel.

Colonel Lake, from Roxton, was Will's resigned guess. This he had tried to avoid.

The man's question was calm. "A little trouble?"

Will nodded taciturnly. He watched silently as the colonel swung easily down, tossed reins to the younger lieutenant, and laid a speculative look on Hansbro, and then on Will.

The same calm tone said, "We heard the shooting."

"He'll not last for the sheriff to arrest him," Will judged briefly.

The colonel turned another critical look on Hansbro. His nod agreed. "Would he be the foreman of Barb?"

"He was."

"I heard he was wanted." Pale-blue eyes estimated the bandage on Will's left hand. "And I judge you're Will Lockhart, whom sheriff Johnson mentioned this morning."

And when Will merely nodded, he was calmly informed, "I'm Colonel Lake, commanding at Fort Roxton."

Will's brief nod let that die flatly, and Lake's gaze hardened.

"This gun fight," said Lake evenly, "together with other incidents, can be serious, should you be a certain man from Laramie."

He's contacted Laramie, was Will's dismal acceptance. He met the blue, boring gaze, and agreed, "No doubt, sir."

Deep gurgles were audible in Hansbro's labored breathing. Will bent over the man again.

"Hansbro, you're going. You know it, and you'd have hung, anyway. Did Darrah have a hand in Dave Waggoman's death and your try at Alec?"

Hansbro glared as he struggled with the shallow, bubbling breaths. Will tried again. "You're not helping Darrah at all. I've cornered him on other crooked business."

After an indecisive moment, Hansbro's thick question countered, "On what?"

"Peddling rifles to the Apaches." Startled interest entered Hansbro's look, and Will asked him, "Did you know that two hundred rifles, shipped from New Orleans as bolt goods, are in Darrah's powder house now? And ten thousand rounds of ammunition?"

Colonel Lake's move to Will's elbow had immediate, alert interest. Hansbro's big, unsteady hand weakly smeared the crimson off his bearded lips.

"Who are you, fellow?"

Will hesitated, and then reluctantly put the future into the hands of this now grim, older man standing at his elbow.

"I'm Captain Lockhart, United States Cavalry."

"Not a mule skinner? A damn' wagon man?" Hansbro broke into coughing, and when his throat was clear, "Peddlin' guns!" came almost as an oath from his smeared mouth. " 'Pach' guns!" Then Hansbro's slow grin shaped incredible malice, from which he seemed to gain strength.

"Sure, Frank Darrah hired me t' kill Alec. He bought cattle, too, that I rustled offa Barb. An' he paid kickbacks on Barb supplies I bought—" Coughing shook Hansbro again, and then he gasped, "But God'll-mighty—'Pache guns! The snake!" He lay quietly, the malice holding on the heavy mouth.

Will's glance crossed Michael Lake's demanding anger. New, brusque authority filled Lake's question. "Explain, sir, this business of selling guns to hostiles!"

"Darrah is the one to explain. You heard me, Colonel. Darrah has a shipment of rifles now, undoubtedly meant for the Indian trade."

"I'll hear what you have to say."

"Not much," Will said, and the old, bitter anger

came back. "I lost a brother in the meat chopper at Dutch Canyon. Someone knew how the Apaches got the new repeating rifles they used at the Canyon. I've been looking for that man."

"Dutch Canyon," said Lake under his breath. "Yes, it was bad. Is this Darrah the fellow who has a store in Coronado?"

Will nodded. The old prodding anger put him past wanting understanding or permission. "I've some more to do about this, at once."

And Will learned now why Michael Lake had qualities which had carried the man's name through distant outposts and garrisons. A gleam entered Lake's frosty look.

"I seem to have missed some of your talk with this man," Lake said thoughtfully. "And since you seem to be a civilian, I've no interest in your affairs. We'll see to this wounded man."

Will had to suppress an admiring salute. He stepped to the rock outcrop and caught up his carbine, and he chose Hansbro's gray gelding for the ride. And as he left without looking back, he was aware that now all friendship with Barbara Kirby would end. Always Barbara would remember him as the stranger who had smashed her future and her happiness.

The thought hung in Will's mind depressingly as he followed the ranch road toward Coronado. It was there when the distant rider he sighted drew nearer and became Frank Darrah.

The man looked as well-dressed as usual, Will noted. Darrah was successful, he was prosperous, and he had a certain florid handsomeness, too. Will could understand Barbara's feeling for the man. He noted Darrah's puzzled scowl at the gray gelding when they met and halted.

"Yes, it's Hansbro's horse," Will said evenly.

Darrah gaped at him. A kind of quick panic and fright put a greenish look on the florid face. Darrah swallowed twice before his angry harshness came through.

"Have they caught Hansbro?"

"For what?" Will asked.

Darrah swallowed again, and Will's tired disgust ended the farce. "I caught Hansbro. I shot him. He talked about your hiring him to kill Waggoman. And a lot more."

"He lied!"

"Did he?" said Will indifferently. "Do you still think you'll get Barb? Or sell those guns in your powder house?"

Darrah looked greenish-sick; he looked ghastly. The question he asked was thick, shaking. "You found Hansbro alone and shot him?"

"Yes."

"I've got five thousand dollars cash here, Lockhart. I can get more. Five thousand more—"

"Now wouldn't that be a bargain buy?" Will said in greater disgust. "Come along to Half-Moon. We'll wait there for the sheriff."

The man's thick desperation urged, "Fifteen thousand! You'll get every penny! Here's the first five thousand now—"

Will's alert watchfulness relaxed as Darrah's hand dragged a bulging canvas money sack from his coat pocket. With shaking hands, Darrah loosed the draw string and opened the sack.

"Look at this, and I'll get the rest!" was his thick

promise as he reached in the sack. "Every d-dollar of it, before night—"

The flat, loud blurt of a gunshot covered Darrah's voice. Will felt the bullet shocking his right side, heeling him back against the cantle. There was no pain. In a kind of marveling surprise, Will gazed at the powder smoke which had spurted from a new, tiny hole in the sack's side.

A derringer hidden in there. He was paying Hansbro, and must have meant to shoot Hansbro! flashed through Will's brain, and the irony of it was supreme. And in the same second, Will was groping back for his own holstered gun, and the arm, the hand, and all his right side felt numb and sluggish.

The greenish fright still held on Darrah's face, but the hand remained in the sack.

Double-barreled! Another bullet! Will guessed as he dragged the heavy Colt's gun from the holster. His shocked, sluggish body bent forward a little, straining unconsciously against the hammer blow of another bullet.

This will kill, and he'll talk out of it someway, and get Barb and Barbara, too! went tiredly through Will's mind.

Then the walloping report inside the sack opened another tiny hole which spewed its mocking vapor. The shock to flesh and bone drove Will reeling, and in some dogged, stubborn way his thumb continued to cock the heavy Colt's gun.

Darrah saw it. A look of frenzied horror came on his face as Will's great effort brought the gun forward. Darrah's frantic snatch of the reins wheeled his horse off the road. When the gun bucked and crashed in Will's unsteady hand, the violent crackling of roadside brush around Darrah's bolting horse did not abate.

Will tried again, cocking, straining the muzzle up in dreamlike, shocked slowness. Darrah was bent low now, kicking his horse into a gallop beyond the belt of brush. This try missed, too. Darrah did not look back as he fled south into the foothills.

Tiredly Will looked after the man. Then slowly, with great effort, Will climbed off the gray horse. He staggered and sat down heavily beside the road.

He was sitting there dully, and the sunlight around him was like a brassy fog when a horse and a big mouse-colored mule took shape in the road. Incredibly the riders were Barbara and red-whiskered Charley Yuill.

And when Charley dropped to a knee beside Will, Charley's knowledge seemed logical. "Was it Darrah, Cap'n?"

Will nodded. Charley spoke hastily over a shoulder to Barbara. "Get the doc from Half-Moon."

"How bad?" asked Barbara's tight voice. She was looking at the blood-soaked shirt. She was pale.

"Ma'am," said Charley, "you'd better hurry."

Barbara's quirted horse pounded away. Charley spread his coat behind Will. "Lie back, Cap'n. What happened?"

On his back, Will dragged his hat forward, with an effort, against the sun glare. His mutter was rueful. "Charley, he was smarter than I thought."

Charley was opening the shirt. Some time later Charley's calloused palm slapped Will's face. "Stay awake, Cap'n!"

Will's drowsy grin held no offense. Past the edge of the shading hatbrim he muttered dreamily,

"Dutch Canyon—and then here— Got both brothers, didn't he, Charley?"

"Dinna speak so foolish!" Charley's worried burr commanded. "The doc'll be here quick!" Charley slapped Will's chin. "Cap'n, get mad! Stay awake!"

Will's faint smile was tolerant. Then a thought made him frown under the hat. "Charley, those guns—"

"Cap'n, I'll track Darrah."

"Good man, Charley—"

Some time later riders were about them and Matt Seldon uncovered Will's face. Smiling slightly at the doctor's serious look, Will let himself drift comfortably into the soft drowsiness. And when he looked up again, Seldon's graying Van Dyke was oddly the broad, concerned face of Kate Canaday.

Will's puzzled frown deepened as he looked past Kate. Her gusty relief was like an invigorating shock. "Made up your mind to stay with us?" Kate demanded.

"Isn't this the Kirby house?"

"Same house," said Kate. "Same bed you was in before. Alec's in the next room. An' why Barbara don't get tired of takin' in beat-up strangers is a miracle."

Will moved cautiously. His middle was swathed in bandages, and under the bandages was more pain. He frowned again. "Very beat up, evidently. Should have taken me to the hotel."

"Ain't a bit of doubt of it," Kate agreed.

"What time is it?"

"Afternoon. Jubal hauled you here yesterday."

Kate was a new woman, dignified in a wine-colored silk dress with puffed sleeves. Her iron-gray pompadour was brushed high and impressively, and rice powder had been discreetly applied to Kate's reddish, weathered face. Marveling, Will murmured, "So Waggoman is here, too."

"Doc wanted him brought to town."

"How is Waggoman?"

"As usual, meaner'n sin. But someone," said Kate with a trace of defiance, "has got to look after the old blowbag."

Will recalled the gray dawn hour and this big, buffeted woman kneeling by Alec Waggoman. Gravely, obtusely, Will wondered, "Do you have to look after him?"

The slightest flush crept into Kate's broad cheeks.

"Who else'd put up with the man?" Kate cleared her throat. "Alec made me a kinda business proposition. Dave's dead, an' Alec won't see his own victuals before long. I ain't got a roof now. So Alec's got an idea I can run both ranches from Barb. Usin' my eyes an' his brain, like he had a brain."

"Mmmmmm," said Will gravely. "You take over Hansbro's job?"

"Wel-l-l, not exactly. Alec was hopin' you'd come over as foreman."

"Impossible. I've business of my own to go back to."

"Colonel Lake guessed so," said Kate with resignation. "He said to stop by the fort before you left an' get your hand shaken."

"Now did he?" Will murmured. His relief came then in a smile. "When," Will asked, "is the wedding?"

Now Kate's face did redden. Bulking beside the bed, big, defiant, blushing, Kate reluctantly admitted, "If I got to stay at Barb, marryin' the old windbag seems the best way. When his eyes give out, this beat-up old face of mine won't turn all his appetite."

Will looked at her long and smiling, marveling that a kind of beauty and shining happiness could come so fully to this big, weather-beaten woman.

"Kate, I'm glad," Will said, and Kate grumbled, "I feel like a fool, at my age."

"You look like a bride," Will said, and he saw that it pleased Kate greatly, despite her indignant snort.

Then a thought narrowed Kate's glance. "I reckon you don't know about Darrah."

"What about the man?" Will asked quickly.

"Charley Yuill an' three of the boys followed Darrah's trail," Kate said. "Later on they found he'd half killed his horse gettin' to town. He loaded grub at the back of his store, cleaned out his safe, an' then drove to his powder house an' loaded cases of guns an' shells."

Will groaned. "I was afraid."

Kate said dryly, "Darrah was more afraid. Charley Yuill spotted the fresh wagon tracks comin' out of the powder house road. The men followed 'em, and met the sheriff's posse comin' from Roxton Springs. Part of the posse went with them. Darrah was heading toward the salt lakes an' the Apache country."

"With new rifles and shells, he'd be welcomed and protected among the Apaches," Will guessed thinly.

"Uh-huh," Kate agreed. "But by trackin' his wagon quick, the boys got a jump on him. They sighted his wagon, and when Darrah saw them, he cut a horse loose and tried to get away."

"Tried?" Will said hopefully. "Did they catch him?"

"In a way. The salt crew at the lakes had just been raided an' killed. Same Indians seen Darrah coming an' jumped him. He turned back toward the posse, but the Indians had good repeating rifles. They dropped Darrah's horse. He was running on foot when they downed him. They got his scalp and got clean away before the posse come up."

Slowly, softly, Will drew a long deep breath. "New rifles— Good repeating rifles— And he was shot by them—and then scalped—"

Will lay thinking about it, strangely not glad, but at peace now, with the long hunt ended. He said quietly, "I'm sorry for Barbara."

"She ain't happy about it, of course," Kate said. "But she'd been to town, given Darrah back his ring, and broken completely with him. They found your gun on Darrah, the one Dave took from you. Ain't any doubt now Frank Darrah killed Dave. And Barbara, and everyone else, knows now all Darrah wanted was to get his hands on Barb quick by marryin' Barbara." Kate's smile was grim. "A woman sure gets cured complete, knowing she was only a cash drawer."

Will lay in astounded silence, hardly hearing Kate's next words.

"Barbara ain't a catch that way now. I mean to make Alec live a long time. But someday she'll have Barb an' Half-Moon, too. She'll need a real man to help." Kate paused. "Got any ideas about that?"

Calmly Will said, "My idea is that you're still a scheming, conniving old woman."

"Now ain't I just?" was Kate's unabashed agreement.

"Where is Barbara?"

"She went to the store." Kate turned her head as her name was called in the next room. "I'm comin' right now, Alec," she answered meekly.

She left hastily, and Will lay quietly, smiling a little as he listened to the two voices murmuring in the next room. Could all the lost years be packed into the remainder for those two, Will wondered. In a way he envied them for what they had found again. And when he heard Barbara enter the house, he closed his eyes again.

Her light quick steps came to his doorway, then moved to Waggoman's doorway. Barbara's quiet voice asked there, "Has there been any change in him?"

"In Alec?" Kate asked.

"You know who I mean."

"I got my hands full with this one," said Kate blandly. "Look after your own man."

"Kate, he's not—"

"Ain't my fault," said Kate.

Barbara's brisk steps went to the kitchen. A few moments later she stepped into Will's room, and came to the bed. Lying quietly with his eyes closed, Will felt her nearness and her silent contemplation. Barbara's hand touched his forehead, pushing back his hair, and rested against his cheek for a moment.

His right hand captured her hand there. Barbara gasped slightly, and Will held the small hand against his cheek. His eyes still closed, he said, "I'll be merely another captain in a hardscrabble fort up the Missouri. A hard life for the army wives and lonesome for the single men."

Barbara said, "Is it?" Her voice was not small or hesitant. She sounded quiet, composed.

He looked up then, into Barbara's steady regard. He knew her now, young, spirited, with pensive depths, with understanding. He said quietly, "Kate loved him like storm in the sunshine—"

Barbara's mouth softened into a remembering smile. She quoted Will's opinion. "Riches for any man—"

Holding her captured hand against his stubble-roughened cheek, Will repeated Barbara's words of that chill dawn. "Or any woman—"

"Any woman," Barbara said now, again.

It was in her eyes, shining in her look, all the years to be not missed as that graying couple in the next room had missed. Will drew Barbara down, and she came to him, her smooth cheek against his rough face—beyond all doubt, Will knew now, riches enough for any man.

The Classic Film Collection

The Searchers by Alan LeMay

Hailed as one of the greatest American films, *The Searchers*, directed by John Ford and starring John Wayne, has had a direct influence on the works of Martin Scorsese, Steven Spielberg, and many others. Its gorgeous cinematic scope and deeply nuanced characters have proven timeless. And now available for the first time in decades is the powerful novel that inspired this iconic movie. (Coming February 2009!)

Destry Rides Again by Max Brand

Made in 1939, the Golden Year of Hollywood, *Destry Rides Again* helped launch Jimmy Stewart's career and made Marlene Dietrich an American icon. Now available for the first time in decades is the novel that inspired this much-loved movie. (Coming March 2009!)

The Man from Laramie by T. T. Flynn

In its original publication, *The Man from Laramie* had more than half a million copies in print. Shortly thereafter, it became one of the most recognized of the Anthony Mann/Jimmy Stewart collaborations, known for darker films with morally complex characters. Now the novel upon which this classic movie was based is once again available—for the first time in more than fifty years. (Coming April 2009!)

The Unforgiven by Alan LeMay

In this epic American novel, which served as the basis for the classic film directed by John Huston and starring Burt Lancaster and Audrey Hepburn, a family is torn apart when an old enemy starts a vicious rumor that sets the range aflame. Don't miss the powerful novel that inspired the film the *Motion Picture Herald* calls "an absorbing and compelling drama of epic proportions." (Coming May 2009!)

"When you think of the West, you think of Zane Grey." —*American Cowboy*

ZANE GREY

THE RESTORED, FULL-LENGTH NOVEL, IN PAPERBACK FOR THE FIRST TIME!

The Great Trek

Sterl Hazelton is no stranger to trouble. But the shooting that made him an outlaw was one he didn't do. Though it was his cousin who pulled the trigger, Sterl took the blame, and now he has to leave the country if he wants to stay healthy. Sterl and his loyal friend, Red Krehl, set out for the greatest adventure of their lives, signing on for a cattle drive across the vast northern desert of Australia to the gold fields of the Kimberley Mountains. But it seems no matter where Sterl goes, trouble is bound to follow!

"Grey stands alone in a class untouched by others." —*Tombstone Epitaph*

ISBN 13: 978-0-8439-6062-4

To order a book or to request a catalog call:
1-800-481-9191
This book is also available at your local bookstore, or you can check out our Web site **www.dorchesterpub.com** where you can look up your favorite authors, read excerpts, or glance at our discussion forum to see what people have to say about your favorite books.

LOUIS L'AMOUR

For millions of readers, the name Louis L'Amour is synonymous with the excitement of the Old West. But for too long, many of these tales have only been available in revised, altered versions, often very different from their original form. Here, collected together in paperback for the first time, are four of L'Amour's finest stories, all carefully restored to their initial magazine publication versions.

BIG MEDICINE

This collection includes L'Amour's wonderful short novel *Showdown on the Hogback*, an unforgettable story of ranchers uniting to fight back against the company that's trying to drive them off their land. "Big Medicine" pits a lone prospector against a band of nine Apaches. In "Trail to Pie Town," a man has to get out of town fast after a gunfight leaves his opponent dead on a saloon floor. And the title character in "McQueen of the Tumbling K" is out for revenge after gunmen ambush him and leave him to die.

ISBN 13: 978-0-8439-6068-6

☐ **YES!**

Sign me up for the Leisure Western Book Club and send
my FREE BOOKS! If I choose to stay in the club, I will pay
only $14.00* each month, a savings of $9.96!

NAME: _____

ADDRESS: _____

TELEPHONE: _____

EMAIL: _____

☐ I want to pay by credit card.

☐  VISA   ☐ MasterCard.   ☐ DISCOVER

ACCOUNT #: _____

EXPIRATION DATE: _____

SIGNATURE: _____

Mail this page along with $2.00 shipping and handling to:
Leisure Western Book Club
PO Box 6640
Wayne, PA 19087
Or fax (must include credit card information) to:
610-995-9274
You can also sign up online at **www.dorchesterpub.com**.
*Plus $2.00 for shipping. Offer open to residents of the U.S. and Canada only.
Canadian residents please call 1-800-481-9191 for pricing information.
If under 18, a parent or guardian must sign. Terms, prices and conditions subject to
change. Subscription subject to acceptance. Dorchester Publishing reserves the right
to reject any order or cancel any subscription.